Y0-CTX-661

THE GUILTY CLIENT

Also by Roberta Rogow

The Problem of the Missing Miss
The Problem of the Spurious Spiritualist
The Problem of the Evil Editor
The Problem of the Surly Servant

THE GUILTY CLIENT

ROBERTA ROGOW

DEADLY INK

Copyright 2009
All rights reserved

Cover Design by D. Cameron Calkins

Interior Design by Debby Buchanan

No part of this book may be reproduced in any form or by electronic means, including information storage and retrieval systems, without written permission from the publisher, except by a reviewer, who may quote passages in review.

This is a work of fiction. Any resemblance to any individual, place, business, or event is entirely coincidental and not intended by the author.

Published by
Deadly Ink Press
PO Box 6235, Parsippany, NJ 07054
www.deadlyink.com

ISBN: 9780978744274

First Edition

For my family

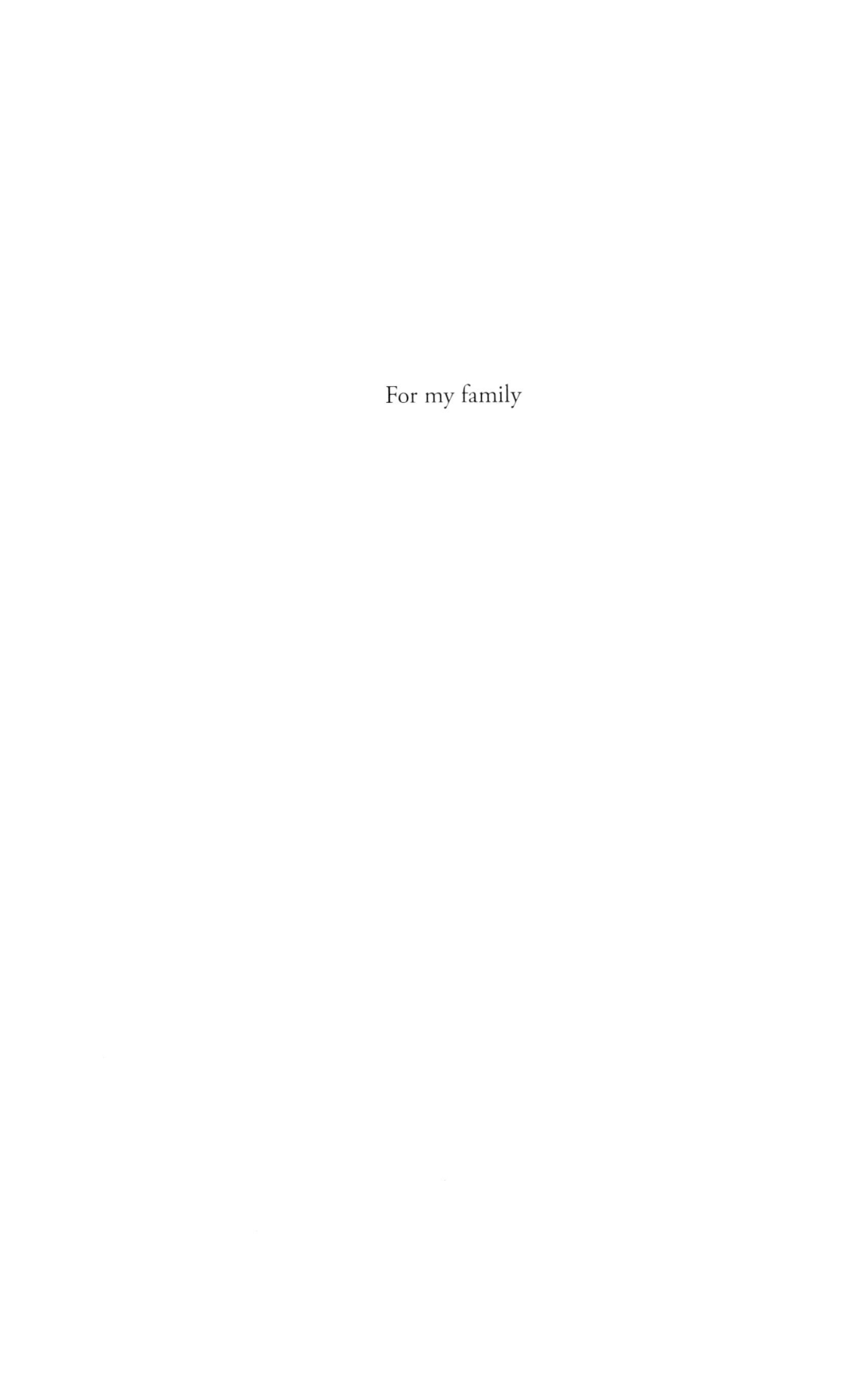

SECTION ONE: PEGGY

CHAPTER 1

It should have been a day of celebration for the firm of Pettigrew and Roth, Attorneys at Law. Our new partner had successfully defended his client, got him out of jail and into the world scot-free, and a substantial fee had been added to the coffers of the firm. I was about to write "Case Closed" to the file: *People vs. Delacorte*. Through the front window of our office we could see the ships on the docks, and between them, the ruffles of waves on the Hudson River under the blue April sky. It was Spring in New York City, the War had been over for five years, all was right with the world. Or so it seemed.

My Uncle Ephraim Pettigrew sat in his enormous leather-upholstered chair, positioned so that he could observe everything on the docks across West Street through the front windows of the small brick building that had once been a pawnbrokers' shop. He is massive rather than fat, an impressive presence, his black frock coat, open to reveal a modest black waistcoat, plain shirt-front, and old-fashioned high collar and stock. He is sometimes called "the Sage of the Docks", and very little goes on along the Hudson River waterfront that he doesn't know about. His particular field of expertise is Maritime Law, and his clients include anyone and everyone with an interest in seafaring and sea traffic, from Captains to lowly seamen. They know that Uncle Ephraim Pettigrew is the one to come to when they need legal counsel, whether it means making out a contract or a Will, or getting a sailor out of the city jail after a drunken spree.

Our new partner, Joshua Roth, stood in the doorway of the office and regarded the brilliant day with an expression of profound disillusion. He is over six feet tall, with a shock of black hair and a short beard that makes him resemble our late martyred President Lincoln, a likeness which he accentuates by adopting the frock coat and tall hat that is already going out of style. The effect is spoiled by the empty right sleeve pinned up to his shoulder. Joshua was wounded in the War, spent time in hospital, was sent to New Orleans to serve there in the military administration of the city, and returned, under difficult circumstances, to finish his legal studies, and pass the New York State Bar.

It was he who had so efficiently exonerated our client, Mr. Bertram Delacorte, of the charge of murdering Mrs. Suzanna Kendall, and seen to it that the said Mr. Delacorte had been released from custody forthwith, without a stain on his character or a police record, thus proving that Uncle Ephraim was right to accept a partner who could cope with the current exigencies of the New York City Criminal Justice system.

As for myself, I am the both the least and the most noticeable member of the firm. I am Miss Margaret Pettigrew, usually called Miss Peggy. According to popular fancy, young ladies like myself should not be sitting in a law office, copying contracts and sorting case files. However, during the War Uncle Ephraim decided that since most of the young men were away fighting, and the ones who weren't were not worth hiring anyway, he might as well let me earn my keep, and since I find the life on the docks much more interesting than Aunt Sarah's round of calls and tea parties, I quite agreed. I suppose I inherited this rebellious streak from my parents. My father was Uncle Ephraim's brother, and he and my mother were journalists, of the most sensational kind, constantly stirring up trouble by exposing wrong-doing in the pages of Mr. Bennett's New York Sun. According to family legend, they sailed off for the gold fields of California, leaving me with Uncle Ephraim and Aunt Sarah, and promising to return with a new stock of stories for the Sun. The last story they filed was from Bermuda. That was over twenty years ago, and while there have been rumors, and various people have said they might have seen one or the other of them, there has been no concrete evidence as to their whereabouts. Although I am well over the age when most young ladies are married, I remain single, and reside with Aunt Sarah and Uncle Ephraim at their home 0n Bank Street.

So there we were, the three of us, in the one-story office, jammed in between a saloon and a chandlery on West Street, facing the docks and the Hudson River, discussing Mr. Bertram Delacorte and wondering why we weren't happy that he was once more out on the streets of New York.

"I feel like I've been sold a bill of goods," Joshua complained. "I just don't know why. It's a kind of itch I can't scratch."

"You can't hang a man on an itch," Uncle Ephraim said. "Facts are facts. Mrs. Suzanna Kendall was found dead in her own bedroom at Mrs. Smith's boarding-house on East Twenty-Third Street. According to a maid, there was a scream, and then the clock struck ten. The maid went upstairs to see what was happening, and found Mrs. Kendall dead. And at that moment, according to our very own Margaret, Mr. Bertram Delacorte was dancing the polka with her at the Veteran's Ball. As you so brilliantly pointed out to Judge Bacon, he could not possibly have gotten from Niblo's Gardens on Prince Street to Mrs. Smith's boarding house on Twenty-Third Street until ten-thirty, by which time the police had already been summoned. Clearly the man was innocent of the charge, and just as clearly, the case was dismissed, and Delacorte went free. Case closed. I don't know why you're unhappy."

"If Miss Peggy hadn't got there on time to corroborate the story, Delacorte might still be in the Tombs," Joshua said. "Thank goodness you got there when you did."

"I wasn't given much notice," I said, a little snappishly. "All I got was that note telling me to get to the court-house as soon as I could. I should have been called in when the investigation started, instead of having to come in and testify at the arraignment."

"The whole Kendall investigation was a botched-up business," Uncle Ephraim grumbled. "Walling's past it. He should have retired after the War, but he's hanging on for dear life."

I ignored Uncle Ephraim's comments on the conduct of the New York City Police Department's leading light. Captain Walling had served well during the War, and had led the police resistance during the Draft Riots, but he was getting on. For that matter, so was Uncle Ephraim!

A thought occurred to me. "I wonder why Bertram didn't let the police know that he had an alibi when he was arrested."

"As I understand it, he was in no condition to say anything," Joshua said, with a sardonic grin. "They found him over at the Devil's Hole, drunk as a skunk, with a couple of his pals in the same condition. He was hustled over to the Tombs without so much as a warning. I suppose we should be glad he was capable of getting a message off to his uncle, Henry Ward Long, otherwise we wouldn't have been called in to handle the case at all, and Miss Peggy's information would never have been entered into the record."

"Slumming, was he?" Uncle Ephraim made a noise of disgust. He's not amused by rich people going to low places to gape at the antics of us peasants.

"He seems to make a habit of it," Joshua said. "He's been seen in some very, um, interesting places."

"Such as the Veteran's Ball?" I countered. "What was he doing there? He certainly wasn't a veteran himself. He was only sixteen when the War started, his mother's a Copperhead, he had relations fighting for the Rebels, the last place you'd think he'd be on a nice Spring night would be at a subscription ball honoring the Union soldiers. He wouldn't even have been dancing with me if that ridiculous little man McAllister hadn't trotted up and practically shoved me into his arms for the polka."

I didn't mention that I wouldn't have been there either except for Aunt Sarah's insistence that I appear at some social functions during the Season. She still has hopes of finding me a husband. I have no such hopes. With so many men gone, there is a surfeit of females in New York, and most of them seem to be in the dark and slender mode that is the fashion these days. Buxom fair females went out with Master Rubens, and I seem to have inherited the Pettigrew coloring as well as the Pettigrew tendency to embonpoint.

The bell over the door (an inheritance from the pawnbroker)

THE GUILTY CLIENT

tinkled, announcing the arrival of the fourth and most unofficial member of the Pettigrew legal team. Michael Riley, Assistant District Attorney, Uncle Ephraim's prize protégé, had come to congratulate his old commander on winning his first criminal case in the City of New York.

There had been a time when I had bitterly resented the red-headed Irish urchin who had been taken off the streets to keep the office tidy, run errands, and generally make himself useful. It was only later that I realized how desperate Michael's lot in life had been, and how profoundly Uncle Ephraim had changed it when he let Michael sleep in the upstairs office instead of under the outdoor staircase that led to it. Uncle Ephraim may have regarded Michael as a son; I came to look on him as a brother, and I was both proud and anxious when he joined the first regiments formed as soon as the War began. It was Michael who had brought Joshua Roth to Uncle Ephraim's attention when he decided to move to the Prosecution side of the courtroom, and it was Michael who had persuaded Joshua to take on the criminal side of the practice which Uncle Ephraim preferred to leave in younger hands than his own .

Michael strutted into the office, showing off a natty new checked suit and derby hat, the very image of the rising young star in the Tweed firmament.

"I suppose I should be upset, letting a murderer out on the streets," Michael said, after tipping his hat to me and shaking hands with Uncle Ephraim.

"You know my rule, Michael," Uncle Ephraim said. "I never take on a client unless I'm convinced he's not guilty."

"That doesn't mean he's innocent," Michael said. "Bertram Delacorte is a nasty piece of work, and no mistake. He's guilty of something, I could swear to it."

"And so could I," I put in. "He looked positively smug, standing there in the courtroom yesterday, even if he hadn't shaved or changed his clothes in twelve hours. As if he'd put something over on all of us, especially me."

"Now, Peggy," Uncle Ephraim said, "you can't let what he said and did when you were children influence your opinion of him as an adult."

"Nasty little boy, was he?" Michael said, with a grin.

"He refused to dance with me at Miss Porter's," I said. My cheeks still burned at the thought of it. "He said I was too fat."

"And he still danced with you at the Veterans' Ball," Joshua said slowly. "My, my, things have changed. You'd think he had some reason to make you notice his being there."

"It's all very odd," I said. "I can't help thinking there was something behind it, but what? Michael, what were you thinking, bringing Delacorte in on such flimsy evidence?"

Now it was Michael's turn to be miffed. "The police found a bloody coat in Delacorte's room at Mrs. Smith's boarding-house. He'd been seen speaking to Mrs. Kendall."

"And that was all?" Uncle Ephraim asked. "Doesn't sound like enough to hang a man. No weapon found, no motive, and a cast-iron alibi for the time of the murder. I don't know why Delacorte was even considered, let alone arrested."

"That's not for me to say," Michael stated. "I was handed the case on the Friday, he was arrested the following Monday, was brought to court for arraignment on Tuesday, and by Wednesday he's free and clear. And I though we might step out tonight, Captain," he said to Joshua. "Kind of a celebration."

Joshua was about to speak, but Uncle Ephraim intervened.

"Not tonight, boys," Uncle Ephraim decreed. "Aunt Sarah's got a new cook, and she's waiting for us to try her out."

"Now I know I'm stepping out," Michael declared. Aunt Sarah's luck with cooks was legendary: all bad. We have had cooks of every description and nationality, mostly recruited from the hordes that stream out of Castle Garden, and each of them has had her own quirks and cuisine. Uncle Ephraim's stomach has been assaulted by strange herbs and spices from all parts of the globe. I understood why Joshua and Michael might prefer boarding house food to whatever awaited them at the Pettigrew dinner table.

Before the situation could be resolved, I saw a commotion on the docks. "Something's going on!" I popped my head out the door, to get a better look.

A gruesome sight it was. The body of a man had been found wedged between two barges, and was now being taken out of the water. It hadn't been in long, by the look of it, and I could see the face clearly.

"It's Delacorte!" I cried out.

And that was the end of our celebrations for a while.

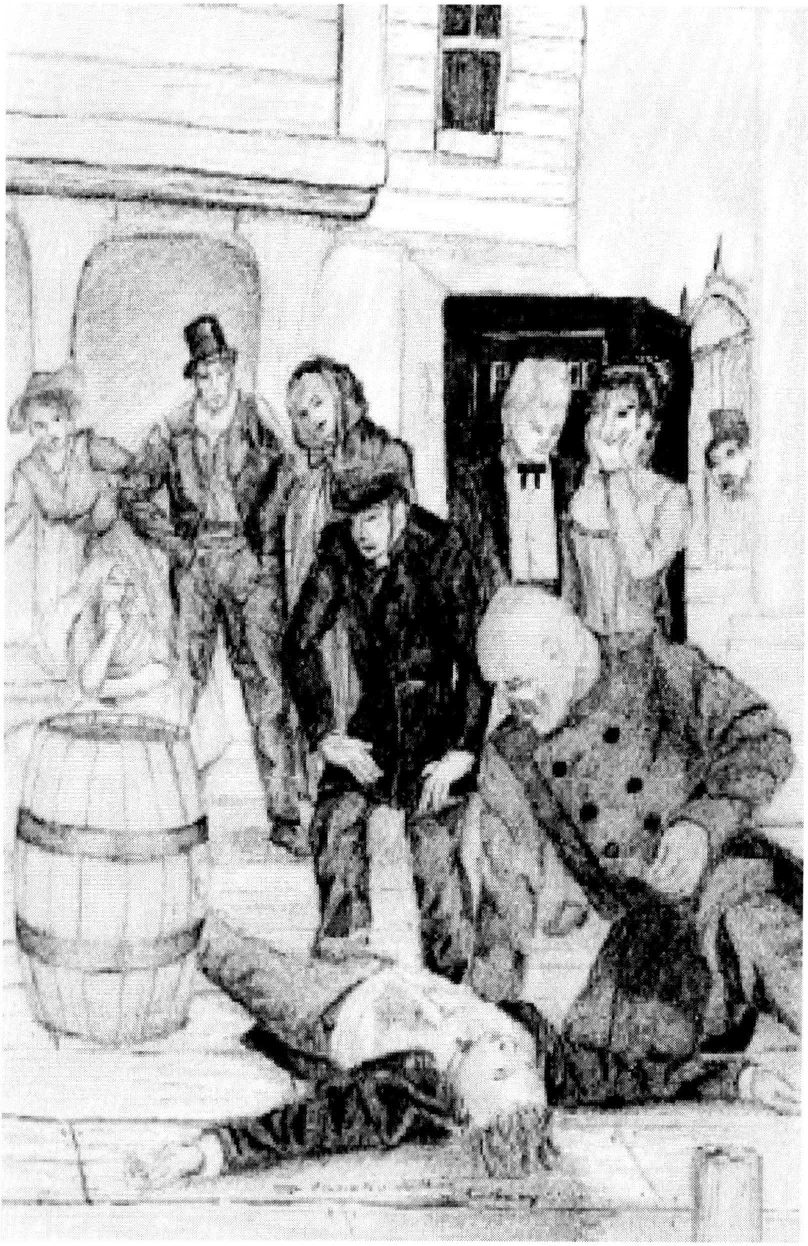

CHAPTER 2

Dragging a body out of the Hudson is common enough on the docks. Sailors are sure-footed at sea, but a drunken man may lose his footing on the slippery wooden slats of the piers or the gangways leading up to the ships. Unfortunate females seeking a better world have been known to cast themselves into the murky waters. There have even been children brought up, little ones who strayed too close to the water's edge, only to be dragged down by the current.

This time, however, there was no question of an accident or suicide. The man hauled out onto the walkway was dressed in evening clothes, with a huge rusty stain all over his once-white shirt front. Great gashes in the man's chest area spoke eloquently of a brutal frontal attack.

The inevitable waterfront crowd had gathered to see the body. Stevedores stopped hauling boxes and bales to and from the ships lined up at the piers. Vendors of hot pies and cold drinks edged their carts closer to the grisly scene. Sailors hung over the railings of their ships to see what was going on. The inevitable gang of street urchins wormed their bodies through the crowd. Undoubtedly, someone would be missing a wallet or a watch by the time the show was over.

"Hey, kid!" One of the men who had taken charge of the body pointed to the largest of the Street Arabs. "There's a dime in it for you if you get the coppers here before the news-hawks." The ragged boy took off at a run.

Uncle Ephraim hauled himself out of his chair to peer out the front window of the office, while Joshua, Michael and I pushed through the gathering crowd to view the body and make the necessary identification as soon as the representatives of the Police and the Press arrived. I carry my sketch pad and pencil everywhere with me, as if I need to have a concrete reminder of what I see, and I record everything I find interesting or amusing or noteworthy. Nothing could be more noteworthy than this! I drew quickly, capturing the condition of the body as it lay on the wooden dock.

Joshua squatted down next to the dripping corpse. "He must have gone back to his rooms to change," he observed. "He was in street clothes when he left the courthouse yesterday."

"Look at them cuts!" someone in the crowd remarked. "Whoever done this was mad for sure."

"Mad crazy, or mad angry?" Michael murmured.

"Possibly both," Joshua replied, in the same low tone. "We've seen this kind of thing before, Michael. This wasn't done with a sailor's knife, nor with the kind of stiletto the gangs use. It was done with a Bowie knife, I'll stake my life on it."

"And where would a New York man find himself an Arkansas toothpick?" Michael's question was rhetorical.

I gave it some thought. "People come home with all sorts of things," I told him. "I've seen Confederate canteens and swords, so why not a knife?"

Joshua stood up and looked down at me with the eyes of one who had been there and seen horrors beyond imagining. "Because, Miss Peggy, the last thing a Confederate soldier would relinquish is his knife. An officer might hand over a sword, a man might abandon his canteen, but those fellows carried their knives until they fell, and then their friends took them and kept them safe. Those Bowie knives cost as much as a soldier made in a month, fine English steel blades and bone or ivory hilts, and they knew how to use them, too. Whoever did this had no idea how to use that knife properly. He just slashed away."

"Or else he was fighting mad and didn't care," Michael added. "Oh, H…." He stopped and looked at me, colored up and amended his expletive. "Hades, here's Williams. Now we're in the soup, but good!"

A carriage marked as New York Metropolitan Police Department drew up at the Bank Street corner of West Street, and Captain

Alexander Williams, better known as "Clubber" emerged, tall and muscular, in his blue uniform coat and cap. He had only recently been assigned the responsibility for Law and Order on the West Side, having made his reputation across town. He was clearly in a mood to assert his dominance in this strange territory. He shouldered his way through the throng, using his night-stick to move whoever did not get out of his way fast enough. I could see why he had got the nickname "Clubber".

The crowd parted before him, as he strode through to gaze upon the sodden object dripping on the boards before him.

"What's this?" he asked.

"The late Mr. Bertram Delacorte," Joshua said. "I'd say he's been in the water since midnight. He's been cut with a Bowie knife, but he may have still been alive when he went in the river. There's a sign of froth on his lips. I'm sure the Medical Examiner will bear me out."

"And who the Hell are you?" Williams tried to stare Joshua down, as he intimidated so many on his beat.

It didn't faze Joshua, who was at least as tall as Williams, and had dealt with the results of five years of military occupation during his sojourn in New Orleans. "I'm Joshua Roth, of the legal firm of Pettigrew and Roth. Our office is right across the street." He gestured with his good arm. "I was this man's lawyer."

"Aha. You're the shyster who got him off, when we had him dead to rights in the Kendall murder." Williams' eyes narrowed, as he assessed Joshua's potential worth as an ally or an antagonist.

"You had false evidence, planted in his rooms. You didn't check his alibi, and I proved that he had one. He had no motive, there was no weapon found anywhere near his person or in his rooms, and he wasn't even there when the murder was committed. You had no case, and you knew it," Joshua said. "If he walked, it was because there was no case against him, and I proved it. The man should never even have been arrested."

"Well," Williams said, looking down at the late Mr. Delacorte, "it don't matter now, does it? He's met his just deserts, right enough, and saved the State of New York the cost of a hangman."

Before further hostilities could be exchanged, a second police vehicle pulled up and discharged a grubby-looking man in a rumpled check suit and new derby hat, bearing the small black satchel that accompanies any medical man anywhere.

Clubber glared at the interloper, who gave him glare for glare.

"What's your business here, Croker?" Williams demanded.

"This is a murder investigations, and as such, is the business of the Coroner's Office, not the New York Police," Mr. Croker said testily.

A third wagon pulled up, this one clearly marked Ambulance. The drivers of the three vehicles jockeyed for position, and their horses added to the din, while growing crowd made for more confusion. A skinny fellow in a well-worn frock coat and battered black felt hat wormed his way to the forefront, armed with a pencil, a notebook, and a gleam in his eye.

"Hallo, Peggy!" he caroled. I recognized Davy Jonas, the most enterprising of the journalists, who would be along as fast as their legs could carry them to chronicle the shocking demise of the scion of one of New York Society's most prominent families. Davy had been a cub reporter when my parents had shocked the city with their "Manny and Specs" articles, and he occasionally regaled me with tales of my parents' adventures. Now he was hot on the scent of an even tastier scandal than the one that had launched Manny's career.

"That's Broadway Bertie Delacorte, right?" he asked, already knowing the answer. He peered over my shoulder and assessed my drawing of the scene. "That's damn' good, Peggy. You got it just right: the copper, the coroner, and the body. What a scoop this can be! I'll bet I can get five bucks for it for you."

"Well…." I demurred. I was flattered by the thought that I might be following in the footsteps of my parents, however modestly, and five dollars is more than Uncle Ephraim pays me per week for my legal duties..

"We may need those drawings ourselves," Joshua said, removing the sketch-pad from my hands. "They may be evidence when this case comes to trial."

By this time Mr. Croker had made his evaluation, which agreed with Joshua's in every particular. He announced that Bertram Delacorte had been murdered approximately ten hours ago, which would have been around midnight. He had been cut with a large-

THE GUILTY CLIENT

bladed implement, and thrown into the river alive. Cause of death was drowning, exacerbated by the knife wounds. A further autopsy would undoubtedly confirm this diagnosis. The body was released into the custody of two burly men, who hauled it unceremoniously into the waiting ambulance wagon, to be taken to the morgue on Mulberry Street.

The rest of the press pack descended on the various official vehicles, but Davy Jonas was already running down Bank Street ahead of them. He had his scoop, and the Sun would be on the streets this evening with a garish headline: Broadway Bertie Slain!

Clubber Williams faced down the reporters with his usual aplomb. "Now, boys," he told them, "this here is unfortunate, but if a man seeks his pleasures in rough company, he's got to take the consequences. Mr. Delacorte was one who liked to go to the shady side of town, so to speak, and he paid the price for it. I'm not going to check every tough customer in New York to see which one had a grudge against this young sprig, for it would do no one any good. I am sorry for his family, who deserved better than this, but this should stand as a warning to those young bloods who feel they should try their hand at out-fighting the gangs."

"Does this mean that the killer of Bertram Delacorte will be let off, free to murder again?" shouted one of the reporters.

"It means that we'll try to find out which of 'em had the worst grudge against him, but it also means that there are very foolish fellows who will go into bad company, and the City of New York cannot be held responsible if their behavior leads to tragedy." Clubber Williams was the very image of outraged propriety.

I could feel my face turning red with suppressed rage. Clubber Williams had more or less told the Press that he would not even try to find the murderer. I had not liked Bertram Delacorte very much, but I resented the idea that he had, in effect, brought his death upon himself.

Uncle Ephraim expressed much the same feelings as soon as Joshua, Michael and I returned to the office and told him what had transpired on the docks.

"Clubber Williams is a corrupt ass," he declared, when we told him what had been said. "He won't make a move unless there's money in it for him."

"There are far too many questions left unanswered," I said. "What was Bertram doing between the time he left the courtroom and the time he went into the river? He must have been celebrating, since he was in evening clothes, but where? And what was he doing near the river anyway? That's not his usual beat; he's not called Broadway Bertie because he hangs about on West Street."

"He could have been killed somewhere else and put into the river later," Michael said.

Joshua shook his head. "He was knifed, and put into the river alive. He was wedged between the barges, so he must have gone in fairly close to here, maybe up near Twentieth Street."

"The, um, establishments, are mostly on West Twenty-Fifth Street," I said. I am not supposed to know that such places exist, let alone where they are, but West Twenty-Fifth Street is known as Satan's Playground for a very good reason. "Bertram was just the sort of man to support them."

Uncle Ephraim nodded sagely. "So, he goes back to his boarding house, changes his clothes, goes to dinner and has some, um, amusement. Then what?"

Another thing occurred to me. "Why was he living in a boarding house anyway?" I asked. "The Delacortes have a perfectly good, large house on Washington Square. His uncle, Mr. Long, has just moved into one of the new brownstones in Murray Hill. Why would he take a room in a boarding house?"

"Could be his doting family had enough of his shenanigans, and threw him out," Michael said, with a laugh. "Coming home at all hours, bringing shame upon the family name by consorting with evildoers. The Delacortes are very much given to Good Works, and the Longs are even bigger sticklers for propriety than the Delacortes.."

"Mmmph!" Uncle Ephraim grunted. The Good Works of the Delacortes were made much of in the Press, but had little effect on the lives of ordinary people. Supporting the construction of the Central Park was all very well, but the ones who used it the most were the Delacortes and the Longs and their set, who drove their carriages there and strolled of a Sunday afternoon.

THE GUILTY CLIENT

The crowd on the docks began to disperse. The office clock chimed noon. I put on my bonnet as I prepared to leave the office to fetch Uncle Ephraim's luncheon from the house on Bank Street.

"I wouldn't go just yet, Miss Peggy," Michael said, with a grin. "You'll want to sit down and look demure. Here comes another client."

I took off my bonnet and sat at my desk. Another carriage had pulled onto the docks, a private conveyance with a gilded crest on the doors and a massively-built coachman tooling the reins. The very sight of it was enough to set Uncle Ephraim's delicate digestive system rumbling. We were about to be honored by the presence of Mr. Henry Ward Long, the most prominent member of the legal profession on Wall Street, the man whose money sat on the desk before us, the man whose nephew had just been hauled out of the river and taken downtown to the Morgue. He would undoubtedly have more questions for us than we were prepared to answer at that moment.

CHAPTER 3

That Mr. Henry Ward Long had descended from the Olympian heights of Wall Street to consult a mere attorney on the West Street docks was unprecedented. He expected lesser folk to come to him, hat in hand, to be instructed or chastised as the case may be. He had summoned Joshua to that office the previous day, to be instructed in the disposition of the case of *People vs. Delacorte*, thus precipitating the events described in the previous section of this report. That he came in his own carriage, complete with coachman, footman, and bodyguard caused a sensation among the crowd still gathered after the removal of the late Broadway Bertie Delacorte.

The carriage alone would have drawn a crowd on West Street. It was not every day that a bottle-green Stanhope drew up on the cobbled street that faced the docks. The pair of gray horses were guided by the hands of a coachman in a green coat and top hat; a footman in matching livery hung on behind, and the presence of a burly man in an ill-fitting street suit and shiny plug hat sitting next to the coachman meant that Mr. Henry Ward Long was expecting trouble and had brought along a personal bodyguard to forestall it.

The coachman scowled at the crowd. The footman hopped down from his perch and opened the carriage so that the august Mr. Long could step forward directly onto the cobbles in front of Uncle Ephraim's office. The bodyguard took up a stand on the other side of the carriage, as if daring anyone to lay a finger on its polished surface.

Mr. Long strode into the office, supremely elegant in a morning coat of understated gray London tailoring, snowy white linen, and high hat. He looked about at the shabby interior of Pettigrew and Roth, Attorneys at Law, and fixed his eyes on me.

THE GUILTY CLIENT

"What is that female doing here?" he demanded.

"You know perfectly well what she's doing. That's my niece Margaret, and she's doing her job, which is more than I can say for that useless youth you wanted to me to take on during the War," Uncle Ephraim retorted. "I suppose you're here because of what just happened."

"What just happened?" Mr. Long looked confused. "I am here because my nephew seems to have disappeared. I had arranged to have a carriage in front of the courthouse, to send him back to his mother after his discharge from official custody. According to my servants, he was not in the courthouse when they arrived with the carriage. I sent someone to that place where he had been residing. He has not been seen there for three days. In short, Pettigrew, he hasn't been seen since he left that courtroom!" Confusion was replaced by anger.

"Oh, he's been seen," Uncle Ephraim said grimly. "He was just taken up out of the river."

The blood seemed to drain out of Mr. Long's face. Joshua slid a chair under him, and Michael helped him into it, then stepped back, into the shadows of what had been the pawn-broker's inner sanctum. It would not do for the Assistant District Attorney to be seen in the offices of the attorneys for the Defense.

"What, exactly, has occurred?" Mr. Long asked, looking hard at Uncle Ephraim and ignoring Joshua completely.

"The body of Mr. Bertram Delacorte has been sent to Mulberry Street for autopsy," Uncle Ephraim said slowly. "We all saw it. I am sorry, Long, for your wife's sake. I know she was fond of the boy. I can't say I'll miss him, though." Uncle Ephraim never minced words, or pretended to emotions he didn't possess.

"To be perfectly honest, Pettigrew, neither will I," Mr. Long admitted, in a rare burst of humanity, the first crack in his armor of self-assurance. He immediately recovered, and resumed his air of superiority. "However, my wife lost most of her family during the War. It's no secret that her brother fought with the Rebels, as did so many of the Virginians from West Point, while Delacorte did his duty for the Union. When he died of his wounds, Bertram was the light of his mother's life. She is a lady of great sensibility, as you may recall."

Uncle Ephraim made a sound that could have been a whistle or a laugh. "I remember she would take on at a moment's notice," he said. "As I heard it, Delacorte was stationed in Washington until the War broke out, and then he sent his wife and son North, to get them out of danger."

"My wife's sister stayed with her husband's family until after the War," Long explained. "Then she decided to take a European tour, with her son, so that he could absorb some of the culture of the Old World. She returned last winter, to make her home with my wife while her son continued his education."

"It didn't seem to do him much good, according to what I've heard," Uncle Ephraim said, dryly. "Broadway Bertie, they call him. He's been seen in some rare places."

Long frowned. "Did someone in one of those places kill him?"

"Now how would I know that?" Uncle Ephraim asked.

"Your man, Roth, let him go, after the arraignment," Mr. Long pointed out. "He might have seen or heard something."

Joshua's face took on the blank look of someone who has just recalled something they wished desperately to forget.

"I must tell you, sir, that Mr. Delacorte was in a great hurry to be away from the court," he told Mr. Long. "No sooner were the charges against him dismissed than he was up and out of there. I didn't even get congratulated for my work. He ran out of the courtroom, and I could not even tell you in which direction he went once he left the courthouse. It was inexcusable, I know, to let him go alone, when the true murderer was still on the loose, but he gave me no choice."

Mr. Long sat silently in his chair, frowning. Then he said, "I want that murderer caught and punished."

"Then go to the police," Uncle Ephraim said.

"I want you to find out who did this."

"Me?" Uncle Ephraim sat up straight in his chair. "This is a legal firm, not a detection agency. Go to the Pinkertons, or the police. You hired us to clear your nephew of the charge of murder, and this we have done. Mr. Roth over here did the work the police should have done, and cleared him. Case dismissed, case closed. Mark it down, Peggy."

THE GUILTY CLIENT

I looked up from my desk, where I had been taking notes of the conversation and amusing myself by sketching Mr. Long as he sat facing Uncle Ephraim: the one so very conservative and fashionable, the other comfortably unkempt and shabby. Mr. Long shot me a look of extreme distaste.

"Why do you permit that girl to continue here? You ought to hire a man to do her work, and release her into the proper sphere."

Uncle Ephraim settled himself back into his chair. "Peggy does what she does very well, and she does it for less than I'd have to pay some young sprig who'll be on his way to your fancy law school in a year or two. Why should I have to train someone over and over again, when I've got a perfectly good law clerk right here to hand? I thought we had this out when you tried to foist that lad of yours upon me back in '63. I told you then that I didn't like his manner, and I haven't changed my mind now that he's no longer in this world to sneer at 'hedge-lawyers'. That was what you called my sort, wasn't it? 'Ill-trained and half-literate, with no more knowledge of the Law than some charlatan who sets himself up as a Revivalist preacher in the back woods of Arkansas has of Theology.' That was what you said before the Legislature, wasn't it? When you tried to get that bill passed, to regulate the legal profession by setting up something called a Bar Association? How did you phrase it? 'A means whereby the practitioners of Law might be held accountable to the Public for their education and behavior.'"

Uncle Ephraim's face was beginning to take on the same tinge of purple as Mr. Long's. I had heard this tirade before. Mr. Long was in the forefront of a faction who were attempting to regulate the professions and weed out those whom they deemed unacceptable. Doctors were to be trained in medical schools, and lawyers were to be college men before they took on the rigors of legal education. This, of course, would preclude the old style of "reading law" or "reading medicine", which amounted to a sort of apprenticeship. Uncle Ephraim had risen to his present position under the old system, by reading law with Aunt Sarah's father, Judge Robert Willson. There were no barriers to women under that system; presumably, I could, after studying and memorizing the legal codes, take the examination and pass the Bar myself. Mr. Long and his cronies would have none

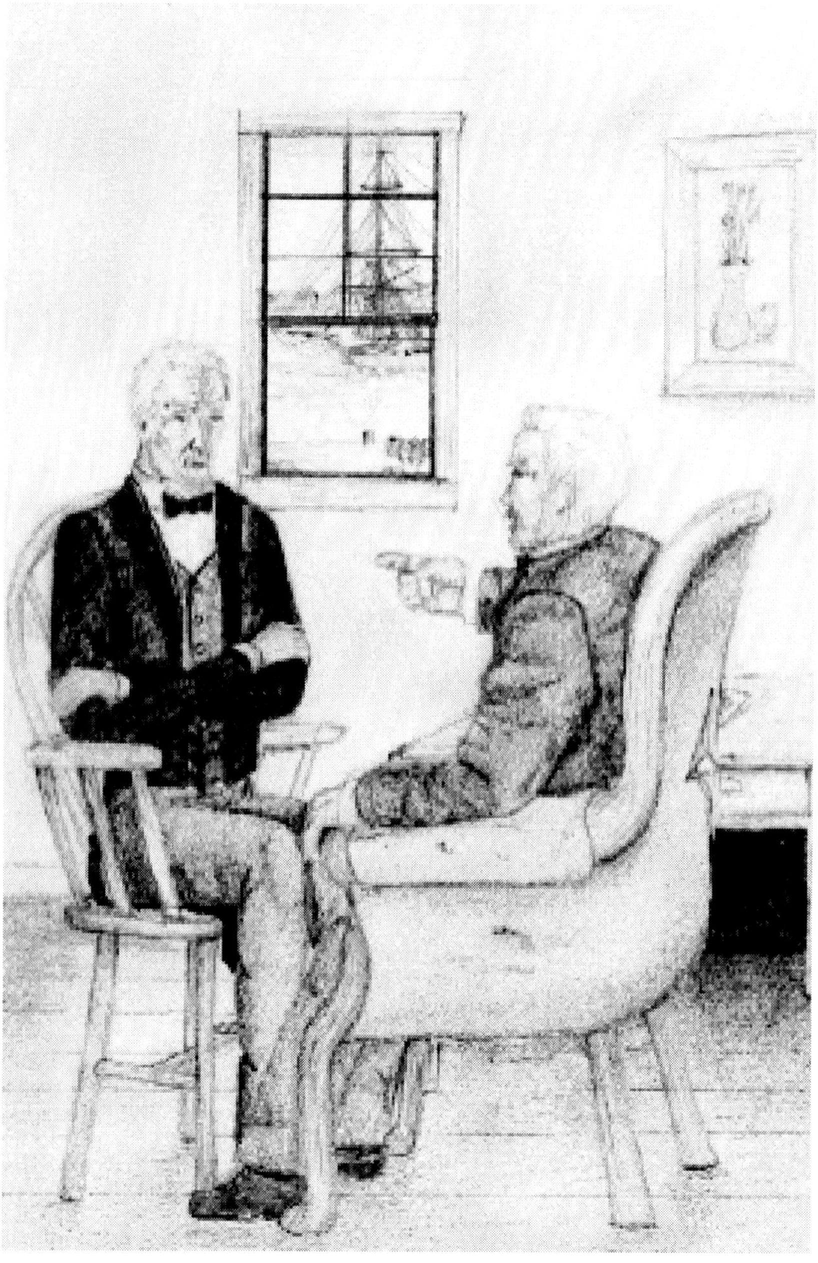

of this, and Uncle Ephraim knew it, and so did I. There would be no women lawyers in New York City or New York State as long as Mr. Long and his associates made the rules. No one would be admitted to the Bar who had not graduated from an accredited School of Law, and no accredited School of Law would accept a female into their halls. Ergo, no woman would be granted the dignity becoming an Attorney at Law in the State of New York. Q.E.D.

Mr. Long drew a deep breath, and willed himself to calm. He fixed his gaze upon Uncle Ephraim, and spoke with sincerity. "Pettigrew, you and I have had our differences over the years, but I came to you in the first place because I know you to be an honest man. None of my colleagues would take Bertram on as a client. All of them believed him to be guilty of murder. Only you, Pettigrew, only you were willing to find the evidence to clear him. Now I ask you, in good faith and in good conscience, to find his killer."

"It's the job of the police," Uncle Ephraim demurred. "Offer Williams a big enough reward, and he'll find whoever did it."

Mr. Long sniffed loudly in disdain. "Oh, he'll find someone, and will probably find evidence to hang him, too, but it won't be the right person, I'll be bound. Pettigrew, I do not ask favors lightly. Name a price, and I'll pay it."

Uncle Ephraim smiled affably. "Well, then, Long, I may be able to assist the police in their inquiries, as my friends in the Press put it. All I ask is that Miss Peggy here be allowed to read law and take the Bar examinations, fair and square, without prejudice."

Mr. Long stiffened in his chair. "I cannot do that! It is against everything I stand for!"

"It's my price, Long, take it or leave it. I nail the killer, you let Peggy read Law."

Mr. Long transferred his steely gaze to me. I could feel myself blushing at the scrutiny of those cold blue eyes. I had been working in Uncle Ephraim's office for nearly ten years, certainly long enough to grasp most of the particulars of maritime law that formed the basis of his practice. I could have written a ship's contract from memory, filling in the particulars of one or another vessel and its captain and its owner, simply from having copied so many of them over the years. I was familiar with the nuances of salvage and

, and what percentage of damaged goods could be charged ḯipping company without too much risk to the owners. I had even accompanied Uncle Ephraim to the Tombs to negotiate for the release of sailors jailed for various sorts of misbehavior, ranging from Drunk and Disorderly to Manslaughter. More than anything I wanted to be able to add Attorney at Law to Miss Margaret Pettigrew, but not this way!

Mr. Long took another deep breath. He rose majestically from his chair, looked at the furnishings of Pettigrew and Roth, and spoke as from on high. "If you find the one who murdered my nephew, I will permit Miss Pettigrew to apply to take the examination for the New York Bar," he pronounced. "More than that I cannot do. I cannot influence my colleagues to extend any more favors for her, or any other presumptuous female who wishes to enter the legal profession."

"Well, it's a start," Uncle Ephraim said. He maneuvered himself onto his feet and offered his hand to Mr. Long. Mr. Long took it with three gloved fingers, and left the office. The footman, who had been lounging alongside the carriage, jumped to Attention and opened the door. The bodyguard, who had been on the far side of the carriage, clambered into the seat next to the coachman. The coachman whistled to the team, and Mr. Henry Ward Long and his equipage headed back towards Wall Street.

Michael emerged from the dark corner where he had lurked during the interview. "Well, Mother of Mercy, what do you think of that?"

"I think it's very interesting that Long should come up to see me, and not send for me to see him," Uncle Ephraim said. "I think it's even more interesting what he didn't say."

Joshua said nothing for a few moments. Then he said, "Michael, I never told you about that last case I had in New Orleans, did I?"

Michael shook his head. "I got word you were pretty cut up about how it turned out. It's why I came down and fetched you back to New York."

"It's not a pretty story. Not for Miss Peggy's ears, anyways. There was a young girl, one of those Free Persons of Color. She was a seamstress, and had to pass by a gang of Regulars who were set to guarding a corner where there had been some activity. The sergeant was a loud-mouthed brute, who forced his attentions on her, and she responded with a pair of scissors. I was told to defend her, and I did, and I proved to those white male jurors that she had every right to take those scissors to the man who tried to assault her. And so she was let go…without any protection."

He stopped and swallowed hard. I could tell how much this had affected him, and how difficult it was for him to tell us this horrible tale.

"They found her the day after she'd been released. Her body was left in the street, with her clothes pulled up, and a pair of scissors…" He could not go on. I pictured the scene and shuddered.

"That was when I resigned my commission. The thought of what had happened to that woman haunted me. I wasn't supposed to get her off, Michael; she was supposed to hang for the crime of defending herself against an assault, because the man doing it wore Union blue, and we had to maintain Order in a lawless city. If you hadn't found me, I would probably have wound up in some river myself." He clutched at Michael's shoulder with his good hand.

Michael blinked away the sudden tears and patted his old commander's hand. "I pay my debts, Joshua. You took a bullet for me, and probably saved my life. I couldn't let you go to Hell…I mean Hades…without trying to stop you. Besides," he added, trying to lighten the seriousness of the moment, "I was able to pay back more than one debt by passing you on to Uncle Ephraim here when I moved into the Prosecutors' offices. He needed a partner, you needed a position. That's the way it was, and all debts are now cleared."

Joshua gave Michael one of his rare smiles. "There are always debts to be paid," he said. "But in this case, I can't rest easy. I must have missed something that would have led to the real killer of Suzanna Kendall, and Bertram knew it."

"If that's so," Uncle Ephraim said, slowly, "then what we have to do is find out who really killed Mrs. Kendall. That'll lead us to whoever killed Bertram Delacorte."

"And where do we start looking?" I asked.

"You go back home, and tell your Aunt Sarah that you'll go with her for an afternoon call at Mrs. Smith's," Uncle Ephraim told me. "When you do, find out all you can about Mrs. Kendall and Bertram Delacorte, and when and where their paths might have crossed. As for you, Joshua, you and Michael get over to Mulberry Street and find out what you can about the Kendall murder, and see if the police have something up their sleeves they didn't bring out when young Delacorte was arrested."

"And what about you, sir?" Joshua asked.

"I'm going to sit here and consider a few things that Mr. Henry Ward Long didn't tell me," Uncle Ephraim said.

He settled back into his chair, laced his hands over his midsection, and smiled benevolently at us, as I put on my bonnet, Joshua and Michael retrieved their hats, and the three of us went our various ways.

CHAPTER 4

I DIDN'T HAVE FAR TO GO. Uncle Ephraim and Aunt Sarah still lived in the house that Aunt Sarah's father had given them when they married, a small brick structure on the south side of Bank Street. It was one of a row of four that had been built when the area had been a pleasant retreat from the hurly-burly of the City, before the dreadful fires of '35 that had engulfed the wooden houses erected before the Revolution. There are not many such private houses left in the city, and this one was already considered a relic, full of odd noises and secrets. I had lived there ever since my mother had put me into Aunt Sarah's arms, as she left for the gold fields, never to return.

New York had grown northwards since the house was built. The Fashionable World had moved to the East Side, and there was little pleasant about Bank Street now. There was a livery stable at the West Street end of the street, a French laundry across the street from Uncle Ephraim's door, and saloons on either end of the block. The houses on either side of ours had already been converted into tenement flats, inhabited by Irish and German families whose menfolk worked the docks, while the women worked the laundry, and the children ran about underfoot without much supervision at all. To the east the clatter and clash of the construction crews building the new elevated railway on Greenwich Street made a mighty din. The elevated had been hailed as a modern marvel. It might be a convenience to some, but it was yet another barrier separating Aunt Sarah from her friends and relations on the East Side.

Aunt Sarah had been trying to persuade Uncle Ephraim to move to the new brownstones on Murray Hill, across town in the 30's ever since the end of the War. Uncle Ephraim will have none of it.

In vain did Aunt Sarah point out that although we do have water laid on, gas lighting has not yet reached the West Side, and we must depend on kerosene lamps for lighting after dark. Our kitchen has a closed stove, but we use wood, and not coal, to fuel it. The necessary facility is a mere shed, attached to the back of the house, and can be very uncomfortable in the winter. Aunt Sarah longed for the comforts of gas lighting and a proper water closet. Uncle Ephraim ignored the inconveniences, and pointed out that he would have to hire a carriage every day to get to his office on West Street if he lived clear across town. As for keeping his own carriage and the horses and driver and groom that go with it, he refuses to even consider the possibility.

I am allowed latch-key privileges, so I let myself in the front door, thinking to take off my bonnet and refresh myself before sitting down to luncheon with Aunt Sarah.

I didn't expect to see our general maid cowering in the hall, waiting for me. Mandy is small and slight, and is of a timorous temperament, a natural consequence of having been hunted down with the rest of the girls from the Colored Orphan's Asylum during the Draft Riots. She is in constant expectation of another lynching mob raging down Bank Street. As a result, she tends to shy away from any signs of conflict, such as loud and angry tones of voice, both of which were in evidence as soon as I opened the door.

"Isn't luncheon ready yet?" I asked.

"It's the new cook, Miss Peggy," Mandy said. "Miz Sarah's trying to talk to her, but she's one of them foreigners, and she don't understand a word you say to her."

"Oh dear." It seemed inadequate, judging from the sounds of battle emerging from the kitchen. "I'd better see what I can do."

"You do that," Mandy said. "I've set the table, but I don't know what there is to put on it. Is Mister Ephraim coming home for lunch?"

"I think he'll have his lunch at Schultz's," I said. Uncle Ephraim was used to taking his midday meal at the saloon next door to the office, where he could indulge in the free lunch and absorb the gossip of the docks at the same time.

I headed for the back of the house. The kitchen is on the same level as the parlor and dining room, unlike the new brownstones that put the kitchen and the servants' rooms in the cellar, below the street level. The parlors are on one side of the stairs leading up to the bed-chambers, the dining room and Uncle Ephraim's den are on the other. The servants' rooms are on the third floor, and the attics are just under the roof. There are fireplaces in each room, instead of central heating, much to Aunt Sarah's discomfort during cold winters.

Aunt Sarah does not usually deal with servants. She leaves that up to me. It must have taken a great deal of effort to get her to descend from her throne and confront a cook in her own kitchen.

Aunt Sarah's shrill voice could be heard all the way into the front hall. "No, no, no! This is a chicken…"

"*E pollo.*" A more musical, deeper tone, a contralto to Aunt Sarah's soprano.

"Yes, and it is to be cooked without too much garlic or pepper. Mr. Pettigrew has a delicate digestion."

"Ees *pollo alla cacciatore.* Ees *buono.*"

I stepped into the kitchen, where Aunt Sarah, small and plump, was trying to explain herself to our latest cook, a large woman in a flowing skirt, laced-up bodice, and embroidered blouse, her hair tied back tidily under a flowered scarf.

"Margaret, this is Maria Luisa," Aunt Sarah said. "She's from Napoli. I think that's in Italy. She was looking for a position, and she says she can cook."

"*Si, di Napoli.*" Maria Luisa nodded, setting her earrings into motion. "I cook."

"What are you cooking for dinner?" I asked, trying to recognize the ingredients. I could see something simmering on the stove, and there certainly were dismembered chickens on the table, but some of the vegetables that would accompany them were not familiar to my untutored eye. I did recognize carrots and cabbages from the little kitchen-garden behind the house, where I try to grow vegetables, not always successfully.

"*Pollo alla cacciatore, con salsa rossa e fettucini. Minestrone.*"

"A red sauce?" I ventured to translate.

"I cook." She folded her arms and glared at us, as if daring us to deny that she could perform her appointed task.

I pointed to the flour and eggs. "Are you also making pastry?"

"*Si, pasta. Fettucini. Molto buono.*" Maria Luisa nodded and smiled happily. "*Per Signor e Signora.* I cook."

"Aunt Sarah, perhaps we should let Maria Luisa get on with it," I said, edging my aunt out of the kitchen. "Is there bread and butter?" I asked, trying to recall the words used by the last Italian cook we'd had. "*Pane?* Cheese? Um, provolone?"

Maria Luisa frowned. "I cook!" She punctuated the sentence by bringing down a cleaver on one of the chickens, neatly removing a leg section.

'Perhaps we should take our luncheon at Mrs. Smith's," I suggested. "Uncle Ephraim thought we might call there today. We have to let them know that Mr. Delacorte will not be coming back to his rooms."

"What!?" Aunt Sarah hustled me out of the kitchen and into the back parlor, where she could sit in her favorite chair and absorb the news.

I explained what had happened that morning. "I assume someone was sent to tell Mrs. Delacorte that her son had met with an unfortunate accident, but no one thought to tell Mrs. Smith. Poor woman, first one boarder gets killed and then another one. It's enough to make people think twice about staying with her."

That was enough to get Aunt Sarah ready to leave. "Send one of the Murphy boys down to the livery," she ordered Mandy, who ran to the front door to call one of the urchins who hung about the streets, waiting for such an errand. "I must go see Phoebe Smith at once. And then, while we're on East Twenty-third Street, we might call on Mrs. Day and Mrs. Roosevelt."

"And dinner?" I asked.

Aunt Sarah smiled weakly. "Maria Luisa seems to know what she's about. I'm sure dinner will be just fine." She looked me over. "Margaret, you cannot go calling in that shabby dress. Mandy, get Miss Margaret into her blue walking dress. And Margaret, don't wear that bonnet any more. Bonnets are completely passé. It's hats, now, straw hats." She bustled off to put on her own hat, leaving me to Mandy's ministrations.

Mandy helped me out of my working clothes and into something more suitable for paying morning calls (which are always done in the afternoon, between three and five.) I much prefer my plain brown dress with three petticoats to the so-called walking outfits with full hoops demanded by Aunt Sarah. Luckily for me, the narrower hoops are now the style, with the fullness in the back instead of all around. There were times during those years when hoops were at their widest, when I was certain that people on the street were wondering whether one of Professor Lowe's balloons had landed whenever I had to pass by. No amount of tight lacing can give me a slender figure, and I refuse to destroy my health and digestion trying to have one. I am what I am, and while corsets are necessary to maintain modesty, I prefer the ones that are stiffened with starch and whalebone to the steel-bound contraptions favored by some slaves to Fashion.

By the time the carriage had arrived, I was properly attired for an afternoon's social intercourse. I had exchanged the brown poplin for a dark blue overdress and lighter blue underskirt. My bonnet was replaced by a small hat, trimmed with blue feathers. I had gloves and reticule, and looked quite the young lady. Aunt Sarah was clad in dark purple, with a larger, more extravagant hat.

"Cards?" she asked.

I checked my reticule. "I have them," I assured her. I also made sure that I had a small sketch pad and pencil. I might see or hear something useful, and a record should be kept on the spot.

A thought occurred to me. "I hope we won't be the first to bring the bad news."

Aunt Sarah would have none of that. "Better that they learn the sad news from us than that they read it in the newspapers," she said. "Come along, Margaret. We can't keep the horses waiting."

Our favorite driver, Reuben, was up on the box. He knew our routines of old, and was willing to put up with Aunt Sarah's fussiness for the sake of the monthly fee Uncle Ephraim paid him to make himself available whenever Aunt Sarah needed him.

"Mrs. Smith's," Aunt Sarah said, and we were on our way.

CHAPTER 5

CROSSING MANHATTAN AT ANY HOUR is fraught with danger. Crossing at noon is the worst possible time for such a trek. Carriages of all sorts, pulled by blooded steeds; large vans and drays, hauled by cart-horses of vast proportions and vaster capacities; little carts, hitched to ponies; even goats and dogs are enlisted in the movement of goods and persons from one side of Manhattan Island to the other. Pedestrians cross the streets at their peril, picking their way around the piles left by the horses, goats and dogs, and trusting that their drivers will occasionally let a foot-traveler pass by.

Aunt Sarah and I were launched into this maelstrom of animals and vehicles, as Reuben steered his way through the traffic. From Bank Street, around the piles of girders for the elevated railroad on Greenwich Street, to Fourteenth Street, and from there across town, around Union Square, and north on Fifth Avenue to Mrs. Smith's boarding house on East Twenty-third Street, between Fifth and Madison Avenues, we jogged along in small increments as the driver found space to insert the hackney-cab. From time to time our journey was enlivened by the exchanges between Reuben and his fellow-drivers. My vocabulary was enhanced, although I doubted whether Aunt Sarah would have approved of some of the epithets used by Reuben to describe the other coachmen and cabbies who dared to impede his progress.

I took advantage of the enforced proximity to Aunt Sarah to plumb her knowledge of the more arcane genealogies and scandals of Society.

"Should we leave cards at Mrs. Long's?" I asked innocently. "Mr. Long called at Uncle Ephraim's office, and said that Mrs. Delacorte and Bertram had made their home with him after they came back from Europe. Won't it seem a bit ghoulish? It's possible that they haven't even been notified that he's dead."

"In that case, it's far better that they get the news from someone who can break it gently," Aunt Sarah said. She peered out the window of the cab, then pulled her head in quickly as a large cart-horse let loose a blast of air that could only add more to the reek of horses and humanity that is the peculiar odor of New York City in the Spring.

"Why on Earth do we even bother to leave cards with the Longs and the Delacortes," I complained. "They're never at home to us."

"I don't let that stop me," Aunt Sarah said. "My Aunt Willson took them up, well before the War, and she would have insisted that I continue the connection. If they choose to cut me, that is their look-out." She sniffed loudly, but whether in scorn or to eliminate the effluvium of New York's streets I could not say. She went on, rambling to herself. "I would have thought those Patterson girls would have forgotten all that nonsense by now, but those Southern belles have memories like steel traps. They never forget and they never forgive. You mark my words, Margaret, the War will never be over until the last of those Southerners is gone, and maybe not even then."

"Forgive what?" I asked, hoping to prompt more reminiscences.

Aunt Sarah's plump features hardened into a stern mask. "It was a very long time ago, Margaret. Before you were even born. Water under the bridge, you might say." There was something there, I knew it, something that had been kept from me for many years. Whenever the subject of what happened before the War came up, the conversation would be cut short, or I would be sent on an errand. This time, Aunt Sarah could not escape. I would find out what it was that no one wanted me to know.

"I know Mrs. Delacorte and Mrs. Long had a brother who was with the Rebels," I said. "Weren't they from Washington, or somewhere like that?"

"Baltimore," Aunt Sarah corrected me. "They'd come up from Baltimore, right after the Panic of '37, to mend their fortunes. Their mother's family was from Virginia, and their father was in shipping, or so they said, and they claimed to be related to that woman who married one of Emperor Napoleon's brothers. They certainly created a stir, the pair of them. The Southern Belles, they were called, and they were taken up by all the best people. Even my Aunt Willson, who was most particular, called on them and had them to one of her cotillion parties. We once formed a cotillion square, the Patterson sisters, myself and Katerina, as she was then. Your mother, my dear," she added.

"Was that before you married Uncle Ephraim?" I ventured.

"We were courting," Aunt Sarah admitted. "He was somewhat slimmer then, and was considered quite dashing, in his way, and my father, Judge Willson, thought he had a good deal of promise, in spite of his connection with journalists, through his brother Emanuel. Emanuel was called Manny, and he was considered a raffish, Bohemian sort, being a writer for Mr. Bennett. Ephraim, of course, was always quite gentlemanly, and my father was proud of the way he conducted himself."

It is always difficult to imagine ones elders as they must have been thirty years before. I've seen the faded daguerreotypes, Uncle Ephraim in a dark suit and high collar, not much different from his current attire, and Aunt Sarah, in a figured dress, standing beside him, her hand on his shoulder. There is a similar daguerreotype of my parents, Manny in checked trousers, his coat thrust aside to reveal the embroidered vest underneath; Specs in a striped dress with a lace collar, her trademark glasses slipping down her nose. I resemble Manny in figure, and Specs in coloring. The result is more suited to the Old Masters than the New Woman: large and fair, with a prominent frontage.

The carriage jerked forward for another few yards. I said, "I assume the beautiful Southern girls got their wishes, and married into New York Society."

"Oh, they did very well for themselves," Aunt Sarah replied. "Nerissa married Henry Ward Long, after I turned him down."

"Mr. Long courted you?" No wonder he and Uncle Ephraim were at odds! Old rivalries die hard, even in New York, where everything changes constantly, and today's rival may well be tomorrow's ally.

Aunt Sarah smiled to herself. "Oh, yes, he did. I wasn't a bad catch, you know. My father was a City Magistrate, and the Willsons had been here since the Revolution. Oh, yes, I could have married him, but there was something about him that I just didn't like. He seemed like a cold fish next to Ephraim, who could set a room rocking with laughter when he chose to speak up. So I chose Ephraim, and my father gave us the house on Bank Street as a wedding-gift."

"So you've said." I'd heard that part of the story often enough, but not that the rival in question was Henry Ward Long. "And the other sister was the one who married Andrew Delacorte."

"Yes. That was Juliet." Aunt Sarah's smile faded. "The more beautiful, it was said, but I never really understood why. Nerissa was beautiful, too, in a cold, hard way. Juliet was temperamental, even then, happy one minute, in tears the next. She carried on terribly until her parents let her have her way and marry her handsome soldier. Lieutenant Delacorte, he was then, and they were terrified that he'd be sent to Mexico, but he was stationed in Washington City, and got promoted to Captain soon after that. They made him a Colonel when the War started, and he led the New York regiment very well."

"Until he was wounded, and died of it," I said.

Aunt Sarah sighed. "It's horrible, the way some of the men died in hospital. As for Juliet Delacorte, I haven't spoken to her in years. She was in Washington City, and once the War started, and Colonel Delacorte sent her North, she wasn't made very welcome here, not even by the Delacortes. They were delighted when she took off for Europe, just as soon as it was safe to travel."

"Which explains why she moved in with her sister and Mr. Long on her return," I said. There must have been a terrible thought in the woman's mind, that her husband had killed her brother, or perhaps vice versa. No wonder she hung onto Bertram so tightly.

"Well," Aunt Sarah said, her voice dropping, although there was no one but the two of us in the cab," I did hear that Mr. Long was not pleased to have both Mrs. Delacorte and Mr. Bertram living with him. When the old gentleman passed to his Heavenly reward, it was suggested that Juliet should return to the Delacorte house to attend to old Mrs. Delacorte as her companion, while young Mr. Bertram Delacorte should find more suitable lodgings elsewhere."

"Such as Mrs. Smith's boarding-house?" I didn't think that was very likely. "You'd think that a young man like Mr. Delacorte would take lodgings, or perhaps find one of the new French flats." I peeked out the window of the cab, to see how far we had progressed in our own trek along Fourteenth Street. My eye was caught by a distinctive bottle-green carriage in the general press of the traffic, guided by a coachman in a dark green livery, with a tough-looking fellow with a drooping mustache and a livid scar running across his face and under his hat, sitting next to him. I had seen that shade of green before, and the tough on the box, shouting down at the rest of the traffic, was certainly the same bodyguard who had protected Mr. Long from the crowd on the docks. I frowned and wondered whether Mr. Long had sent his carriage ahead of us to send his wife and her sister the sad news of Bertram's passing, and whether he was in it himself.

I realized that I had missed several paragraphs of Aunt Sarah's monologue.

"It was the money, of course," Aunt Sarah burbled on. "It's all money these days, not Family, the way it was then, before the War. Most of the really well-connected people lived near Washington Square, and we all called on each other regularly, and had each other to dine. My Aunt Willson made sure that I was invited to all the parties and dinner, and we all knew each other: the Delacortes, the Longs, the Van Horns, the Schuylers and the Schermerhorns."

"Really?" I tried to picture Aunt Sarah as a girl, in the wide sleeves and elaborate hair styles of the '30's.

Aunt Sarah seemed to be lost in contemplation of her glorious days as a debutante. "Katerina Van Horn was my dearest friend. She met Manny, through me and my connection with Ephraim. Old Gustave Van Horn was outraged when the pair eloped, but to hear Katerina tell it, the second Mrs. Van Horn was the sort of stepmother one finds in Herr Grimm's fairy-tales. And Manny insisted that he was playing the chivalrous knight, getting her away from a pair of ogres. And so he and she became Manny and Specs, and they wrote stories together for Mr. Bennett at the *Sun*."

I'd heard part of this story, of course. I knew that Specs was really Katerina Van Horn, of the Staten Island clan, whose current representative was challenging Commodore Vanderbilt for supremacy in the shipping field. It was interesting to note that I might well be have a claim on this moneyed family, but since I no contact with them nor they with me since my birth, I ignored the possibilities, and concentrated on the present case.

Aunt Sarah went on and on. "I was rather in awe of Katerina, you know. She was quite intrepid, and as long as Manny and Specs wrote only for the newspapers, no one paid them much attention, because none of our set ever read that sort of scandalous stuff anyway."

I nudged Aunt Sarah into the Present, even as the carriage lurched into a gap between two pony-carts, and turned into Fifth Avenue. The bottle-green carriage veered into another gap and shot ahead of us, evoking a roar of rage and some choice language from Reuben.

"What happened to change all that?"

Aunt Sarah closed her eyes, as if considering all aspects of what she was about to reveal. Then she opened them and said, "Have you ever read 'Belle of New York'?"

"My parents' book?" It was known as The Book, the one that changed everything. It came out just after I was born, and the story I was told was that Manny and Specs had written it while Specs was unable to perform her journalistic rounds, because of my imminent arrival.

"Yes. That book. It was considered quite racy, you know."

"Really? Of course, I suppose all the characters are really people in New York Society, but that was over twenty years ago, and no one knows or cares about that now."

"They certainly cared about it then," Aunt Sarah said. "Part of the plot had to do with a young woman from the South, her brother, who was an Army officer just out of West Point, and a servant who resembled her mistress quite closely."

"Oh. I see." And suddenly I did. The mating habits of the Southern aristocracy were considered scandalous in those days before Emancipation. There were whispered rumors of male travelers to Southern plantations who were offered their choice of female slaves, much as in an Oriental harem, and of Southern mistresses, who treated their husbands' concubines with terrible ferocity. "And the Patterson sisters. . ."

"Thought that the book referred to them and their brother," Aunt Sarah finished for me. "They even brought suit, claiming defamation of character!"

"That was stupid of them," I said bluntly. "If you really want people to read a book, tell them it's about some kind of scandal. Was the book about them?"

"As to that, who can say? Katerina insisted that none of her characters were based on specific individuals, but only on general types who could be seen in New York Society. The book sold very well, as scandalous books will sell for a time, and Ephraim insisted that some of the money should be put away for you. But just then the news came that gold had been discovered in California, and Manny thought that it might be a good idea for the two of them to go there, and let the fire die down, so to speak."

"How old was I? Two or three?"

"You were three years old, and a little dear," Aunt Sarah said, patting my cheek. "The two of them were terribly fond of you, but there was no taking you with them on such a dangerous trip. Katerina put you into my arms and said, 'Take care of her, Sarah, we'll be back next year with a story that will blow the roof off!'"

"And that was the last you saw of either of them," I finished the tale. "And the scandal died down because a new book came out."

"Mrs. Stowe's book surpassed anything that Specs ever wrote," Aunt Sarah agreed. "Ephraim was very glad that he'd made his brother put the royalties for 'Belle of New York' in your name. It'll be a nice portion, when you marry. I only wish your parents were here to see you now!" She sniffed loudly, but that might have been at the sight of a dead goat lying in the road.

"I'm not about to marry someone who wants to marry me for my fortune," I said firmly.

"It's not a fortune," Aunt Sarah said. "A competence, really."

"Enough to live on?" I asked.

"I suppose so," Aunt Sarah said, with another sigh. "If you insist on dwindling into an old maid."

I regarded the ruffled front of my afternoon dress. "I am hardly dwindling, Aunt Sarah, and if that new cook has her way, I will have to go on one of those new reducing regimens in order to fit the new styles."

Before Aunt Sarah could respond, the carriage lurched once

THE GUILTY CLIENT

again, and our driver announced, "We're here."

He climbed down from the box to open the door so that we could get out on the Fifth Avenue side of East Twenty-third Street, since Aunt Sarah insisted that we must not be seen leaving a hired carriage. She would have the driver pick us back up in two hours at the same place, in front of Mr. Stewart's store. I used the time we spent in walking that long block to Mrs. Smith's boarding house in digesting the information I had received. Somewhere in that mass of gossip I was certain must be a clue to what had happened to Mrs. Suzanna Kendall and Mr. Bertram Delacorte.

Out of the corner of my eye I saw the bottle-green carriage making its way up Fifth Avenue. Mrs. Long and her sister would soon receive word of what had happened to young Bertram. I only hoped I could find out what I needed to know before the doors of New York Society closed for good on what promised to be another sensational scandal.

CHAPTER 6

New York is full of boarding-houses of all sorts, ready to provide lodgings and meals for people who, for one reason or another, do not wish to have the burden of home ownership, and are well enough off to avoid the noisome tenements of slums like Five Points. There are sailors' boarding houses, which are little more than way-stations; theatrical boarding houses, whose proprietors are often members of the profession who have fallen out of favor with the public; run-of-the-mill boarding houses, such as the one that accommodates Joshua and Michael, usually run by a widow who opens her home to transients; and then there is Mrs. Smith's.

Mrs. Smith has established herself in what was once an elegant mansion, whose previous owners decided to move farther uptown, away from the commercial establishments of Fifth Avenue. Her clientele is restricted to persons who can provide references, often from the former Confederate states, who may not be welcome in other places. How she and Aunt Sarah came to be acquainted I have no idea, but there is genuine friendship between them. I can only assume that Aunt Sarah gives Mrs. Smith a certain cachet; Mrs. Smith gives Aunt Sarah a place to ferret out information about doings on the East Side, and both of them enjoy each others' company. It seems to work very well, but I had my doubts about whether Aunt Sarah would be quite so welcome at Mrs. Smith's after we gave her our sad news about Mr. Bertram Delacorte and his shocking demise.

Mrs. Smith is a slender woman, given to much fluttering and sighing, with that slurring of the vowels that denotes the women of the South. Mr. Smith is a mysterious figure, seen fleetingly from time to time in the back parlor. There are three Smith daughters and two Smith sons, all enjoying the benefits of education in New

York's finest schools. They inhabit the highest story of the house, in a separate apartment, where they may live their lives apart from the boarders. The only Smith child allowed to come down to the general parlor was Miss Alva, a sharp-eyed miss of seventeen, who was not in evidence that afternoon.

Aunt Sarah was greeted with modified enthusiasm. "We were just sitting down to luncheon," Mrs. Smith explained.

"Oh dear," Aunt Sarah said, eyeing the long table. "I hadn't realized the time. We haven't eaten yet. Our new cook is still unused to the American way of dining, and she is still preparing our evening meal."

Mrs. Smith made the best of it. "You must join us," she said. "There is always a place for you here, Sarah." She looked down the table. "Mr. Lawton and Mr. Donovan take their midday meals away from here, as do Miss Dawson and Mrs. Mears. As for Mr. Delacorte, he does keep odd hours, but this time he has outdone himself. He went out on Monday afternoon, and has not been seen here since!"

"How odd," I remarked.

"I don't know what to say, Sarah," Mrs. Smith said. "Imagine, Mr. Long actually sent a carriage for him yesterday, and I had to tell his coachman that Mr. Delacorte was not here, and had not been for at least twenty-four hours."

"Most distracting for you, Phoebe," said Aunt Sarah, as we joined the Smith family at the communal table.

We partook of cold ham, pickles, corn bread, coffee, and pie. Aunt Sarah could not give her vital news over the table, but had to wait until the servant started to clear and Mrs. Smith led us into her back parlor before coming out with it.

"You must prepare yourself for a shock, Phoebe," she told her friend. "Mr. Delacorte will not be returning this afternoon. Or ever." Aunt Sarah dove into her reticule for a handkerchief.

"Whatever do you mean?" Mrs. Smith's cap fairly quivered with alarm.

I could see that Aunt Sarah would take all day to give the news. "Mr. Delacorte has met with an unfortunate accident," I said bluntly. "I saw him taken up out of the river this morning. I am surprised that the police have not been here yet."

"I'm not," Aunt Sarah said, with a scornful sniff. "They'll have to go to the Delacortes first, to give them the information. Then they'll come here to get his things."

Mrs. Smith started to cry. "Oh, no, not more trouble. First that wretched woman, now this! My guests will leave! How could he do such a thing?"

"I don't think he meant to do you any harm," I said. "He seems to have been attacked by some ruffians while he was out celebrating his release from jail."

"Jail?" she squeaked out.

I could see she had no idea of what Mr. Bertram Delacorte had been doing in the last forty-eight hours since his departure from the boarding house.

"He was arrested for the murder of Mrs. Suzanna Kendall Monday afternoon. Yesterday he went before Judge Bacon, but was acquitted of all charges, because I provided evidence that put him far away from the scene of the crime at the time of the murder. It is assumed that after he left the courtroom he came here. Did he?"

Mrs. Smith sat up straight in her chair, trying to assimilate all this information. Then she said, "Mr. Delacorte left this house on Monday afternoon, after taking luncheon with us. It was two o'clock, exactly."

"Are you sure?" I asked.

"Of course. The chimes were ringing the hour."

She indicated the elaborate long-case clock that stood on the landing of the stairs that led to the sleeping-chambers on the second and third floors. The ladies' rooms were on the lower floor; the gentlemen had the upper, with the staircase between them. There would be no hanky-panky in this boarding house, to be sure.

"You must have been the last one to see him before he left that day," I said. "He didn't keep a servant, did he?"

"Clem is here for those gentlemen who require assistance with their attire," Mrs. Smith said loftily. "Most young men are not so particular these days. Mr. Lawton does not seem to need too much attention, and he and Mr. Donovan patronize the barber down the street. Clem obliged with Mr. Delacorte's wardrobe and other requirements."

"I wondered that Mr. Delacorte should have left Mr. Long's house," Aunt Sarah said. "I did hear that there was a disagreement..." Her voice trailed off, expectantly.

Mrs. Smith raised her eyebrows and said," I never ask questions of my guests, Sarah. Mr. Delacorte explained that he was considering setting up his own establishment in one of the French flats that are going up, but that the building itself is not quite ready for occupancy. Of course, I knew his family, and since I had a room available, I decided to accommodate him until my next boarder showed up. Now I see that I was mistaken."

"You couldn't know that Mr. Delacorte was violent," Aunt Sarah said. "And there was no suspicion of him when that wretched woman was killed, was there?"

"Not then, no," Mrs. Smith said slowly. "Of course, the police were here, and asked questions of all my guests, but Mr. Delacorte walked in the front door while the questioning was going on, and had clearly been away during the time that the . . . the crime had been committed. The policeman seemed to think that the. . . the person who did it was a burglar, and that Mrs. Kendall had surprised him while he was trying to rob the house."

"That sounds like a possible explanation," I said. "But it does seem odd that a burglar would choose this house instead of some of the ones down the street, on Gramercy Place."

Mrs. Smith declared, "This is a most respectable household, Miss Peggy. We do not encourage burglars!"

"Of course not, Phoebe," Aunt Sarah said soothingly. "But then Mr. Delacorte was arrested for the crime, which sounds even more unlikely."

Mrs. Smith considered this, then said, "I was, at first, somewhat reluctant to have Mr. Delacorte here. However, Mr. Long prefers not to accommodate lengthy visits by his wife's relations, and often sends them to my establishment when they visit New York. It was only natural that Mr. Delacorte would come here when his relationship with his uncle became strained."

"I heard that he had a quarrel with his uncle over his, um, choice of companions," Aunt Sarah hinted.

"One usually discounts such things. Evil gossip, I thought, and not worth repeating," Mrs. Smith said. "However, Mr. Delacorte was not an ideal boarder."

"I shouldn't think he was," I murmured.

"He was not used to some of the requirements of communal living. He could be somewhat inconsiderate of the other guests with regard to certain amenities." Mrs. Smith had kept all this to herself. Now, with a willing listener, she unburdened herself of a month's resentments.

I didn't quite understand, but Aunt Sarah did. "I did hear that the new houses have very lavish bathing facilities," she hinted.

"I had to explain that we have only one," Mrs. Smith said. "And then there was the matter of his behavior towards my female guests."

"Really?" Aunt Sarah leaned forward.

"Young men these days are dreadfully rude," Mrs. Smith said. "Mr. Delacorte made insinuating remarks at the table, and cast glances at the ladies."

"Do you mean that he actively pursued Mrs. Kendall?" I asked.

Mrs. Smith was torn between her love of gossip and her professional reticence. Gossip won. "The policeman who came last week to question my guests more thoroughly about the unfortunate incident seemed to think that the only reason Mr. Delacorte came here was to scrape acquaintance with Mrs. Kendall."

"That sounds even more unlikely than the burglar story," Aunt Sarah exclaimed. "I think I met Mrs. Kendall at one of the Musical Evenings you had last year. She sang some very moving melodies by Mr. Foster. Do you remember, Peggy? The tall, dark woman? You probably have a sketch of her somewhere. She must have been quite a bit older than he."

I tried to recall the occasion. Mrs. Smith's Musical Evenings were pleasant enough, and Aunt Sarah dragged me to them in hopes that I might attract the attention of one of the up-and-coming young men who boarded with Mrs. Smith while seeking their fortunes in New York City commerce. Now I remembered that there was a woman who sang, in a moving contralto. If this was the infamous Suzanna Kendall, then she was at least ten years older than Bertram Delacorte, and possibly more. At the arraignment, Bertram was accused of

THE GUILTY CLIENT

murdering her in a fit of thwarted passion. The Bertram I knew had never been thwarted of anything, and was totally incapable of passion, but people do change with time.

"Who was she, anyway?" I blurted out. The two older ladies stared at me. "I mean, Mrs. Smith, you always require some sort of reference. This is not a hotel, where people check in and out constantly," I said, turning to the landlady. "Mrs. Kendall must have told you something about herself."

Mrs. Smith sighed. "She came here three years ago, with a story about having lost her husband in the War. She seemed a quiet, reliable sort of woman, and she paid her rent without fail."

"Then she must have had an income," I said.

"I believe she received some kind of pension, or annuity," Mrs. Smith told me. "She also did fine sewing. She was always ready to oblige when one of the ladies needed a dress altered, and she was a dab hand at hair, too."

"Did she have any friends? Any callers?" I asked.

Mrs. Smith shook her head. "I could not say. She went out in the afternoons in all weathers, but she always returned before dark, even in the winter. She rarely went out of an evening, and when she did, it was usually in the company of one or another of my guests, to the theater or to the Academy of Music for a concert or lecture. As far as I could tell, she was a quiet woman, she kept to herself, and did not put herself forward in any way. I cannot imagine why anyone would want her dead, and so brutally!" Mrs. Smith resorted to her handkerchief once again.

Has anyone come for her traps?" Aunt Sarah wanted to know. "What's to become of them?"

Mrs. Smith shrugged. "After the police were finished, I had the room completely cleaned. There was blood, you see, and I couldn't let people know what had happened there. They might think the poor creature would Walk!"

"A ghost might be something new in a boarding-house," I ventured, but Mrs. Smith was not amused.

"I do not wish my establishment to have that sort of reputation," she corrected me, icily. "Ghostly visitations are not conducive to repose! I run a decent house, where people may be comfortable in home-like surroundings. Mrs. Kendall's death was shocking, and I only hope that it will soon be forgotten."

"If Bertram didn't do it," I said, "then someone else did. She may still be here, waiting for someone to avenge her death."

"Don't be melodramatic, Margaret!" Aunt Sarah snapped out. To Mrs. Smith she said, "You know, Phoebe, Margaret is quite clever. Perhaps she can find something in Mrs. Kendall's belongings that will help us find out who she was."

"The police went through everything when they did their investigation," Mrs. Smith said, as she led us up the stairs, past the infamous clock that was loudly marking the time. "I packed everything she had into the trunk she brought with her, and put it into the hall cupboard, just in case someone came to claim it. I was going to have Clem put it into the attic, if no one did by the end of the month."

"Let me take a look anyhow," I said. "The police are all men. Someone like me might recognize something a man wouldn't notice."

Mrs. Smith hesitated. "Are you sure?"

"You can watch me, if you like. I assure you, I won't steal anything valuable."

"She didn't have anything valuable, poor woman," Mrs. Smith said, as she pulled out a small trunk. " Poor creature, she didn't have much. Only her clothes, and not many of those."

Mrs. Suzanna Kendall had not had much in the way of earthly possessions. I made an inventory of her clothes: one black silk dress, for special occasions; three bodices with matching skirts, for day wear; a gray woolen pelisse, trimmed with black braid, which wouldn't give her much warmth in a New York winter; a gray bonnet, trimmed to match. No widows' veils or jet jewelry, so I had to assume that if she was a widow, she was out of full mourning, and into colors. Under the day clothes were her underthings, plain linen drawers and chemises, carefully stitched and unadorned by lace or other insertions. I frowned when I saw her corsets, neatly tied and poked alongside the underdrawers.

"What was she wearing when…um, it happened?" I asked.

"Her nightdress, and a wrapper," Mrs. Smith replied. "I cannot understand what happened at all. You see, it was a Saturday night, and most of the guests had gone out for various reasons. I believe the two ladies, Miss Dawson and Mrs. Mears, were attending the theater. Mr. Lawton had told me that he was dining with the family of a young lady with whom he was fixing his interest. Mr. Donovan was out on his own business, and Mr. Delacorte had informed me that he would dine out and then go to the Veteran's Ball, for which he had acquired a ticket. Mr. Smith and I had retired to our own apartments, which are on the top floor, where we were able to have a little time with our children.

"Cook, that is, Lacey, was in the kitchen, which is two floors down, in the basement, with Biddy and Clem and the kitchen girl. They all said that they heard the clock chime ten, which is natural, because that clock is set to chime loudly. We all set our watches by that clock!" Mrs. Smith glanced at the object in question with great pride. Then she returned to her tale. "As I said, the clock chimed and then they heard a scream, and they ran upstairs to see what was about. I heard the scream, and ran downstairs. We all met in front of Mrs. Kendall's door. We knocked, to see whether she was all right, and the door opened before us, and there she was! Oh, Sarah, it was terrible! Lying there, her hair all unbound, blood all over her her! I was completely overset! It was Mr. Smith who had the presence of mind to call for the police."

"And then what happened?" I asked, while Mrs. Smith caught her breath.

"The police came, a man called Captain Walling. Biddy said that she'd seen a man running out of the back garden, going over the wall," Mrs. Smith explained. "So Captain Walling said that it must have been a burglar, and that was that. After all, Sarah, it was very unfortunate, but you know how dreadful those gangs are, and no one is safe anywhere, not even here on the East Side! And so we went about our own affairs, and went to Divine Service for Good Friday and Easter Sunday, and then another policeman came, and said he was acting on Information Received, and had a warrant to look in Mr. Delacorte's room."

"I don't think Mr. Delacorte would like that," I commented.

"Mr. Delacorte was not there. As I have told you, Mr. Delacorte

kept very odd hours, and was rarely in this house, except to change his clothes, bathe and sleep, and that he did when other folks were at their businesses. The policeman noted that Mr. Delacorte had the room directly above Mrs. Kendalls' and they found a greatcoat, smeared with blood, jammed into the wardrobe. I was never more shocked in my life, Sarah, for I could not believe that a young man from such a fine family would do such a horrid thing, particularly not Mr. Delacorte, who was something of a milksop, to tell you the truth! and know tou twll me he'd been arrested!" She finally collapsed under the strain of the last two weeks, and burst into tears on Aunt Sarah's shoulder.

"You poor dear!" Aunt Sarah patted her friend's back, and looked at me as if to say, I thought she knew more than she let on.

"You have no idea, Sarah! My whole reputation is in ruins! And now this!"

I continued my search through Mrs. Kendall's belongings. "Didn't Mrs. Kendall keep a diary or journal?" I asked. "Most women do."

Mrs. Smith wiped her eyes and considered the matter. "I don't think so. I know she could write, at least, she signed her name, but do you know, Miss Peggy, I don't think I ever saw her read a book, or even a newspaper. Do you think she could not read?"

"It is possible," I said slowly. And idea was forming in my mind, as to the possible identity of this mysterious woman from the South, but I didn't dare voice it just yet. My eye was caught by a small scrap of paper at the very bottom of the trunk. I slid my fingers down and under the lining to touch what proved to be a small piece of cardboard. I thought it might be a carte de visite, one of those photographs taken by soldiers prior to their leaving for the battlefront, but I could not be sure. I slipped it into my reticule, to be examined later. If the police had missed it, that was their lookout, I reasoned.

Mrs. Smith closed the lid of the trunk just as the maid called up, "Mrs. Smith, you've got callers!"

"Now what?" Mrs. Smith asked crossly.

I went to the hall window and peered down into the street. I saw a brougham with the emblem of the New York City Metropolitan Police Department, a green Stanhope carriage and a nondescript cab all lined up in the street in front of Mrs. Smith's boarding-house, and the inevitable New York crowd beginning to form.

"The police have arrived," I said, and followed Mrs. Smith as she descended majestically to confront them.

I wondered if Michael and Joshua had discovered anything more than I had, and when we could get together to compare notes. It was clear to me that the deaths of Bertram Delacorte and Suzanna Kendall were connected, but at that time I had no idea how, or by whom.

However, the next portion of this report belongs to Michael, and I will allow him to tell it in his own words.

SECTION 2: MICHAEL

CHAPTER 7

    Miss Peggy wants me to include my own information on the Guilty Client case with hers, her point being that Joshua and I could go where she couldn't, and what we discovered led to the conclusion of the case. I asked her whether it wasn't too much to ask, me not being one for literary endeavors. She told me, "Dictate to me, I will write it down as you tell it."

    I says, "And what about the cussing?" In that some of the language used by working men is not fit for a lady's ears.

    She says, "I leave that to your discretion."

    That being the case, here's my tale. My Pa brought us over from County Cork, me and Ma and my two sisters, in one of those coffin ships, before the steam packets took over. Ma died on the trip. No one would give him work but the railway men, so off he went, leaving me to fend for myself while the gals found men who would care for them, or at least, pay them for what they could give. If Uncle Ephraim hadn't found me under the stairs to his office and taken me in to mind the place, I'd have wound up dead on the street. That was before Miss Peggy went to work for him, when Uncle Ephraim's law office was in the rooms over Schult's Saloon. Aunt Sarah wouldn't have Miss Peggy going up an outside stair, not in her hoops, and she said that a saloon was no fit place for a young girl. It was move house or take on someone else. By that time Uncle Ephraim had had enough of climbing stairs himself. He took the old pawnbrokers, and settled in, while I went off to fight the Rebs with Duryee's Zouaves. That's where I met Joshua, and we've been friends ever since.

So that's me, Michael Riley, Attorney at Law thanks to Uncle Ephraim getting me through the Bar examination, and Assistant District Attorney for the County of New York, City of New York, if you please, thanks to Uncle Ephraim calling in a few favors that some people owed him. I'm not too proud to take a hand when it's offered, but I pay my debts. When Joshua needed healing, I got him back to New York. Don't ask how. It wasn't pretty, what had happened to him. He said he wanted a place where he could sit and practice law without being called on to defend murderers, and Uncle Ephraim's practice was just the ticket, being mostly ship contracts and sea captain's wills and salvage rights, with a sailor to bail out of pokey for a barroom fight for a change of pace. I warned him that the practice was so slow, I'd jumped at the chance to see some action on the Prosecution side, but Joshua says he needs peace and quiet, and sitting by the river will give it to him. And then along comes Broadway Bertie, and here he is, up to his neck in murder again.

When Uncle Ephraim dismissed us, and Miss Peggy went back to Aunt Sarah's house on Bank Street. Joshua and I headed over to Mulberry Street, to see what the police left out of their reports. They're supposed to hand over all evidence to the District Attorney's office before we go to trial, but men like Clubber Williams like to hold back a thing or two, just in case they need to hold it over some nob's head.

At that time of day it was easier and faster to walk across town than it would be to take a cab. Joshua's long legs ate up the distance. I'm a bit shorter, and boarding house food puts on the pounds, especially when the cook is German and the board is mostly potatoes, so I did a bit of puffing while Joshua did the talking..

"I don't like the smell of this case," says Joshua, as we skirted the piles of rubble thrown up by the builders on Greenwich Street. He could have meant the street itself, which was as nasty as any in the parts of New York not frequented by the Pillars of Society.

"No more do I," says I, and I meant it. I don't like to go before a judge without having all my facts straight, like Uncle Ephraim says, "like ducks in a row". When Joshua trotted out Bertram's alibi, I was knocked for a loop. I was used to shysters like Hummel and Howe pulling that sort of rig, but I didn't expect it from my friends. I'm not saying that Joshua should have told me, I'm saying that the police should have known about that alibi before they ever made the arrest. No point in their arresting someone if they can't make it stick!

We got a quick bite from a German sausage-wagon, with a cup of cider to wash it down, then headed over to Mulberry Street, to see what the police surgeon had to say about young Bertram.

We found them both at the dead-room, and a fearful place that is. Dank as the dungeon, and about as cheerful, with a smell of death that brings back memories that I'd prefer not to dwell on. Let's just say, I did my share of the fighting, and leave it at that.

The police surgeon was a cheerful old goat named McNaughton, a fellow I'd seen far too often for my taste. He's good at his job, but I wouldn't have him near me if I wasn't dead already. He's short and round, and he's got a beard full of tobacco bits from those cheap cigars he's always smoking, and he's got an apron that's got blood on it from the Mary Rogers case.

"You here again, Riley?" he says, by way of greeting. "Don't you trust anyone any more?"

"Not since I was a pup," I says. "Has Bertram Delacorte come in yet?"

"Who's he?" asks McNaughton.

"Brought in off the docks this morning," says I.

"Aha." McNaughton glances over at the body next to him, on a slab, with a sheet draped over it, for decency's sake. "I was just getting to him. Death by drowning."

"Eh?" Joshua had said that, but I hadn't really believed it. "Look at all them wounds on him!" I pointed at them.

"Don't mean a thing," says he, waving a nasty-looking instrument in my direction. "Those cuts didn't do more than break the skin." He pointed down at the body. "See that? He was wearing a corset. The whalebone on that was as stiff as any armor."

"Well, I'll be jiggered," says I. "If I'd have known that, I'd have laced up before I took on the Rebs."

"Whoever did this didn't know about the corsets," McNaughton says. "He just slashed away, until the lad fell into the river. The wounds were enough to sap his strength, and the current did the rest."

"So this could be ruled an accidental death," Joshua spoke up. I could see the little wheels turning around in his head. He was already preparing a defense, even if he didn't know for who yet.

"Hardly an accident," says the Doc. "Death was the intention, and death was the result, whether by knife or by water."

"Are you trying to teach me the Law, Doctor?" Joshua says, really soft. He don't like anyone implying that he's not as good as anyone else, just because he left his right arm in an army hospital.

"What kind of knife made those cuts?" says I, nipping that argument in the bud. "I would say, a large knife, of the type known as Bowie," says McNaughton.

"Are you sure?" says I.

McNaughton gets huffy. "Young man," he says, "I have seen more knife wounds than you have hairs on that chin of yours. I can tell just by looking at 'em what made 'em, and who used the knife that did 'em."

"Is that so?" says I. "Then you tell me who did this, and I'll stand you to a drink when we put him on the gallows."

"Now, now," he says, backing off. "I can't give you a name. What I can do, is give you something to go by. I'll tell you what he looks like, but you have to go out and find him."

"Indeed," says I, "What does he look like, then?"

"I'd say, a tall man. Six foot or more. Right-handed, not left."

"From the direction of the cuts?" Joshua puts in.

"Yes," says theMcNaughton. "And a strong man. Some of those knife-cuts cut right through the starch and whalebone to the skin. And I'd guess, from the depth and number of the cuts, that he was in a state of extreme emotional turmoil."

"Excitable chap, then," I says. A picture was forming in my mind, and not a nice one, either. Whoever did this did not like Bertram Delacorte at all.

"As to that, I wouldn't like to state on the stand. All I can give you is probably weight and height, and the type of weapon used." McNaughton is a cautious man. I've seen him giving evidence, and he's not one for suppositions.

"I only wish I'd known that much when I got the notes on Suzanna Kendall," I says, with a sigh.

McNaughton draws himself up, haughtily. "That was not my doing," he says. "I was not the examiner on that case. Mrs. Kendall was brought in on a Saturday, and I believe in Sabbath observance. I do not work on Sundays. I leave that to heathens like Oberdonk."

There's a bitter rivalry between McNaughton and Oberdonk, as to who is the more efficient medical examiner. To my mind, McNaughton has the experience, but Oberdonk claims he studied in Vienna, and he's more up-to-date. Also, cleaner; he washes his hands with hard soap after every examination he does.

I says, "I got the barest facts on Kendall. Death by exsanguinations was all Oberdonk wrote, by which I suppose he meant that the poor woman was cut and bled to death. Time of death was given as between nine and ten in the evening. Nothing more."

McNaughton gives a snort. "Humph! Nothing more indeed. I hear the accused was released at his arraignment on the grounds that there was nothing worth holding him on."

"I should have been more careful with the case," I said. "I took what I was given, and didn't look for myself." As I usually do, in cases of murder, which is how I come to be acquainted with the medical examiners. Most of the Assistant District Attorneys don't go to the dead-rooms, but that's not my way. Tammany Hall doesn't pay my salary, the People of the City of New York do, and I believe what Uncle Ephraim taught me, give honest value for honest pay, and you'll never go wrong.

"Where is she?" I asks.

"She's still here," says McNaughton. "If no one claims her by next week, it's Potter's Field for her."

Suzanna Kendall was lying in one of the cold drawers, stark and stiff. It had been three weeks, and there had been some decay, but it's cold enough and damp enough down in that dead-room to keep a body fresh for a time. Still, she'd have to be put underground soon, although who'd do it I could not say.

I held back my rising stomach and took a good look at her. She must have been a handsome piece in life, regular features, clear skin, dark waving hair. In death she was just another lump of lifeless flesh, to be put away and forgotten.

Joshua had been silent while I was chatting with McNaughton.

Now he came over to take a look at what had been Suzanna Kendall.

First he looked closely at the knife wounds. Then he lifted each of her hands, then took a peek at her feet.

"She wasn't a country girl," he says at last. "But she's done domestic service. You never get rid of the burns on the hands from the lye soap. There's a mark on her middle finger where the thimble presses, so she probably did sewing for a living. And she wore good shoes. There are no bunions or corns on her feet, as she'd have from badly-fitting shoes."

McNaughton came over to take took a look at the woman himself. Then he gave a yelp, like he'd been stuck with a pin. "That's the same knife," says he. "I would have spotted it, if I'd done the first autopsy."

"The same knife as what?" says I, confused.

"See for yourself," says McNaughton. "Here's this young fellow, and here's this woman. It's the same knife killed them both."

"Will you swear to it?" Joshua says, all excited.

"I will," says McNaughton. "Dang me, if you hadn't been here, Riley, I never would have caught that."

"You weren't looking for it," says I. "And we thought we had the one who did for her."

"Well, whoever it was, it wasn't that youngster on the slab," McNaughton says. "He's too short, for one thing, and too slight for another. These are deep wounds, driven by a very heavy arm."

"And are you certain about the blade being the same in both cases?" Joshua says.

McNaughton points to a tiny tear in one of the wounds on Delacorte. "D'ye see that? There's some kind of nick in that blade, that produces a tiny tear when it does in and comes out. Now, look at the wounds on the woman, and you'll find exactly the same tear in exactly the same place in each wound. It's the same blade, and yes, I'll give you a sworn deposition whenever you like." He folds his arms over his belly, and nods his head.

"So now we have a connection between Mrs. Kendall and Bertram Delacorte," says I. "But who it is we still have to find out."

"Well, do it somewhere else," McNaughton says, testily. "I have to make young feller here presentable for his family, which, as I understand it, is well-placed in Society. There won't be a Potter's Field burial for him, to be sure."

So Joshua and I took our leave, and happy we were to get out of that horror-hole.

We stood on Mulberry Street, breathing in the Spring air of New York City, and I says, "What now?"

"Now," says Joshua, "we find out what did happen to Suzanna Kendall, and why Broadway Bertie Delacorte wound up on that slab."

"And how do you propose to do that?" says I, knowing full well that Clubber Williams was probably questioning everyone up and down the Hudson River docks, looking to find someone to nail for the murder, whether he'd done it or not.

Joshua thinks for a moment, then says, "Michael, where's your file on *People vs. Delacorte*?"

"Didn't you get it?" I says.

"I did not," he says, with a nasty look in his eye. He'd got that look when one of our men tried to run out, just before we went into the line, and it meant that someone was trying to put one over on him, and that someone was going to rue it. "I was handed the case that very morning, and all I knew was that Delacorte had been arrested, on very little evidence, and that he claimed to have an alibi for the time of the murder. As to the particulars of the case, I knew nothing, and still don't understand how someone could get into a house in a decent neighborhood like East Twenty-third Street, kill a woman in a brutal manner, and get away clean."

"Then let's step into my offices," says I, and we'll go over it together.

So off we goes, him in his high hat and frock coat, me in my brand-new suit that I'd only just bought, so as to wear something new to the Easter Service at St. Patrick's, as odd a pair as every you'd want to see, even in New York. For it's the custom that the Defense and the Prosecution sides never fraternize, but in this case, the cause of Justice overran Custom, and Riley and Roth were both on the hunt for a killer.

CHAPTER 8

JOSHUA AND I SHOOK THE DUST of the morgue off our shoes and headed back to my office in the brand-new County Court House on Chambers Street, and a grand building it is, thanks to Mr. Tweed and his pals at Tammany Hall, all marble and brass on the outside, that part that's finished, that is. There's plenty of polished wood and fancy painted walls on the inside, and that's not finished either. There's a roof on the building, and four walls, and that's enough to keep us warm and dry. Gas laid on, water closets, all the comforts of home, and all paid for by the taxpayers, and didn't they get their money's worth? No one seemed to care, except for Mr. Nasty Tom Nast, who was spreading his poison all over the pages of the New York Times. Thanks to his pictures, some people were starting to realize that all that money wasn't just being spent on bricks and mortar and tables and chairs, and that this beautiful Court House was going to cost the City of New York a good deal more than they bargained for.

I didn't think there was any chance of us running into any of the other Assistant District Attorneys after two in the afternoon. One of 'em's Eddie Flynn, and he'd be over at Tammany Hall, playing up to the big bugs around Senator Tweed. Another's a Conkling man, and he'd be over at the Union League Club, pretending he's a gent. Then there's William Marcy Tweed, Junior, who's got his own office a flight down from my little cubby-hole, at the express request of his influential Papa. None of them does a lick of work if they can get away with it, which means I get to appear in court a lot more than I would if any of them did what they was paid for. All to the good, says I, because that's the way reputations are built. The more cases I win, the more gets reported in the papers, and the more likely I am to stay here when the wheels of political power turn and the ins go out.

We climbed up the three flights to what I use as an office. It's about as big as a broom-closet, down a hallway and well out of the sight of any of the big muckey-mucks, but I've made sure it's mine alone, and I keep it locked when I'm away. It's got one of the round windows, so I get a breeze in summer; it's got a stove, so I've got heat in winter; there's gas laid on, so I've got light. I've got my roll-top desk in it, and the law books, and a standing file cabinet with my case notes. The other fellows have their desks in a bigger room down the hall, and they're welcome to them. I mean to keep my notes secret until I'm ready to use them.

I don't keep whiskey in my desk, either, like those other two do. I'm not teetotal, nothing like it, but whiskey's killed more careers than I care to think. I'm bound it won't kill mine! What I do indulge in, and I'll have to beg Miss Peggy's pardon for it, is a good cigar now and again, and I keep a box of those and some matches in my desk, with a spittoon on the floor for anyone who insists on chewing tobacco.

I took one of the cigars out, lit up, and sat down at my desk, while Joshua made himself comfortable in the one leather-bound chair I keep in case someone actually comes in to see me at my work.

"Well," says I. "What do you make of all this?"

Joshua scratched at his chin-whiskers. "I think we'd better look at the Kendall case again," he says slowly. "It's beginning to dawn on me that your office doesn't usually have fellows like Bertram Delacort hauled in for murder, and when you do, there's a lot more to go on than what you presented."

"I used what I was given," says I, not liking to be put down as a slacker. "Is it my fault that I wasn't given time to prepare a case?"

"No, it's not," says Joshua. "Nor was I. The first I knew of Broadway Bertie was when Mr. Henry Ward Long called me into his office and told me that I was hired to defend his nephew, who was being arraigned on that very day. I barely had time to get a note off to tell Miss Peggy to get herself over to the courthouse, and then I got to the Tombs to see my client. And I can't say that he was pleased to see me, either. He grumbled and groused, and complained that he thought his Uncle Henry would have got Hummel and Howe for him instead of some crippled critter like me. I told him that I was the lawyer he'd got, and that he should tell me his story, and I'd do my best for him."

"And what did the lad tell you?" I asks.

"Not much, only that he was at the Veterans' Ball that night, as he told the police when he saw them at Mrs. Smith's."

"So they had his alibi?" I ran my fingers down the pile of case-files on my desk *People vs. Delacorte*, April 26, 1870. "Let's see. Here's the police report." I pulled it out of the paper file box. "No mention of it here. According to this, he was arrested on April 25, at 4 PM, at a saloon called Devil's Hole, where he was in the company of two other young men."

"Kendall was killed the night of the Veterans' Ball. That was Saturday, April 9, in celebration of it's being five years since the signing of the surrender at Appomatox," says Joshua. "And they let it go for two weeks until they arrested him?"

I looked through the papers, trying to make out the scrawls on the police reports, which looked to be written in pencil by men who weren't used to writing at all. "According to this report, the murder of Suzanna Kendall was reported to Captain Walling. He caught it, East Twenty-third Street being in his precinct. He examined the body, determined that it was of a woman of about thirty years of age, and that she'd been cut severely and bled to death. Investigation indicated that the woman had interrupted a robbery in progress, and that the robber had then fled the scene, leaving the woman dying. Servant reports seeing a man escaping over the back garden fence. No one else reports seeing such a man."

"A robbery?" Joshua says, with his eyebrows quirking up, the way they did when one of the men tried to come up with a good excuse for being late to camp after a night off on the town. "Anything taken?"

I checked the reports. "Not that anyone could notice," I says.

"Then how did they hit on Delacorte?" Joshua asks, which is exactly what I was thinking.

I read the next report, which was in another hand, not Walling's.

THE GUILTY CLIENT

"Acting on information received, a warrant was issued and a search performed in the room used by Bertram Delacorte at Mrs. Smith's boarding-house. During said search, a great-coat was found, with bloodstains upon it. On this evidence, Mr. Bertram Delacorte was arrested at a place of entertainment known as the Devil's Hole, on Monday, April 25, at four P.M., after which he was taken to the New York City jail commonly known as The Tombs."

"Stupid of him to keep that coat for two whole weeks after he got it covered with blood," says Joshua.

"Well," says I, "a coat's a coat, and a man don't throw away a good coat for the sake of a little blood on it."

"Perhaps you might not, but Delacorte could afford a new coat," says Joshua. "And there are places where it could have been cleaned, and no questions asked as to how the blood got onto it."

There was a silence between us while we thought about what had been said. Then I spoke what I was thinking. "I wonder why we didn't spot Delacorte at the ball ourselves. He'd be in soup-and-fish, not in blue like the rest of us, who'd taken the old uniforms out to make a show. You'd think he'd stand out like a sore thumb."

Joshua shook his head. "Not so," says he. "Some of the boys have come up in the world, and don't fit the uniform any more. And some want to show off for the ladies. You can rent a tail coat and topper for a dollar or two, if you want to make a splash."

"All right," says I, "then why didn't we spot Bertie?"

"We weren't looking to see him," Joshua says. "Nor was Miss Peggy, come to think of it. She said she was surprised to see him there. Now, how did he come to be there?"

"Anyone can buy a ticket," says I. "It's a subscription ball, not a private one. I had to buy a couple myself, to help the Cause, and give support to the Widows and Orphans of the Grand Army of the Republic. I gave them to Aunt Sarah and Miss Peggy, which is why they were there. And I know you bought one for yourself, even though you're not up to dancing." There was an awkward moment there. Joshua don't like to be reminded that he's like to tip over if he's forced to go round and round, as in a waltz or a polka, and he can't hold onto a lady for a quadrille. Me, I like to trip the light fantastic, as they say, and there were plenty of pretty gals at the ball whose Mamas wouldn't look too hard at a man who could claim a steady job and a position in the city government, even if his name was Riley. I'd done my duty by Miss Peggy for the first waltz and the promenade, then taken a few gals round the floor myself. I don't bother learning all the steps, so I skipped the quadrilles and had a bite at the supper table. I tried to recall if I'd seen Bertram Delacorte, but the Veteran's Ball is a grand turnout, and I wasn't looking to see him in any case.

"Write this down, Michael," Joshua says, sharply. He don't like not having the use of a writing hand. Miss Peggy does his writing for him in the office, and she's usually on hand when he sees clients, privately or in court. This time she was off with Aunt Sarah, so I drew up a piece of paper, dipped my pen in the inkwell, and prepared to take notes.

"Suzanna Kendall was killed on the night of the Veterans' Ball. That was on April 9, to mark the fifth anniversary of the signing of the surrender at Appomattox.

Bertram Delacorte was arrested on April 25." He stopped, and says, "Why wait two weeks?"

I gave him a grin. "Easter," I says. "April 10 was Palm Sunday, and then there was Holy Week. You can't expect an Irish Catholic to work a murder case during Holy Week, can you?"

Joshua was took aback. He don't make a deal of it, but he's a Jew, and as such, wouldn't have known about such things as Holy Week. He gives a snort, and says, "You can't tell me the all the coppers in the East Side precincts were good Catholics and in church, Michael."

"Maybe, maybe not," says I. "But there wouldn't be too many left to cover for those who were, and Kendall was supposed to have been killed by a burglar in any case."

"Indeed," says Joshua, to show that he don't believe a word of it. "So then someone tips the police off that there's something in Delacorte's rooms, and they get the warrant and they find the coat. He's arrested on April 25, is put into the Tombs, and is called up for arraignment on April 26, which is when Uncle Ephraim got the note from Mr. Long that sent me off to Wall Street to handle the matter."

"Not with Miss Peggy?" I says.

"Not at Long's," Joshua says, with a grin. "Uncle Ephraim's no fool. He sent me alone, because he knows Long's dead set against females in law offices, and he wanted me to nail Long for at least a hundred bucks in fees before I'd touch the case."

I let out a whistle. "And he paid it?"

"Without a whimper," Joshua says. "So I sent word to Miss Peggy to come down to the courthouse, where she gave her evidence, and Bertram Delacorte was set free. And you, Michael Riley, were left with egg on your face, wondering why no one had checked to see if Delacorte had an alibi before they even touched him."

"And so I did," says I. "It's not as if the police didn't have time to do it. After Easter, they waited another five days before going ahead with the arrest."

Joshua gave his chin-whiskers another scratch, as if to coax some more thought from that direction. "It seems to me," he says slowly, "that someone didn't want Broadway Bertie to get off."

"Indeed," says I. Both of us know that young men of Bertram Delacorte's stamp never pay for whatever it is they might do to the Lower Sorts, whether it's running little kiddies down if they get in the way of a carriage race, or ruining gals on the streets. Over the two years I've been in this office, I've had plenty of notes from on high telling me that such-and-such or so-and-so is a "a fine lad, of a good family" or "one of the old neighborhood lads", meaning, "Back off, Riley, he's not to be touched." But no such word came down to me about Bertram Delacorte, and I'm not such a fool as I didn't wonder why.

Joshua got a look on his face that I remembered well. It was the look that meant someone had tried to put one over on him, and that someone would learn better before long.

"I think we'd better go back to the beginning," says Joshua. "And that's with Suzanna Kendall. What do we know about her?"

I looked over the file again. "Not a thing before she turned up here in New York," says I. "According to information received by Mrs. Smith, she came in the Spring of 1867, said she was looking for the relations of her husband, who was supposed to have served in one of the New York regiments. Mrs. Smith says she was quiet and unassuming, paid her shot on time, and didn't cause trouble with the other boarders."

"What did she pay with?" asks Joshua. "Where'd she get the money?"

"Did some fancy sewing," I says, checking my notes again. "Maybe got a pension. Otherwise, it don't say."

"Who was she?" Joshua asks. "What was she? Why did Suzanna Kendall have to die, and who wanted Bertram Delacorte to swing for it?"

"Questions with no answers," says I.

"Then let's go find some," says he, " and I know where to start. Get your hat, Michael, and let's get up to Mrs. Smith's boarding house, before the police and the Press get there."

"We?" says I. "In case you've forgotten, Captain Roth, we're fighting on opposite sides here."

"Not this time," says he. "You don't like being diddled any more than I do, and whoever is behind all this is laughing up his sleeve at the pair of us. I intend to make him laugh on the other side of his mouth. How do you feel about that?"

I gave him my best salute. "Lead on, Captain, and I'll follow you, like I always did."

Down the stairs we went, and there was Young Bill Tweed, for a wonder, coming in just as we were going out.

"Riley!" he calls after me. "Where do you think you're going?"

I stopped, because it's never a good idea to get the Boss angry at you for slighting his son. "You've heard by now that Bertram Delacorte's body was taken out of the river," I tells him. "I've got information that will lead to his killer, and it's related to the Kendall case. Mr. Roth is involved because he was present when the body was discovered."

Young Tweed gives a pull on his mustache, and says, "Riley, you're going off half-cocked. Clubber Williams is already working the Delacorte murder. You'll only get in his way."

"We think the same person killed both Mrs. Kendall and Mr. Delacorte," says Joshua.

Young Tweed ignores him, and says to me, "Riley, you're not supposed to be chasing murderers yourself. Your job is to see they get hanged."

THE GUILTY CLIENT

"That may be," says I, "but in this case, Mr. Tweed, I think the wrong man's going to be indicted. I'm not going to be left hanging again. If I prosecute the man who killed Bertram Delacorte, I want to be damned sure that it's the one who did it, and not some poor fellow who's been beaten into a confession."

Young Tweed gives Joshua a nasty look, then says, "There's more than one case on your desk, Riley."

"And there's more than one Assistant District Attorney in this courthouse," I says, just as nastily. "I'll be back by four, be assured, Mr. Tweed."

And off we went, Prosecution and Defense, in the Cause of Justice, to Mrs. Smith's boarding house on East Twenty-third Street.

CHAPTER 9

THIS TIME WE INDULGED IN A CAB, since it was important that we get up to Twenty-Third Street in good time. The traffic on Fifth Avenue was such that I felt we could well have walked, but then we'd have had the expense of shoe leather.

By the time we got to East Twenty-Third Street I saw that we'd already been fore-stalled. There was a police brougham at the door, and Long's bottle-green Stanhope carriage had pulled in beside it. The police and the Long family would be going at it right smartly, I thought, and I decided on a flanking attack.

I led Joshua around the alley I'd spotted between two houses, that led to the back door. The new brownstones are built in a row, cheek by jowl, so to speak, and the only way into the kitchens downstairs is through an areaway, in plain sight of the street, but this was one of the old mansions, built like Uncle Ephraim's place on Bank Street, with an alley that led through a little garden to the kitchens. I was sure I'd see the servants there, and it was the servants I wanted to question before the coppers got to them.

I was right on the money there. The cook was big and black, a woman in a checkered dress and a red head-wrap. There was a skinny little girl, who was probably the kitchen-maid, and the older gal, the house-maid called Biddy, who was of a light complexion, and then there was Clem, the manservant, who presided over the table like the master of the house.

I tapped on the kitchen door, and peeked into the kitchen. "Good afternoon," says I, most politely.

"What you doin' heah?" That was the cook, and I'm not going to try to put down exactly how she talked. I could just about make out what she meant. I'd have put her down as a Contraband, probably came North with Mrs. Smith after the War.

THE GUILTY CLIENT

"You've heard about Mr. Delacorte," Joshua says, letting himself in after me.

"What's he gone and done now?" says Clem, with a sigh.

"Got himself knifed," says I. The reaction was a scream from Biddy, and a sniff from Cook.

"That boy was trash," she says. "I said so, didn't I, Mr. Clement? He didn't belong in a nice house like this."

"And what makes you say that?" says I, with a look at Mr. Clem. He was a light-colored Negro, with hair that was just starting to grizzle gray, and I could see him struggling within himself, between his feelings for the Family and his proper sentiments regarding young sprouts and their rackety ways.

Clem glanced at Cook and Biddy, then led us outside, into the kitchen-garden. "Ahem," he gives a cough. "I have served Mrs. Smith for several years."

"Before or after the War?" Joshua asks.

Clem struggles, and says, "Before Emancipation, I was with Mrs. Smith's family." What he left out was probably, that he was related one way or another to that or another white family, and that when he said 'with' he meant that he was bought and sold. Plenty of slaves stuck with their masters after Emancipation, but I could tell this fellow really cared about Mrs. Smith. That would make him a hard nut to crack, but I knew Joshua. He'd do it in the end.

"Only her name wasn't Smith," Joshua says, with a knowing grin. "Not that it matters now, of course. The War's over, and bygones are bygones."

"Not for some," Clem says. "Lacey and I came North with Mrs. Smith, when Mr. Smith decided to remove from his previous place of employment."

"I see," says I, thinking, the Smiths, or whatever they were called, were probably caught between Union and Sesesh, and decided to go with the winning side. "So, Clement," I says, "I suppose you know how to take care of a gentleman's clothing, and such-like. What did you think of young Delacorte?"

"It's not my place to comment upon the habits of Mrs. Smith's guests," he says, prim as a parson.

Joshua gets that look that made little privates shake in their boots and get into the line.

"A man's been killed," he says. "The police are already at the door. It's not going to do him any harm, and may do him some good if we can find his killer. Now, Clement, you probably had the best opportunity to observe Mr. Delacorte during his stay here. It was Napoleon who said that no man is a hero to his valet, and Broadway Bertie was no hero to anyone. So, I ask you once again, what was your opinion of Mr. Bertram Delacorte?"

Clem eyes the two of us and makes up his mind to come clean. "He was, as Lacey says, high-born trash," says he, his face showing his disgust at such proceedings. "He'd sleep until noon, then roll out of bed and demand a shave and bath, every day. He spent a great deal of time about his toilet. He changed clothes twice a day, from a day suit to evening clothes. I was expected to retrieve his discarded garments and see to their laundering, also every day."

"Used to having his own way, was he?" I puts in.

"Undoubtedly," says Clem.

"And did you oblige him?" asks Joshua.

"For a consideration," says Clem, with dignity. "But I had other gentlemen to attend to, whether they paid or not. Such are my duties in this household. I serve at table at dinner, I purchase any beverages that might be needed for the table, and I provide whatever services may be required by the gentlemen staying here. Mr. Delacorte arrived with one small portmanteau, which contained a change of undergarments, his toilet articles, night-wear, and some shirts."

"No other suits?" I says, not thinking that a dandy like Delacorte would travel without at least a spare suit or two.

"None," says Clem, looking like he'd swallowed a lemon and a pickle both.

"Then where'd he get the soup-and-fish?" Joshua asks.

"I believe he had his clothing sent from his previous lodgings," Clem says.

"A day suit, a set of evening togs, shirts and night-shirts, underclothing, stockings, that sort of thing?" I could see more wheels turning in Joshua's mind. More questions than answers, thinks I. No one comes to a boarding house and sends back home for clothes. It don't make sense. Nothing about Bertram Delacorte's stay at Mrs.

Smith's boarding house made sense.

Joshua was off on another tack. "Did Mr. Delacorte take any of his meals here?"

"He breakfasted, if you can call it that, when he rose, and had a cup of coffee and perhaps some toast, sent to his room. He occasionally had a midday meal with the other guests," Clem says, "although one might call it a breakfast, since he had only just risen at noon. He usually took his dinner elsewhere."

"What about Mrs. Kendall?" I asks.

Clem's face seemed to shut down. One minute he was all helpful smiles, the next his face was blank. "What about her?"

"What can you tell us about her?" It was like drawing teeth, trying to get a work out of that man on that subject.

"I have no opinions about Mrs. Kendall," says Clem.

"Surely you must," says Joshua. "She's been living here for nearly three years. What sort of person was she? Did she have any habits that might have cause discord among the other boarders?"

"Mrs. Smith prefers to term the persons who come here, guests," says Clem, with great dignity. "As for Mrs. Kendall, she arrived with a small trunk. She was given the back bedroom, which she occupied with no complaints. She spent her mornings in that room, doing fine sewing, which, I should say, is how she earned her living. She would go out in the afternoons, presumably to deliver the items, possibly to get more. She had good manners, was not quarrelsome, did not put herself forward or intrude in any way."

"You served her at table," Joshua says slowly.

"I did. She was sitting with the other guests, and I served her."

I caught something under his careful tones. "You didn't like her."

"It is not my place to like or dislike one of Mrs. Smith's guests," says Clem. "Mrs. Kendall was quite genteel. She kept to herself, she did not intrude."

"Where did she come from?" asks Joshua.

"I could not say. Certainly she did not," Clem says.

"She received no letters? No communications?"

"Only those connected with her sewing, such as messages concerning this or that item, and where it was to be delivered."

Nothing more could we get out of that man.

"What about the other boarders? I mean, guests," I says. "Did Mr. Delacorte speak with her?"

"Only the merest pleasantries," Clem says. "Mr. Delacorte's habits were such that they did not meet. As I said, he spent his mornings abed, whereas she was in her own room in the mornings. She would come down for a midday meal, at which time Mr. Delacorte might join the company, or might not, depending on the state of his health."

"Meaning, he was having a morning after," I says, with a grin.

Clem raised his eyebrows, but didn't disagree. He went on, "I saw them meet exactly once in the week before she met her untimely end." He frowned a little. "I have already given this deposition to Captain Walling."

"Well, he didn't give it to me, so if you will be so kind, please tell me what was said," says I. I would have to have a word or two with the old boy, thinks I to myself. How is the Prosecution supposed to do its duty if the police don't forward their depositions in a timely manner? Not that anyone expects a mere Assistant District Attorney to do his duty, but that's not the way Michael Riley goes about things. Maybe Tweed, Junior can slack off, but I'll not be tarred with his brush when the house of cards comes crashing down about them. Anyone who thinks Tweed will last forever is living in a Fool's Paradise, and that starts with the Boss himself.

Clem looks from Joshua to me and says, "It was the night before she was. . ."

"Killed," says I, deliberately brutal.

"The night before her unfortunate demise," Clem says. "They were in the parlor, just before the clock rang the hour for gathering before dinner. Mr. Delacorte must have been waiting for her, because he positioned himself at the bottom of the stairs, just outside the parlor door. It is the custom in this house for the guests to gather in the parlor and march discreetly into the dining room, rather than descend in an unmannerly scramble, as is known to happen in less orderly places."

I grinned at Joshua. Mrs. Baumgartens' boarding house could answer that description right enough. If you didn't look sharp, you didn't get dinner at all!

Clem goes on: "Mr. Delacorte took Mrs. Kendall by the arm, and led her off, away from the rest of the boarders. I could not quite hear what was said, but Mrs. Kendall was not pleased to hear it. I could see that she was upset. Mr. Delacorte did not join us for dinner, but took himself off elsewhere."

"And what did Mrs. Kendall do then?" asks Joshua.

"Mrs. Kendall did not partake of dinner as heartily as some of the other guests. I could hear her crying in her room when I went upstairs to set the clock." I could see Clem struggling with some kind of inside emotion. "I suspect that Mr. Delacorte accused Mrs. Kendall of being other than what she claimed to be."

"And what did she claim to be?"

"A widow, of course," Clem says, without blinking. "Many women claim to be such, and claim their late husband's pensions, without ascertaining if the man is actually deceased."

"Or if he's actually a husband," I says, with a wink and a grin. "It could be that Mr. Kendall might very well be alive and kicking, and if so, he might have a word to say about someone claiming his pension." There's a line of investigation that bears looking into, I thinks to myself. So why didn't Walling follow up on it?

"Now how would a youngster like Delacorte know anything about who's a war widow and who's not?" Joshua says, more to himself than to Clem.

I had another thought. "I never saw Mrs. Kendall in life," I says. "She looked to be of a creamy complexion. Dark hair, dark eyes, and skin of a sallow shade. Is that correct?"

Clem gives me a narrow-eyed look. "That is a fair description, sir," he says.

"Would you say that she was from one of the Rebel states?" I had an idea by the tail now.

"She had that turn of phrase that I have heard in my own country," Clem says.

"I see." And I did. No one says another word.

There was a tapping at the kitchen door. "There's police at the front door!" Biddy looked out and waved at Clem. "What do I do?"

"Let them in," says he. He turned to us. "Get out of here!" he hisses at Joshua and me. "Go in at the front door like gentlemen! If you can call yourself such!"

He draws himself up, and becomes the proper butler, and marches off to let the police into the house.

Joshua and I ducked back through the alley and into the street, where the police brougham and the Long Stanhope were already discharging their passengers.

"Let's get inside," says I, and the two of us made our way around the crowd to the front stoop, where we could see Miss Peggy standing by the front door, as if she knew we were there.

"Where have you two been?"" she hisses at us.

"Following up on Mrs. Kendall," says I.

"Come inside, quickly, before they post a guard," she says, and lets the two of us into the hall, before Biddy could stop her.

And so, there we were, the three of us, and I'll let Peggy go on from here.

SECTION 3: PEGGY

CHAPTER 10

When we came downstairs, I saw that three vehicles had pulled up in front of Mrs. Smith's boarding-house: a black police brougham, an elegant Victoria, and a lowly cab, all jockeying for position, with drivers yelling imprecations, horses stamping and jibbing at the reins, and passers-by being drawn to the scene.

I saw Michael and Joshua edging through the crowd that had gathered, as always happens in New York, whenever something looks interesting. Aha, I thought, they've been to the back of the house to speak with the servants.

"Where have you two been?" I asked.

"Following up on Mrs. Kendall," Michael said.

"Come inside, before they post a guard," I told them, and let them in the front door, through the hall, and into the front parlor. "Well, what did you find out?"

"We've had a good look at the late Mrs. Kendall, and managed to get some more information on the movements of the recently departed Broadway Bertie. We've also had a word with the servants. We didn't know we'd be part of a circus parade." Michael grinned at me, then jerked his head towards the front hall.

"I've got something for you to look at, too," I said. "But it will have to wait until we can be private."

By this time Clem had reached the front door, and was doing his best to maintain the dignity of Mrs. Smith's establishment.

"Whom shall I say is calling?" he intoned.

Clubber Williams would have none of this ceremonial claptrap. "Tell Mrs. Smith this is police business," he snapped out.

Clem looked past Williams and recognized Mrs. Long and Mrs. Delacorte. His priorities were clear: Society first, Police second (if ever!).

"Mrs. Smith is at home," he announced. He led the ladies into the front parlor, the one used largely for ceremonial gatherings, and saw to it that Mrs. Long and Mrs. Delacorte were seated on the throne of honor, the horse-hair-covered sofa. Clubber Williams stood by the fireplace, glowering at them, while his men stamped up the stairs and Mrs. Smith fluttered about, wringing her hands. Aunt Sarah had taken a position behind the two ladies, as a kind of guardian angel. I backed out of the way, into the doorway, my hoops barely missing upsetting the china-laden whatnot, and got out my sketchpad. This was too good an opportunity to miss. My pencil danced over the page, capturing Williams' bulldog face and the icy profiles of the two ladies, who regarded the police captain with the expressions usually found in persons who have discovered a large multi-legged creature on a picnic tablecloth. Michael and Joshua lurked just outside the parlor door, next to me, where they could see and hear without being noticed..

"I'm sorry to tell you, ma'am, that your son's death was no accident," Clubber Williams said, as gently as he could. Not even Clubber Williams could daunt the reserve of these two grande dames of New York Society.

"So I was informed," Mrs. Delacorte said.

"By who?" Williams demanded.

"Mr. Long sent his people to inform my sister and myself of what had occurred," Mrs. Long answered. "It was shocking news." Well, I thought to myself, that explains the green carriage following our cab across town. Mr. Long had lost no time imparting the information about Bertram's demise to his wife and her sister.

"So much for breaking it to her ourselves," I muttered to Michael.

"You couldn't expect Long to keep it quiet," Michael murmured back.

Mrs. Delacorte clutched her sister's hand as she regarded Clubber from behind her black veils. "You will release my son's belongings to me at once!" she ordered. "I will not have them pawed about by your disgusting creatures!"

"Juliet!" Mrs. Long tried to stop the diatribe. "The police must do their duty. It is possible that there is some clue in Bertram's rooms that will lead to the discovery of his killer."

"He should not have been here," Mrs. Delacorte exclaimed. "She did this, I know she did!"

"Who did?" Williams asked.

"Suzanna, of course. She did this!"

"If you mean Suzanna Kendall, she can't have done this. She's dead," Williams stated brutally.

"No, she's not. She's here, I can feel her. That wretched creature is here!" Mrs. Delacorte fumbled for a handkerchief. Joshua stepped forward from his place of concealment to supply one.

Mrs. Delacorte peered up at him. "Thank you sir. Do I know you?" "I'm Joshua Roth, ma'am. I represented your son at his arraignment, at the request of Mr. Long. I may inform you that all charges against him were dismissed."

Mrs. Delacorte sniffled into the handkerchief and tried to pull herself together. "I suppose I should be grateful to you for getting Bertram released. He never should have been taken up in the first place. Persons of our standing do not get taken up by the police."

"Once the facts of the case were brought forward, ma'am, your son's release was inevitable. I only wish he'd have stayed longer, so that I could have seen to his protection." Joshua bowed his head. "I witnessed his removal from the river this morning. I am sorry for your loss, ma'am."

Mrs. Long gave Joshua a long, hard stare that might have been hatred or appraisal. "You didn't go with Bertram after he left the courtroom?" she questioned.

"No, ma'am, I did not. I wish I had been quicker, but there was legal business to do, and by the time I had seen to it, he was out of sight. I've been trying to follow his trail after his release, and it has led me here."

"Mixing into police business, Councilor?" Williams sneered.

"I've got the Prosecutor's investigator with me, to keep me straight," Joshua responded. Michael stepped forward and grinned at the irate policeman.

"And I'm here to keep you straight, Williams," he told him. "Now, let's have a look at Mr. Delacorte's room, shall we?"

Williams ignored him and turned to Mrs. Smith. "How long had he been staying here?" Williams asked her.

"He paid a month's rent, and his time's nearly up," Mrs. Smith said. "I was on the point of requesting him to leave. I am very sorry to say it, Mrs. Delacorte, but your son was not an ideal guest."

Williams turned to the bereaved mother. "Why'd he leave home?"

Mrs. Delacorte resorted to tears. Once again her sister answered for her. "That is none of your affair, Captain, but if you must know, there was a difference of opinion about a family matter. Bertram decided that he should have his own establishment."

"So he came to a boarding-house?" I couldn't blame Williams for his scorn. You don't leave the Long mansion to live in Mrs. Smith's boarding-house on your own, not if you're a young man with foppish tastes and a private income.

"I supposed he had his reasons." Mrs. Long wasn't giving anything away. She swallowed hard, then tried a different strategy. "Captain, my sister has had a dreadful shock. Bertram was her only surviving child. I realize that you have to do your duty, but I do not see why you have to do it so harshly." Another concession. "Please. Let us have Bertram's clothing and other belongings, and let us bury him with some dignity."

"Hey, Cap, looky here!" The uniformed policeman who had gone upstairs to Bertram's room called down to the parlor.

There was a general exodus from the front parlor, as everyone streamed up two flights of stairs, past the clock on the landing, and up to the room lately inhabited by Bertram Delacorte.

It must have been a dreadful come-down for a young man about town, to go from the luxurious chambers found in the new brownstones to this single room, furnished with an iron frame bed, a tall wardrobe, and a washstand. There was gas-jet near the door, and a kerosene lamp on a small stand near the bed, to provide light at night.

Bertram's belongings were strewn about the room, shirts crumpled on the floor, cravats hanging on the end of the bed, stockings next to the shirts. I peeked into the wardrobe, and only saw a dark coat and a pair of trousers looped up on a wooden hanger, with a silk hat tossed onto the upper shelf of the wardrobe. Obviously he'd always had a servant to pick up after him. I wondered how he had lasted as long as two days without one, let alone three weeks, counting the two after Mrs. Kendall's death. Joshua and Michael had hinted that they'd had a word with that manservant. I burned with the desire to get out of this crowd find out what they had learned.

Mrs. Long gave a cry. "How dare you!"

The uniformed copper had found a piece of paper at the bottom of the wardrobe. He handed it to Williams, who unfolded it to see what it was.

"How dare you paw through my son's letters!" Mrs. Delacorte cried out.

"Evidence, ma'am," Williams told her.

"Evidence of what?" Mrs. Long reached for the paper.

Michael got it instead. "The Prosecutor's office will want to have this, ma'am," he said. "It may give us a motive for your son's tragic death."

"Motive?" Mrs. Long echoed. "Bertram was killed by ruffians on the docks. Mr. Long said so."

"Did he now." Michael looked at Joshua, and the two of them nodded at Williams. There was an unspoken assumption that the Mr. Long would try to shield his wife and her sister from the nastier realities of Bertram's choice of playmates.

"Is there anything here that you don't recognize, or that is out of place for Mr. Delacorte to have? Is there something missing, that should be there?" Williams was trying to be conciliating. It was an awesome sight, watching the mighty Clubber Williams truckling to the Quality.

Mrs. Delacorte looked at the shirts, the cravats, and the tie-pin and shirt-studs on the wash-stand. "This is all Bertram's," she said, trying to stem her tears. "I don't see anything that isn't his. Oh, Nerissa!" Her reserve cracked, and she flung herself into her sister's arms.

"What about this?" The man at the wardrobe reached in and took out a small pistol, the sort called a Derringer, a tiny object carried by some gentlemen who go into rough places for their amusements.

Mrs. Delacorte screamed and fainted. Mrs. Long shouted for assistance. Mrs. Smith called down to Biddy, who came running up the stairs with a glass of water. Mrs. Long found her vinaigrette, and applied the smelling salts to her sister's nose.

I got Joshua and Michael out of the bedroom and down to the next floor. "Now's our chance to check out Mrs. Kendall's room," I said. "They're all busy tending to Mrs. Delacorte."

Mrs. Kendall's room was directly below Bertram's, furnished similarly. The floor had been scrubbed and waxed, the bed had been re-painted, and there was nothing left to show that there had been a violent crime committed in that room. A small rug had been placed next to the bed, but that was the only difference between the furnishings of Bertram's room upstairs and this one a flight below. The wardrobe and chest of drawers had been emptied, made ready for the next guest, who would not know the story of the previous tenant of this room.

"That's where it happened," Michael said. He lifted the rug. Sure enough, a faint stain showed against the wooden floor. "You never get the bloodstains out of wood," Michael said, as one who had seen it far too often.

"It certainly soaked in," I remarked. "I wouldn't have thought it would have the time. Not if Mrs. Kendall had been killed just before her body was found."

"Do you mean she could have been killed earlier?" Joshua thought it over. "In that case, Bertram's alibi doesn't hold up."

"But how could he have killed her earlier?" I pointed out. "I can swear that he was at the Veteran's Ball. They opened with the Grand Promenade, and Michael led me in that, and then we danced the first waltz. Then I sat out the next few dances, and then along came Bertram for the polka, and McAllister grabbed me and practically thrust me into his arms. That was around ten. And you saw that there was no weapon in his rooms except that little pistol, and he didn't even take that with him when he went out on the town last night."

Joshua frowned. "There's something wrong here," he said. "Something's missing."

It came to me in a flash. "His dress-suit is in the wardrobe, but his day clothes aren't," I said. "When he was arrested, he was wearing his day clothes, and he spent the whole night in the Tombs in them. He looked a sight at the arraignment, half a day's beard, clothes stained . . ."

"And this is the fellow who had a bath every day?" Michael shook his head at the extravagance of a Gentleman of Leisure.

"I know what I'd want if I had spent a night in the Tombs," I said. "I'd want a bath, and a change of clothes."

"So, where did he get them?" Joshua said slowly.

"Not here," I said. "His tie pin and shirt-studs are right here, with his evening coat and hat."

"Didn't he say something to you before he ran out of the courtroom?" Michael asked.

"I think he muttered something about going home," Joshua said. "I supposed he meant here."

"I had to copy all the forms and fill out the papers," I said, by way of excusing myself. "But Mrs. Smith's isn't Bertram's home, and never was. He'd have gone to Mr. Long's house, where he had rooms with his mother, before he'd quarreled with Mr. Long. I wonder what that was all about?"

I heard the tramp, tramp, tramp of feet coming down the stairs and back to the parlor.

"I think we'd better join the others," I said. "Clubber's finished, but there's a lot more to be learned here."

We slid into the rear of the procession as it filed down the stairs, with Clubber in the lead, followed by Mrs. Smith, protesting all the way; Mrs. Long and Mrs, Delacorte, waving vinaigrettes and moaning; Aunt Sarah, cooing soothing phrases; and a pair of policemen in uniform carrying a small trunk.

As the parade reached the bottom of the stairs, Clem opened the front door to admit two more ladies: a tall, angular woman in a severely-tailored jacket and mannish-looking hat, and a younger, plumper woman in a round-hooped walking dress and straw bonnet. I recognized the two women who had been at the Musical Evening when Mrs. Kendall had performed so movingly. These were Mrs. Smith's two female 'guests'.

"What on Earth is going on, Mrs. Smith?" demanded the taller woman, Mrs. Mears.

"Police business!" snapped out Williams.

"Oh, not again!" That was the shorter lady, Miss Dawson.

"I think we may need the front parlor," Mrs. Smith said, opening up the sliding doors in the hall, " and perhaps we can finish this unhappy business before dinner."

And once again, the group assembled, with the two additions, for more questions, to which there were unsatisfactory answers.

CHAPTER 11

After the group had assembled in the front parlor, the Society ladies appropriated the horsehair sofa, while Aunt Sarah hovered behind them. Clubber Williams took up a commanding position in front of the fireplace, flanked by his uniformed minions, while Mrs. Smith fluttered here and there, and the two female boarders found places on side chairs. Joshua, Michael and I stood near the door, to see if anyone else might come to join the festivities.

Clubber Williams glared at the two new arrivals. Mrs. Smith explained, "This is Mrs. Mears and Miss Dawson. They are teachers at Miss Porter's School, on Fifth Avenue." In other words, they are ladies, and should be treated as such.

Williams took this in, then stated, "Ahem! Ladies, I have sad news. Mr. Bertram Delacorte is no longer with us."

"Good riddance," exclaimed Mrs. Mears forcefully. "Mrs. Smith, I warned you about that rackety young man."

"I don't think you understand, ma'am," said Williams. "What I meant was…"

"He's dead!" shrieked Mrs. Delacorte.

"Oh, dear," moaned Miss Dawson. It seemed inadequate to the occasion.

"When did this happen?" Mrs. Mears asked.

"We think some time last night," Williams said. "Mr. Delacorte had been arrested…"

"What!" Another shriek and moan from Miss Dawson. "That nice young man?"

"Nice? Balderdash!" Mrs. Mears would have none of polite fictions. "He was a well-bred lout, in my opinion."

"Please, Mrs. Mears," Aunt Sarah put in, "his mother is present." She indicated Mrs. Delacorte, weeping on the horsehair sofa.

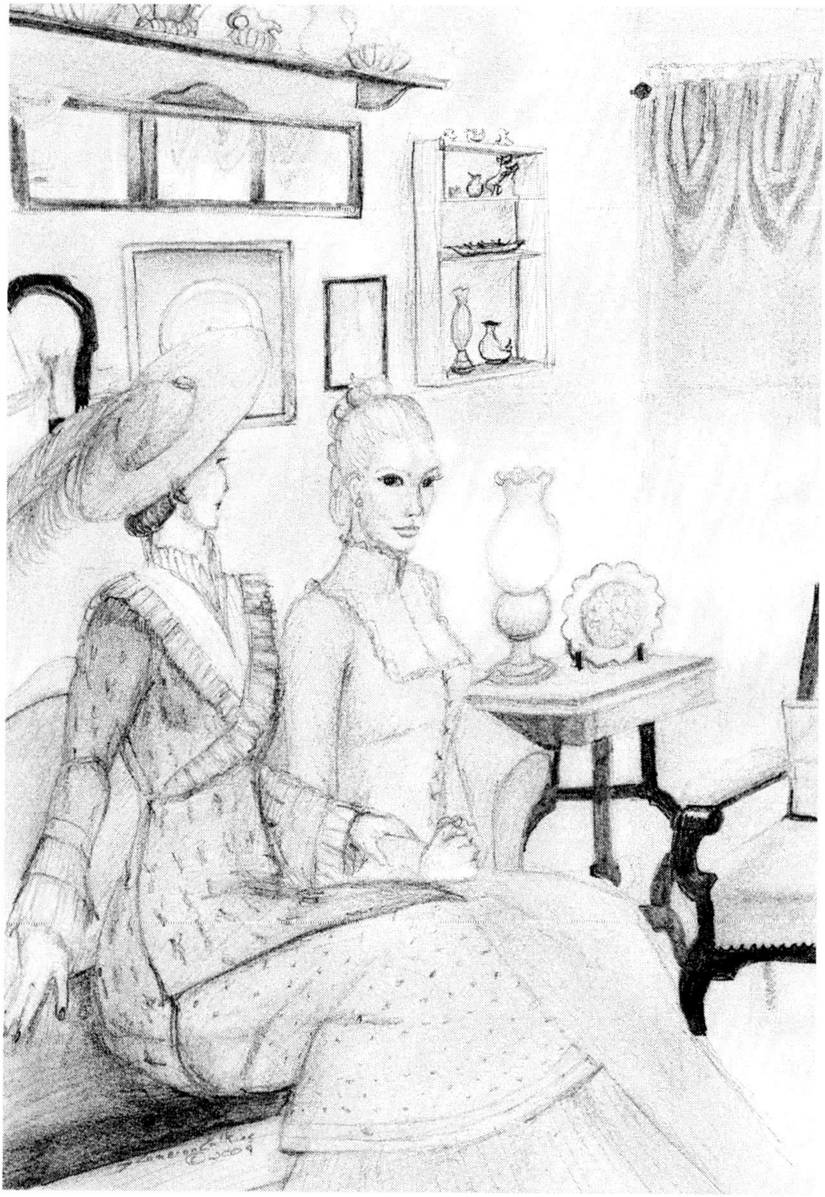

THE GUILTY CLIENT

"Then I am sorry to tell you, ma'am, that your son was a person of intemperate habits, and worse speech, and that you undoubtedly indulged him beyond belief." Mrs. Mears ended with a scornful sniff. I could see that here was a woman who would not stand for any nonsense, and very glad I was that I had left Miss Porter's school before Mrs. Mears had joined the faculty.

"And you are, ma'am?" Clubber Williams gave her the look that usually had miscreants shaking in their shoes. It didn't faze Mrs. Mears in the least.

"Rachel Mears. I teach mathematics and geography to the older students. This is Miss Anne Dawson, who teaches the primary class." Mrs. Mears looked Williams over. "If you are a policeman, I must assume that Mr. Delacorte's death was not an accident, and that you require all the information we have about him. I fear I cannot oblige you to any extent. Miss Dawson and I must leave for school very early, and do not return until late in the afternoon. Mr. Delacorte showed up in his evening clothes at least twice, at the hour when we were at breakfast, presumably after having been on the tiles all night. I assume he slept during the day, and changed his clothing at some time. He re-appeared early in the evening, when he dressed for his evening activities, whatever they were." Another scornful sniff, leaving no doubt about Mrs. Mears' opinion of Bertram's 'evening activities'.

"He came in at all hours," Miss Dawson added. "I do believe I heard him banging on the door just as I was waking up. We are due at the school quite early, so that we may give some of the little ones a bit of breakfast."

Williams looked at Mrs. Smith. "Didn't he have a latch-key?" he asked.

"Certainly not," Mrs. Smith stated, folding her hands over the bunch of keys that clinked at her waist. "My guests are ladies and gentlemen, and they are let into this house by a servant. None of them have the keys to the front door."

"That must make for inconvenience when folks are out late," Williams commented.

"None of my guests are so inconsiderate as to keep late hours," Mrs. Smith said loftily. "Except for Mr. Delacorte. He was, as I have said, a difficult person."

"Difficult? Mrs. Smith, you understate the case," Mrs. Mears broke in. "He was thoroughly obnoxious. He had no care for anyone's comfort but his own. As Miss Dawson said, he came and went at odd hours, and he was not congenial company when he arose. I strongly suspect that he suffered from over-indulgence."

Clubber nodded sagely. "Hangover," he deduced.

"And he was most inconsiderate about the, um, personal facilities," Miss Dawson whispered, blushing.

"Hogged the bathroom, did he?" Clubber boomed out.

"I suppose he was used to a more luxurious life than the one we lead here," Miss Dawson said, with a shy look at Mrs. Delacorte and Mrs. Long.

"All right then." Clubber put his hands behind his back and rocked back and forth, trying to look official. "When was the last time any of you actually saw Mr. Bertram Delacorte? Not you," he added, nodding at Joshua, Michael and me, standing in the doorway. "I know Mr. Riley, Mr. Roth and Miss Pettigrew were in the courtroom yesterday, when Mr. Delacorte was let go. Did any of you see him after that?"

The ladies looked at each other. Mrs. Long spoke up: "I did not see Bertram. However, I heard someone come into the house…"

"Which house is that?" Clubber took out his notebook and a pencil, to jot down whatever facts would come to light.

"We have recently taken residence on Thirty-Second Street," Mrs. Long said, with some pride.

"Didn't wait for First of May?" Williams was referring to the New York custom of renting a house from year to year, and moving on May first. Moving in April was considered premature.

"Mr. Long saw no reason to wait, as long as the house was ready for occupancy," Mrs. Long explained. "My sister and her son were to have rooms, of course, but there were some differences of opinion between Bertram and his uncle that led to his removing himself from our home."

"And I'll bet Mrs. Delacorte had a conniption fit when Bertie moved out," I muttered to Michael.

"No takers," Michael replied, and I nearly gave myself a choking

THE GUILTY CLIENT

fit suppressing my giggles.

Williams continued his questioning. "Did you actually see Mr. Delacorte in your house yesterday?"

Mrs. Long looked down at her sister and sighed. "I could not swear that I did," she said. "I heard someone coming up the stairs, and I heard water being run."

"Only the best for the Longs," Joshua commented, under his breath, to Michael and me. "Hot and cold running water, gaslight in all rooms, and a servant to take care of you at all hours."

"Not the life of this Riley," Michael answered. "And that explains where Bertie changed his clothes."

"What about you, ma'am?" Williams tried to tone his voice down, to accommodate the grieving mother. "Did your son pay you a visit, just to let you know he was safe and out of jail?"

"I didn't see him," Mrs. Delacorte said. She started crying again. "I was very cross with him, you see. I had heard that he had seen That Woman at This Place, and I had told him not to do so. I did not want him to move from the house. He was my only hope! I had such plans for him! But he wouldn't listen to me, and he would go out, and he wouldn't give up his pleasures for his mother's sake…" Once again she dissolved in hysterical tears.

"If this is what he had to put up with, I can see why he'd go anywhere, even here, to get away from his Mama," Michael murmured, and I had to agree with him. Living with that family situation must have been galling to a man of Broadway Bertie's tastes.

Williams summed it up: "Then none of you saw Mr. Delacorte after he left this place three days ago?"

"I certainly did not," declared Mrs. Mears.

"Nor did I," added Miss Dawson.

Williams nodded, then said, "So much for Mr. Delacorte."

I said, just loud enough to be heard, "And what about Mrs. Kendall?"

Everyone turned to stare at me. I felt my face grow red, but I persevered. "Well, he was arrested for killing her, but he couldn't have, because he was dancing with me at the Veterans' Ball when the clock struck ten here. And if he didn't kill her, then who did?"

"It was a burglar, they said," quavered Miss Dawson.

"It must have been one of those dreadful gangs," Mrs. Mears agreed with her.

"Miss Pettigrew, I am conducting this investigation!" Clubber Williams shouted. "Your statement has already been noted."

"No one questioned me when Mr. Delacorte was first suspected," I argued. "Otherwise, he would never have been arrested at all."

"Who is that dreadful young woman?" Mrs. Delacorte came up for air from her handkerchief.

"That's Margaret Pettigrew," Mrs. Long told her sister. "Katerina van Horn's child."

"Whatever happened to Katerina?" Mrs. Delacorte asked. She seemed to be off in some world of her own.

"Don't you remember, Juliet? She married that journalist and went to California," her sister told her.

"Then why is she here?" Mrs. Delacorte looked around her in confusion. "What is this place? This is not our home, Nerissa."

"No, Juliet, it is a boarding-house, where Bertram lived."

"Where is Bertram? He should be home by now." Mrs. Delacorte stared blankly about her. "Nerissa, I do not feel well at all." She applied the handkerchief and the vinaigrette to her nose once more.

Mrs. Long stood up. "Captain Williams, I see no reason to continue this inquisition. As you see, my sister is unwell. I wish to take her home at once. You may continue to do your duty here, and when you have finished, you may call on my husband and inform him of your progress in bringing the murderer of my dear sister's son to justice. Good day, Mrs. Smith. You may send a reckoning of Bertram's expenses to Mr. Long, and he will see that you are paid whatever Bertram owed you."

With that, Mrs. Long gathered up her sister, and swept regally from the parlor, pointedly ignoring Aunt Sarah and me, and marching past Michael and Joshua as if they did not exist.

She nearly knocked over the two men who were being let in the front door as she descended the stoop. The street urchins and assorted passers-by watched as the two ladies were arranged into their carriage, and the whole equipage drove off.

Aunt Sarah, Joshua, Michael and I watched the scene from the front hall. Mrs. Smith hovered behind us.

THE GUILTY CLIENT

Aunt Sarah shrugged and looked at me. "I think we have done all we can here, dear," she said with a sigh. "I told Reuben to pick us up at the corner. Joshua, Michael, please come to dine tonight."

I added my own pleas. "It's the Italian cook," I explained. "Uncle Ephraim might not appreciate her cuisine. Besides, we've got a lot to talk about, and not much time to do it in if we're going to beat Clubber Williams to the gate."

Michael and Joshua exchanged looks, then nodded. "I'm going back to Chambers Street," Michael said. "I told Young Tweed I'd get back to the office, and I'd better make good on that before someone else gets my cases."

"And I have a few errands of my own," Joshua added. "But I'll be there for dinner. Seven o'clock?"

"Seven it is," Aunt Sarah said. She turned to Mrs. Smith. "Phoebe, I am so sorry all this happened."

"I didn't expect one of my guests to be murdered," Mrs. Smith said. "Nor did I expect to have another of the guests arrested for the crime. I do not know whether my current guests will remain past the First of May. This is just dreadful, Sarah. Perhaps this was not as good an idea as we thought."

"Phoebe, you must bear up!" Aunt Sarah told her. "I will come back tomorrow, and then we can sort all this out. Margaret, the cab is here!"

Reuben had tooled the cab right up to the front door, thanks to Michael's directions, and I let Aunt Sarah and Mrs. Smith make their goodbyes while I pondered what I had discovered about Bertram Delacorte…and what I was beginning to surmise about Suzanna Kendall.

CHAPTER 12

The ride back to Bank Street was a somber one. Aunt Sarah was uncharacteristically silent, and I had a good deal to think over after the visit to Mrs. Smith's boarding house. I had had only a glimpse of the small pasteboard from Mrs. Kendall's trunk before I slipped it into my reticule. More than anything I wanted privacy to examine the thing before I turned it over to Uncle Ephraim and the others.

We pulled into Bank Street and into the middle of what looked like a small riot. Our neighbors were waiting for us, led by Mrs. Murphy, an Irish woman with a deceptively small frame that held a mighty voice. Mrs. Murphy and her brood had taken over the brick house next to ours, which made her a major power amongst the neighborhood women. Mrs. Murphy's rental of a whole building trumped the other women on Bank Street, who rented one or two rooms for their families in the houses whose owners had decamped to the East Side. Mrs. Murphy's husband, long deceased, had been one of those volunteers who took up the paid position of Fireman, and had died heroically in the line of duty, leaving Mrs. Murphy with several children and a small pension. Mrs. Murphy's son Thomas had moved up the social scale, and was now the Democratic Party's Ward Heeler for Bank Street and environs. Between her son's prestige and her own personality, Mrs. Murphy was the de facto ruler of the distaff side of Bank Street, and considered herself the neighborhood spokeswoman when necessary. Apparently, she now felt it was necessary.

Behind her were ranged the rest of the inhabitants of the shabby tenements that lurked behind the more respectable facades of the brick houses built by tradesmen in the days when Bank Street was a green and leafy retreat from the noisome atmosphere further downtown. The City had grown around these houses, and their owners were now comfortably ensconced in new brownstone residences in the East Thirties, leaving their houses to be partitioned off into smaller and smaller apartments. Nevertheless, the inhabitants of Bank Street still considered themselves a cut above the wretches in the tenements of Five Points, in that they often had an entire floor to themselves in those houses that had been abandoned by the gentlefolk of Aunt Sarah's generation. The streets might not yet be gaslit, but they were cleaned once a month. The summer breezes off the river cooled down the steaming July and August heat waves. The snow was cleared in the winter. All told, Bank street was not a bad location for a family in modest circumstances that intended to rise to better things.

Aunt Sarah, conscious of her superior social standing, did not speak directly to the women of the laboring classes. Instead, she looked at me, and asked, "Margaret, what is going on?"

I turned to Mrs. Murphy, and inquired politely, "Is there something amiss, Mrs. Murphy?"

Mrs. Murphy came directly to the point. "It's that smell," she stated.

I took a deep breath. True, there was a distinct odor wafting from the rear of our house, overpowering the familiar scents of New York city streets: horse droppings, grease, and the tangy salt of the Hudson River making its way across Manhattan Island.

"It seems to be garlic." I identified the aroma.

"It's pizining the neighborhood," Mrs. Murphy declared.

"I wouldn't go that far," I said. "It must be our new cook. She's from Italy, I believe." I didn't really want to deal with cooks or Mrs. Murphy. I wanted to go to my room and look at that pasteboard whatever-it-was. Mrs. Murphy was not to be mollified.

"Miss Peggy, we understand that Mrs. Pettigrew is a lady, and as such, she must hire someone to do for her, and we also understand that some of them that do for her don't know our ways, but this is too much! We been smellin' that stink all afternoon, and it won't do, Miss Peggy. It just won't do!"

"I believe the Italians use garlic," I said. "Apparently, this one does, quite a bit of it." I was beginning to resent Mrs. Murphy's hectoring tone and her attitude of righteous indignation. I could have mentioned that the aromas of boiling cabbage and soiled infants' garments were not particularly pleasant either, and both were emanating from her back door.

"You tell that cook of yours that this is a decent neighborhood, and we'll not have them Dagos here. Tell her to take herself off to Little Italy, if she's goin' to use them heathenish tricks." Mrs. Murphy planted herself in front of me, arms folded, clearly aiming to assert her supremacy on Bank Street.

"I don't think she understands much English," I told Mrs. Murphy. "She has not been in this country very long. She speaks Italian."

"Greenhorn, just off the boat?" Mrs. Murphy relayed this back to her minions. The women behind her muttered amongst themselves. "Anyone of yez talk Dago?"

A hand went up in the crowd. A girl was thrust forward, much to her embarrassment, followed by a short stout woman, apparently her mother.

"I know some Italian," the girl admitted.

"And who are you?" Mrs. Murphy looked the girl over.

The girl dropped a curtsy towards Aunt Sarah, then said, "If you please, I'm Rose Fenster, two doors back. I study at the Academy of Music, and I sing in the opera chorus. A good many of the musicians are Italian, and the operas are in Italian, so I've picked up a bit of the lingo."

I saw my salvation. "How fortunate for us that you are here. You must come and act as translator." I started towards the back door of our house, while Aunt Sarah tried to make her escape through the official, i.e., front entrance. Alas, Mandy was not holding the door open for her, as she should have been. The front door remained closed.

Mrs. Fenster saw her chance to get a glimpse into the forbidden Pettigrew territory. None of the Bank Street residents had gotten farther into our house than the front hall, when Uncle Ephraim doled out New Years' wassail to any who cared to knock. Aunt Sarah might allow an immigrant into the kitchen, but the parlors were most definitely a bastion not to be breached by the likes of Mrs. Murphy, no matter how high her son might rise in the Tammany firmament.

Mrs. Murphy and Mrs. Fenster consulted in undertones.

"My Rosie don't go into no kitchen," Mrs. Fenster stated, in a heavy Germanic accent. "She's gonna be in the opera. She's gonna be a star!"

"Mamma!" Rosie protested. "Miss Peggy's a lady. She wouldn't ask me to do something that wasn't decent."

I decided to bring this drama to a halt, and take it off the public stage. "Mrs. Fenster, if Rosie can use her gift for languages, which she clearly has, for the betterment of the entire neighborhood, I'm sure you'll agree that she should do it. And since the cook is in the kitchen, perhaps we should let her do it there. There is nothing untoward about lending a hand to a neighbor." I smiled at the assembled women. A few smiled back.

There was a general murmur of approval amongst the women. I added one more bolt to the quiver: "And of course, you must come with her, Mrs. Fenster, to lend her your support." Mrs. Fenster looked at Mrs. Murphy. Mrs. Murphy nodded briefly.

"I'll go along, too, just to see things is done right," said the Queen of Bank Street.

Aunt Sarah looked around helplessly, then did the unthinkable. She let herself into her own house, leaving me to cope with the irate delegation.

I led Mrs. Fester and Rose through the alley and to the back garden, where I tried to grow a few herbs and vegetables for the pot. The kitchen door was open, to allow the air to circulate into the kitchen, and the smell of garlic to evaporate into the atmosphere of Bank Street.

Mandy's defection from door duty was explained. She stood at the stove, stirring something brown that seethed like a witch's brew. Maria Luisa was instructing her in loud and incomprehensible Italian terms, while rolling out something that might have been cake or pie dough.

"*Che' la?* Who dis?" Maria Luisa turned around, rolling pin in hand. Her face was scarlet from the heat of the stove, and strands of hair had escaped from her head-kerchief, giving her the look of one of the wilder hags in an Italian opera.

Rose took one look, and backed away. Her mother was made of sterner stuff. "Rosie, Miss Pettigrew vants you should talk to dis voman. You talk!"

"*Buon giorno.*" Rosie quavered out.

Maria Luisa's grim expression relaxed into a grateful smile. "*Parla Italiano!*" She continued in a babble of liquid sounds that clearly bore no resemblance to anything Rosie might have heard in the chorus at the Academy of Music.

"*Andante, andante!*" I could tell that Rose was trying to remember any and all words of Italian that might be useful. Few operas deal with such realities as cookery, and while her fellow-musicians would have known food-related terms, it is most unlikely that they would have used them in her company.

Rose tried again. "*Signora, che facie?*"

Maria Luisa stated once more, "I cook." I began to realize that this was more or less the extent of her English vocabulary, which could be taken either as a description of her profession or a verbal statement of activity.

"Um, *e aiolo?*," Rosie said, recalling at least one Italian word that would apply. "*Ritardando, per favore.*"

Maria Luisa frowned, then seemed to grasp that something was amiss. "*Aiolo, si.*" She pointed at the cloves on the kitchen table.

"*Troppo aiolo,*" Rosie said. "*Il signor Pettigrew* has a stomach *molto delicato.*" She patted the appropriate portion of her anatomy, which was considerably less than Uncle Ephraim's. "*Aiolo, ma non troppo.*" She turned to the rest of her audience. "I'm trying to tell her not to use too much garlic."

Clearly the concept of too much garlic never occurred to Maria Luisa "*Non troppo!*" She brought the rolling pin down on the table for emphasis.

Rosie glanced at her mother and made one more attempt to mollify the cook. "Signora Pettigrew doesn't like garlic," she said. "*La signora no amo aiolo.*"

"*Bah!*" Maria Luisa turned back to the pan simmering on the stove. It smelled very interesting, but heavily spiced. I didn't think Uncle Ephraim would enjoy eating it.

I smiled at the two older ladies, then said, "You did your best, Miss

Rosie. I think we'd best let Maria Luisa get on with her cooking." I herded them out into the garden, and back down the alley, to the waiting crowd.

"I spoke to her," Rosie told them. "I told her she was using too much garlic."

"And?" One of the other women asked.

"She didn't think so," Rosie told her.

"She's got to go," Mrs. Murphy stated.

I knew what Aunt Sarah would say to that, but I put it more tactfully. "Mrs. Murphy, I understand your objections to this cookery, but you can't expect Mrs. Pettigrew to hire her servants to your liking."

"I sent her one of my own," Mrs. Murphy pointed out.

"Yes, you did," I agreed. " As I recall, one of your relations applied for the position of cook and was not acceptable because she had never seen a closed stove before, let alone used one. I thank you for your efforts, Miss Fenster, but I think I will have to deal with Maria Luisa from now on."

"This don't sit well, Miss Peggy," Mrs. Murphy warned me. "My Tom will hear about this."

I didn't think anything Tom Murphy said or did would affect the Pettigrew position one way or another. Uncle Ephraim was a Stalwart Republican, not one of Tammany's minions, and if he owed allegiance to any political boss, it would be to Mr. Conkling in Albany, not to Boss Tweed. Still, the neighborhood women could make life difficult for Mandy, and for her sake I tried once more to mollify the situation.

"You know how Mr. Pettigrew is about cooks," I said, with a rueful smile. "I suspect that Maria Luisa will be on her way to someone else's kitchen by the end of the week."

"She better be." With this Parthian shot, Mrs. Murphy retreated to her own kitchen, which was contributing its own pungent aromas of boiling cabbage to the evening air.

The crowd dispersed, and I mounted the three steps up to the front door. I saw Uncle Ephraim rounding the corner of West Street and making his way homeward, stopping now and again to observe the youth of Bank Street as they whooped and ran and did what youngsters always do, getting in the way of their elders.

Uncle Ephraim stopped and sniffed the air as he approached the house. His affable expression began to coalesce into a frown.

"What sort of cook has Sarah got this time?" he exclaimed.

"It's a long story," I said. "And I think I have something for you that may tell us who and what Mrs. Kendall was."

We entered the house together, ready for whatever Maria Luisa would serve up. I only hoped that Uncle Ephraim could eat it.

CHAPTER 13

Dinner was not a success.

Michael and Joshua turned up, in fresh shirts and collars, willing to partake of whatever delights Maria Luisa had decided to set upon the table, but nothing could make that meal remotely palatable.

The soup was a thick brown concoction with vegetables and noodles, called minestrone, strongly flavored with garlic. The fish course was a platter of roasted peppers and onions, with small salty objects in between slices of sausage, all flavored with garlic. The *pollo alla cacciatore* turned out to be pieces of chicken covered with a bright red sauce made from tomatoes and garlic, served with the flat noodles that Maria Luisa had been rolling out when we saw her in the kitchen. The only bright spot on the entire menu was the sweet, and even that was odd: a sort of crispy pancake stuffed with cheese, sweetened with almonds, that Maria Luisa called *cannolli*.

Uncle Ephraim tasted one dish after another, and rejected most of them. Aunt Sarah gamely ate what Mandy set before her, and I did my best, but the garlic that permeated the entire menu nauseated me, and I could only take a few bites before I had to resort to the bread and butter to soothe my palate. As for Michael and Joshua, they ate what they could and agreed that whatever it was, it was better than the camp food that they had endured during their wartime years. The conversation was limited to the food, since Aunt Sarah had banned business talk from the dinner-table, and there was nothing we all wanted more than to go over what we had learned about our Guilty Client.

At last, Uncle Ephraim stood up and stated, "Sarah, that woman has no business in this kitchen. She goes tomorrow!"

"But Ephraim," Aunt Sarah protested, "I can't let her go. I don't know if I can get another cook by tomorrow night."

"There are agencies," Michael pointed out.

"But they ask a fee," Aunt Sarah said.

Uncle Ephraim made the supreme sacrifice. "Pay it!" he ordered. "Do what you have to, but get that ...that person out of this house!" He stamped off to his sanctuary, his own den, the front room that had once been his father-in-law's office.

The house on Bank Street had been built with a central staircase that led up to the bedchambers on the second floor. The front and back parlors were to the left of the front hall; Uncle Ephraim's den and the dining room matched them on the right. The kitchen was at the back of the house, with only a small pantry in between the kitchen and the dining room. Usually this was a good arrangement, since the food could be served hot from the kitchen. Alas, there was one grave deficiency in placing the kitchen so close to the living-quarters. On this night the aroma of garlic permeated the dining room, and made its way forward and upward, to the bedchambers above.

The usages of Polite Society meant that the ladies (Aunt Sarah and myself) were supposed to remove ourselves to the back parlor after the sweet had been eaten, leaving the gentlemen (Uncle Ephraim, Joshua and Michael) to sit and drink and smoke. Aunt Sarah rose to her feet and signaled me that I must join her. I sighed, gathered my skirts and got ready to follow her into the back parlor, as Society demanded. I have always felt that this custom was ridiculous, but Aunt Sarah insisted that whatever else I did during the day, in the evening I was a lady, and I would obey the dictates of Society.

On that night, however, I was reprieved. "Peggy, I want you to come and take notes," Uncle Ephraim ordered, and I gratefully joined the gentlemen as they left the dinner table for Mandy to clear.

Uncle Ephraim's den was crowded with books and furniture. Three shelves along one wall held his law books and the codes of the State of New York and the City of New York, along with the much-thumbed Blackstone and books on Constitutional law. Another bookcase contained atlases and books of travel and adventure, together with the works of Mr. Dickens and Mr. Thackeray. There were some new books, too, including the one about whaling by Mr. Melville, and a brand-new author about whom I'd heard a good deal, a Mr. Mark Twain, who had been lecturing about his adventures on a guided tour of Europe and the Holy Land.

The furnishings were old and shabby but comfortable: Uncle Ephraim's favorite easy chair, a roll-top desk, and several small side chairs that could be moved to make room or make a cozy circle around the fireplace. I had my own small chair across from Uncle Ephraim's large one, with a wooden sewing table beside it. I had removed the usual threads and notions from the sewing table drawers, and replaced them with pen, ink, and sketch pad. Since gas had not yet come to Bank Street, two kerosene lamps shed a soft glow in the room, one on my small table, another on the desk.

The focal point of Uncle Ephraim's den was the shrine on the mantelpiece over the fireplace. Here he had placed a signed photograph of Mr. Lincoln, given to him in recognition for his efforts in assisting General Arthur in supplying the troops by keeping the waterfront bullies in check during the War. There was a copy of the newspaper with the shocking headline of the assassination, and another with the funeral procession arrangements. The entire assemblage was surmounted by a mourning wreath and bow. It was the first thing anyone saw when they entered the room, and I always felt I should genuflect before sitting down at my rightful place underneath it.

Uncle Ephraim dropped into his chair with a grunt and looked us over. Joshua had taken a position near the fireplace, where he could rest his bad arm; Michael drew up a chair next to my little table. I took out my pen and lined paper, to make notes. The three of us looked at Uncle Ephraim with the expressions of eager school children ready to recite for the teacher.

"So," Uncle Ephraim began. "Where do we stand?"

Joshua and Michael looked at each other, as if to decide which one should speak first. I jumped into the breach.

"Aunt Sarah and I went to see Mrs. Smith," I said. "We learned a little about the Kendall murder, and a little about the character of Bertram Delacorte."

"Not a nice fellow," Michael commented. "And what he was doing at Mrs. Smith's I cannot tell you. He had been living at Long's with his mother since they came back from Europe. There was some sort of quarrel, and Long put him out of the house."

"Mr. Long mentioned that quarrel this morning," I said.

"Mrs. Delacorte seems to be a very emotional woman," Joshua said carefully.

"She's had a good deal of trouble in her life," Uncle Ephraim said. "It can't be pleasant knowing your husband and your brother are shooting at each other, especially when neither of them comes back from the War."

"She certainly indulged Bertram," I said. "It must have taken a major upset to get him out of Long's house."

"And he didn't go far," Michael put in. "Long's house is only a few blocks away from Mrs. Smith's. He must have gone back to Mama after he finished with us, because he left all his clothes at the boarding house, including a set of tails and all that goes with them, shirt studs and tie-pin."

"His watch wasn't there," I pointed out. "But he left his pistol. He would have taken that if he was going off to the Points or somewhere else dangerous."

"Pistol, eh?" Uncle Ephraim raised his eyebrows.

"One-shot derringer pop-gun," Michael sneered. "He'd be lucky if he even got a shot off before some bully-boy clubbed him down."

Joshua frowned. "Seems to me he'd have taken it with him if he was going to a place like the Devil's Hole," he said. "Why'd he leave it behind?"

Michael shrugged. "Another mystery?"

Uncle Ephraim summed it up. "He left the courthouse, he went to Long's house on Thirty-Second Street, where he bathed and changed his clothes. I suppose he had something to eat, too."

"We can find out when we interview the servants at the Long residence," Michael said.

"That don't matter," Uncle Ephraim told him. "I want to know where he went after he left Long's."

"And what the quarrel was about," I added. "He left Mr. Long's household to live at Mrs. Smith's because of the quarrel, and he met Mrs. Kendall there, and a few days later she was killed. I still don't understand why the police waited two whole weeks before they arrested him."

THE GUILTY CLIENT

"It was Holy Week," Michael reminded us, and thought that explained it all. "Walling had already put the Kendall killing down as a failed burglary, so there wasn't much interest in it. Croker wasn't about to waste his time investigating the death of some woman in a boarding-house who'd surprised a burglar and got stabbed for her pains."

It seemed to me that New York City's political squabbles between the Coroner's office, who were responsible for investigating suspicious deaths and the New York City Metropolitan Police, who were supposed to protect the public, did not lead to either good policing or more protection for anyone.

"And then someone alerted the Coroner's men that there was a coat with blood on it in Delacorte's room," Joshua said.

"A man who changes his clothes twice a day leaves a coat with blood on it in his wardrobe?" I said. "I don't think so."

"My thought exactly," Joshua agreed.

I went over it again in my mind. "I still don't understand why Bertram would continue to live at Mrs. Smith's after the murder," I said. "Unless he thought that he was safe. After all, the murder had been put down to some anonymous burglar, and he did have an alibi. Unless, of course, he had changed the clock, but that would mean that he had planned the murder, and that's impossible."

"Eh?" Uncle Ephraim's eyebrows went up again.

I tried to think it through. "You see, everyone in that house goes by that particular hall clock. They know what time it is because they hear the chimes. But suppose someone wanted to make it appear that a murder had occurred at ten o'clock that had really happened at nine? He'd move the hands of the clock, then do the deed, and move them back when he got back into the house."

"Sounds complicated," Michael objected.

"But it does make sense," Joshua said. "The blood soaked into the wooden floor boards, and the body was stiff when the police came by. Mrs. Kendall hadn't been killed a few minutes before they arrived; there had to have been time for the blood to congeal, and to soak into the floor."

"And that would explain why no one heard it, either," I said. "Mrs. Smith and her family would be upstairs, on the top floor, and there are so many of them, all talking at once, it's impossible to hear anything. As for the servants, they would be banging about in the kitchen, cleaning the pots and pans. They might have heard something, but they wouldn't know what."

"But they did hear someone cry out as the clock struck ten," Michael said. "That's when they all came running up the stairs, and that girl Biddy says she saw someone going over the fence in the back garden."

"How could she see anything?" I asked. "There's no lighting in the garden."

"She said there was enough light coming through the kitchen window to make out someone going over the fence, and that's all she said." Michael waved his hands as if to clear the air of all the lies and fabrications that went with a murder investigation.

"So, the police do what they always do, which is not very much," I said with a sniff. "They probably asked the servants if they saw any suspicious characters lurking about, and whether Mrs. Kendall had any enemies."

"And the answer to both of those is No, and No," Michael said. "I went over that when I got the case. There was the note, pencil on plain paper, stating that they'd find something interesting in the wardrobe in Bertram Delacorte's room at Mrs. Smith's. There was a warrant, it was duly served, and Walling's men found a large overcoat covered in blood, jammed into the back of the wardrobe. That was all the evidence they had, but it was enough to issue the arrest warrant."

"Sounds like a put-up job to me," Uncle Ephraim said.

"And so I stated in court," Joshua said. "I didn't get more than a few minutes with Mr. Delacorte, but he told me that he'd been arrested at the Devil's Hole on West Fourteenth Street, where he'd been having a small drink or two with some friends."

"A drink or two? At four in the afternoon?" Michael shook his head. "That lad was on his way to becoming a drunkard, if he wasn't one already."

I burst out, "Why does everyone call him a 'lad' or 'a boy'? He was twenty-five years old, which, I may add, is just as old as I am! And I'm considered an Old Maid, and he's still a Boy? It's just not fair!"

THE GUILTY CLIENT

The men stared at me as if I'd just burst into flames. Then Uncle Ephraim said, "Peggy, you're right. And you knew Bertram better than any of us. You were in dancing class with him, weren't you?"

"He one of the Young Gentlemen who were brought around to Miss Porter's to be our partners when we had our dancing classes," I said. "He'd been brought North when the War started, and he was always bragging about how the Rebs were going to win. I thought it was horrid of him especially when his father was at the Front. And then his uncle Long brought him around to you when he'd been let off the Draft. He told you to take him on, and you refused to do it."

"I told him I already had a clerk, which was you, Peggy, and that I didn't need some youngster who would be called up at any moment. At which, Long told me that he'd already arranged for a substitute to serve for Bertram if need be, and that the youngster needed the practical experience of a law office under his belt before he took on the classes at Columbia School of Law."

"And he couldn't take his nephew into his own firm, lest he be accused of favoritism," Michael said. "That's nonsense, and we all knew it. Plenty of young men in their relatives' businesses."

"Boys younger than Bertram were serving their country," I said. "I always felt that he was a slacker, who wouldn't do his duty." I tried not to look at Joshua, who had done his duty, and had paid the price for it.

"Not so," Uncle Ephraim said. "Bertram was only eighteen, and his father was serving, so he could have gotten a staff position. The thing of it was, his mother was making no end of a fuss, and Long just paid some bully-boy to take Bertram's place when his number was called to have a little peace at home. That's the way it was, and I'm the one who should know, being that I was on that Lottery Committee."

Joshua had been silent while we thrashed all this out. Then he said, "As I see it, we have to find out more about Suzanna Kendall. No one seems to know much about her life before she came North to New York."

"I have a few ideas about that," I said. "I'll have to go through my sketchbooks and see if I can find that picture I drew of her at the Musical Evening. It's a pity that so many records were destroyed in the South during the War."

"You think Mrs. Kendall was hiding something?" Michael asked.

"I found at least one thing she was hiding," I replied. I finally produced the small pasteboard object that had been in my skirt pocket all during dinner. "This was under the bottom lining of her trunk."

"That's concealing evidence!" Michael snatched the pasteboard from my hand.

"It's something the police missed," I corrected him. "I think it's a carte de visite photograph." It was a picture of a man in Union uniform, his cap set at a rakish angle, grinning at the camera.

"So it is," said Michael. He passed it to Uncle Ephraim. "What do you make of it?"

Uncle Ephraim scrutinized the photograph, then handed it over to Joshua. "There's a magnifying lens on my desk," he said. "See if you can make out what regiment this fellow is from?"

Michael took the photograph, I brought the lamp closer, and the three of us peered through the lens.

"I make it out to be Infantry," Michael said at last. "And he's not an officer, that's for sure."

"He's got a Kearny badge on his shoulder," Joshua said, "and that means he joined after '63."

"Not one of our boys, then," Michael said. "A Draftee?"

"Possibly," Joshua mused. "Not a boy, but still young. Maybe, twenty, twenty-two, would you say?"

"Could be one of the Bounty Boys," Michael said. "You know, Captain, there are some people who might be able to tell us who this fellow is. I've kept up with some of the boys who stayed on after you went to New Orleans and I got mustered out. I'll go have a drink with them tonight. Do you mind if I take this with me, sir?" he asked Uncle Ephraim.

"You go right ahead, Michael," Uncle Ephraim said. "Joshua, I want you to talk to those two young men at Mrs. Smith's. Find out what they were doing the night Mrs. Kendall was killed. Then drop by the Fifth Avenue Hotel, and see what the word is there. Our friend Henry Ward Long is known to step by there, and he might even drop a word in your ear as to his feelings towards his nephew."

THE GUILTY CLIENT

Joshua grinned sardonically. "I do not think Mr. Long will want to converse with so lowly a person as the lawyer who let his darling Bertram walk free, only to be set upon twelve hours later."

"That soon, eh?" Uncle Ephraim

"So it would seem," Joshua said. "He was out of the courtroom by two; give him a few hours to bathe and dress, go somewhere and dine…"

"Delmonico's? Rector's?" Michael guessed.

"Or somewhere else," Joshua conceded. "Then he goes… where?"

"Somewhere on the West Side," Uncle Ephraim said. "You might try some of the, um, places on West Twenty-Fifth Street."

"And what am I suppose to do?" I asked rebelliously. "Sit here and wait until you come back victorious?"

"Exactly so," Uncle Ephraim said. "I want you to finish writing these notes, and then go have a word with that cook."

"My mother would have put on trousers and gone out with Michael," I grumbled. "It's just not fair."

"With all respect to Specs, she had Manny with her," Uncle Ephraim reminded me. "And she was of a slimmer build than you. I must tell you, Peggy, no one could ever mistake you for a boy, trousers or no trousers."

I could not deny this. I had to watch as Joshua and Michael retrieved their hats and went out into Bank Street. Then I went over Michael's notes and re-copied them.

Finally, I went through my sketch-books, looking for the drawings I had made some months before of the people at Mrs. Smith's Musical Evening. I found the picture of Mrs. Kendall: a strikingly handsome woman with a regular profile and lustrous dark hair gathered into a chignon at the back of her neck. I tried to recall whether or not she had spoken more than a few words to anyone, but all I could remember was her very beautiful voice, a throbbing contralto with a most poignant sound. What had she sung? Oh yes…Mr. Foster's "Old Kentucky Home". She would have, wouldn't she? I thought to myself, as I prepared to do battle with Maria Louisa. It would be a fitting climax to one of the most stressful days I had spent since the mob had come raging up Bank Street in '63.

SECTION 4: JOSHUA
CHAPTER 14

I SHALL DICTATE THESE NOTES to Miss Peggy, at her request, to complete this record. I can write after a fashion with my left hand, but it is difficult. At first I was somewhat uncomfortable with having a woman as amanuensis, but I have become used to Miss Peggy's presence in Mr. Pettigrew's office. I must add, for the accuracy of the record, that certain adjectives have been deleted from this report, and certain nouns have been revised. The language of men is earthy, and not always fit for ladies' ears.

That said, I resume the narrative of the Guilty Client.

"We won't melt in a bit of water," he told me. "I'm off to see a few of the lads, and I'd be laughed out of a saloon if I came in with a bumbershoot and a mackintosh coat."

"I've been wet and cold often enough not to want to do it again," I said. "But this can't last too long. You go check your saloons, Michael, and I'll have a word with the gentlemen boarders at Mrs. Smith's. It's not too late for an evening call, I think."

"Where will you be if I find out something you should know?" Michael asked.

"If I'm not at Mrs. Smith's, I'll be at the Fifth Avenue Hotel, probably at the bar," I told him. "And if I'm not in the bar, I'll be upstairs, at the Union League Club. You can send a runner down there." We paced together, and I said, "You know, we may be going over old territory here. Walling must have been down this road before us."

Michael shook his head. "I've read his report," he said. "All he did was follow that anonymous tip. Once he found the greatcoat with the blood on it, he decided he had his man, and Bertram Delacorte was arrested within the day."

"They didn't give you much to go on," I said. Both of us knew that Bertram Delacorte had been set up. The question in my mind was, who hated him so much that they wanted the man hanged for a murder he didn't commit?

To that end I caught a cab and got over to Mrs. Smith's boarding house once again.

The manservant, Clem, answered my knock. He looked me over carefully before allowing me to enter the front hall.

"Good evening," I greeted him. "You remember me. The lawyer who represented Mr. Delacorte."

Clem nodded briefly. "Indeed, sir." He had been well trained, for there was no sign of emotion on his face.

I said, "I would like to speak to the two gentlemen who board here, Mr. Lawton and Mr. Donovan, I believe their names are."

"Is this an official visit?" Clem asked.

"Not precisely," I said. "There are a few points I have to clear up before I can call this case closed."

"I should think, sir, that with Mr. Delacorte's death the case would be considered closed," Clem said.

"It is not," I said. "Will you please ask Mr. Lawton and Mr. Donovan to join me? Otherwise, I will have to join them in the parlor, which might upset the ladies."

"If you will wait here, sir, I will see if they wish to join you." Clem moved off, leaving me to contemplate the hall rug and a piece of furniture covered with damp coats and hats.

I recognized the two men who followed Clem into the hall as the two who had arrived just as Michael and I were leaving that afternoon. One was a tall, thin fellow with a straggling mustache who walked with a decided limp; the other was a shorter, stouter man with mutton-chop sideburns and the air of confidence that goes with success.

The taller, younger man introduced himself as Roger Lawton; the other was Jerome Donovan. Both produced cigars as soon as they got into the hall.

"I could have blessed you, man, for interrupting us," Donovan said, as he lit up. "Mrs. Smith don't allow smoking in the parlor, and I wasn't about to stand outside on the stoop tonight."

"Do you care to join us?" Mr. Lawton offered me his cigar case.

I had to turn them down. I've gone off the weed since my injury, and I'm probably the better for it.

I got right to the point. "My name's Roth. I was hired by Mr. Long to represent Mr. Bertram Delacorte when he was arrested two days ago. You have heard by now that Mr. Delacorte met with an untimely death only hours after he was released from custody. I will tell you, gentlemen, that does not sit well with me. I cannot close out this case until I find out what happened to Mr. Delacorte."

"Probably some gink he'd insulted," Donoval said, blowing a smoke ring. "If ever a man was asking to be murdered it was that one."

"You didn't like him." It wasn't a question, it was a statement.

"I did not. He didn't belong here, Mr. Roth, and that's a fact. I make my living selling, sir, and I've learned to size up a customer right quick. That young man was trouble waiting to happen. I'm only sorry it happened here."

"Do you agree, Mr. Lawton?" I asked.

The younger man took his time before answering. When he did, it was in a soft Southern accent. "I barely spoke to the man. He kept very odd hours, coming home when the rest of us were up and about for our day's labors, and leaving in a dress-suit when we were preparing to retire for the night."

"So neither of you had any reason to attack him," I said.

"Attack him?" Donovan let out a laugh. "Why should I bother? The only conversation I had with him was about investments, and I could tell you, Mr. Roth, that boy had no sense at all. None at all!" He repeated it, and punctuated it with another puff on his cigar.

"How so?"

"He found out that I work on Wall Street, and he told me he had a sure-fire investment for me. He was trying to raise the coin to start a new theater, if you please, all the way up by Long Acre Square. Forty-Second Street at Broadway! Now I ask you, Mr. Roth, who's going to go all that way to see a show? Particularly the kind that youngster was thinking of producing!"

"The Show Business is very risky," I said.

"And this sort of show wouldn't last a day!" Donovan exploded with laughter. "Have you seen 'The Black Crook'?"

I admitted that I had, indeed, seen that extravaganza, which featured several female dancers wearing tights and not much else.

"Delacorte wanted to mount a production just like it, only without the fleshings, if you get my drift."

I did, and I could see where young Delacorte would have a good deal of trouble getting anyone to invest in such a production, let along putting it on in a remote area like Long Acre Square. Forty-second Street marked the northern boundary of New York City as far as most people were concerned. I'd heard of a scheme to build French flats as far as Seventy-Ninth Street, but that was as remote as the Dakotas to Society. No horse-cars went past Fiftieth, and most of the car-barns were just past Eighth Avenue, on Fifty-Seventh Street. Bertram Delacorte's theater would have been a disaster without his mounting a scandalous show. If he intended to mimic the French, with nude dancers, it would have meant financial and social ruin for his family.

I wondered if this, then, was the source of the quarrel between Mr. Long and his nephew. Broadway Bertie wanted to become another Barnum, and Mr. Henry Ward Long would have none of it. Bertram insisted; Long threw him out of the house. It still didn't explain why Bertram chose Mrs. Smith's instead of one of the better hotels, but it made a kind of sense.

Donovan went on. "I told him, like I'm telling you, that he should put his money where it will do some good. Railroads, I told him. That's where you put your money these days, not the Show Business. You follow the Commodore's lead, I said, and invest in railroads. That's where the money's going to be, I told him. Railroads. That's the future!"

Mr. Lawton nodded sagely. "I may be only a counter-jumper at Stewart's, as Mr. Delacorte so contemptuously put it," he said. "I don't have any money to invest, but even if I had, I certainly wouldn't put it into some theater that puts on vulgar plays, and leg shows."

I had to agree with them. The Show Business is notorious for promising fortunes and usually delivering bankruptcy.

I tried another topic. "I was called in to represent young Delacorte, but I never really got the gist of the case against him. What actually happened here when Mrs. Kendall, um, met her end?" Both men stopped puffing and looked at me with alarm. "I don't mean to distress you, gentlemen, but Delacorte had an air-tight alibi for the time of the murder, and if he didn't do it, someone else must have."

"I wasn't here," Donovan said quickly. "That is, I was out that night, with some friends, as I told that policeman who took down our statements. I dined out, had a few drinks, and played euchre until nearly midnight. Mrs. Smith is pretty strict about our comings and goings, but I'd tipped Clem the wink that I'd be up late, and that he should leave the door on the latch for me."

"Does he do that often?" I asked.

"Oh, I don't abuse the privilege," Donovan said, with another jovial wink. "Not like Delacorte, anyhow."

"He was in and out at all hours," Mr. Lawton added. "And he was very inconsiderate about using the bathing facilities."

"As Captain Williams put it, he hogged the bathroom," I said. "Were you in the house that evening, Mr. Lawton?"

"It was the anniversary of Appomattox," Lawton said. "Not a day I wish to celebrate."

The two of us exchanged looks that said a lot. There's something about a fellow who has seen action that makes us more like than unlike, even when we were on opposite sides of the fight. "You're a little young to have seen the elephant," I said at last.

"I was a guidon-bearer, artillery," Lawton said. "After the War, there wasn't any artillery, so I packed up the guidon and came North to seek my fortune. I have no hatred of Yankees, sir. We both fought for causes we believed were just. You won; we lost." He sighed, bleakly, but not bitterly. He was a lot more resigned than many I'd seen in my time in New Orleans.

"Then you weren't at the Veteran's Ball," I said.

"Hardly!" Lawton said. "On Appomattox Night I dined with a young lady and her family, and after dinner we had some music. I arrived back here at about the same time as the police, so I can tell you nothing about the murder."

"What about the two lady boarders?" I asked. "Surely everyone wasn't out?"

"They had gone to the theater," Donovan said. "Wallack's, I think."

"So the only people in the house were the Smith family, and the servants," I summed it up. "And not one of them heard Mrs. Kendall crying out?"

"One of them did," Donovan said. "That girl, Biddy, kept crying, saying that she'd seen someone going over the back fence."

"That is, the fence between the back garden and the alley, where the trash is put out for collection," Lawton explained. "The Smith's sometimes sit out there in fine weather."

I let that slide. "What did you two think of Mrs. Kendall?" I asked.

Donovan took a long draw of his cigar and eyed Lawton, as if to judge how much he could say in front of such an innocent youngster. "Not a bad looker," he admitted. "A mite long in the tooth, but good years ahead of her. Considerably better on the eyes than either of the school-ma'ams." He grinned, as one who appreciates female pulchritude.

"A widow, I've been told," I said.

"War widow, more likely," said Donovan. "Didn't wear weeds, didn't wear a ring."

"From the South," I said. "A good many records were lost when various armies went through. It is possible that her marriage lines might have been among them."

"I thought her a quiet, friendly person," Lawton said. "Not stand-offish, but modest. She did not intrude herself on the company."

"I also heard she had a fine singing voice. Perhaps that's what attracted Mr. Delacorte to her, if he was thinking in theatrical terms." I looked from one man to the other, to see if they agreed.

"I did not see any such attraction," Mr. Lawton said. "They barely met."

"The whole affair don't make sense," Donovan said, stubbing out the butt of his cigar. "Mrs. Kendall wasn't the kind to make enemies. Of course, there are some who would have faulted her for coming to this house, instead of the ones downtown, but I'm no bigot, and if a person decides to pass, that's their lookout."

"What!" Lawton was taken aback. "Are you saying…I mean, really! How could she…"

"Pass for White?" Donovan shrugged. "Probably had a White papa, and maybe a grandpa, too. Most of them high yaller gals are at least half white, if not more. You can't tell the difference just by looking at 'em."

Lawton was really upset. "But she dined with us…sat in the parlor…"

"Awful, ain't it? Just like real folks!" Donovan jeered. "I don't know what you Rebs have against Negroes. They serve you dinner, why not let 'em set with you to eat it? I've got no problem with it. Hell, Clem there's got better manners than some of the brokers on Wall Street."

"What would happen if Mrs. Smith found out about Mrs. Kendall's, um, past?"

I asked. "Would she do something, well, violent?"

"Do you mean, would old Smith knife her?" Donovan shook his head. "I don't think so. Word gets out as it is. I don't know as I'd stay here past First of May, if I was squeamish about those things, but I'm suited here for the time being, and I'll stay."

Lawton took a deep breath. "I didn't tell this to the police," he said, "but I did see something odd. When Mr. Delacorte arrived with his portmanteau, I was just arriving from my work. I passed Mrs. Kendall as I went up the stairs to my room. She was standing on the landing, next to the big clock, and she was staring down at Mr. Delacorte. She had a look of absolute horror on her face."

"You think she recognized him?" I asked.

"I could not say. I thought I heard her murmur something to herself, something that sounded like, 'Billy'."

"What happened then?"

"The man who brought Delacorte's traps into the hall looked up and stared at us. Then Delacorte gave him a gratuity, and he left.

Mrs. Smith called for Clem to take the trunk upstairs while she dealt with Delacorte. As for me, I went upstairs to wash up for dinner."

"And that was all?" It didn't seem like much.

"All I can tell you, Mr. Roth," Lawton said, finishing his cigar. "I am quite stunned that I did not recognize Mrs. Kendall for what she was, but I cannot hold it against her now. I guess she was just another one of those adventuresses I was warned against when I told my family that I was coming to New York."

"So it would seem," I said. "Thank you, gentlemen, for your time. You've given me a good deal to think about."

"But do you know who killed Delacorte?" Donovan asked.

"I am quite sure it was not either of you," I said, to the relief of both men. "Delacorte was killed by someone who was both tall and strong. Mr. Donovan, you're too short, and Mr. Lawton, you're not strong enough. He's out there, though, and I will find him."

And with that, I took my leave.

CHAPTER 15

I HAD A LOT TO THINK about when I walked over to the Fifth Avenue Hotel from Mrs. Smith's. It's not all that far from East Twenty-Third Street off Gramercy Park to West Twenty-Third and Fifth Avenue but it's all the difference in the world to Society. East Twenty-third is where respectable people live. The West Side isn't that respectable, and Sixth Avenue marks the borderline between them. The Fifth Avenue Hotel straddles the line, so to speak, being on the west side of Fifth Avenue.

The Fifth Avenue Hotel is considered one of the grandest edifices in the city, almost the equal of the venerable Astor House for luxury. Its management can provide public and private dining, and a set of rooms on the top floor is rented out to the Union League Club, for our particular use. I am not what is popularly termed a clubman, but I was allowed into the Union League Club by virtue of my having been an officer (and by extension, a gentleman) in the recent conflict. I find most of the members to be reasonably intelligent, and it's a good place to find a game of poker free of sharks and other annoyances.

My destination on this evening, however, was not the private but the public sector of the hotel. In particular, I wanted to talk to a few of the younger fellows who hang about at the Union Bar. Tammany Hall doesn't hold sway here; it's Republican Territory, and Roscoe Conkling's the one who calls the tune for the men who line up at the bar, not William Marcy Tweed. The older fellows drop by for a drink before they have to go home to their fine wives; younger ones, unencumbered by domesticity, may stay for an hour, then go on to a ball or something less respectable.

I must also qualify some of my previous statements. I have given the impression that I had never seen or heard of Mr. Bertram

Delacorte until our meeting at the courthouse before his arraignment. This was not strictly true. I had seen him from a distance at the Union Bar, usually in the company of other young men of his stamp: sons or grandsons of wealthy men, who had no profession of their own, and who seemed to pass the time spending their fathers' money indulging in such pleasures as billiards, horse-racing, and chasing after notorious women.

It was one of these men that I saw sitting at a small table at the edge of the barroom, with a bottle of whiskey in front of him and a glass in his hand. I noted the hastily-sewn black band on his sleeve and the long weed in his hat.

"Johnny Ellison," I said. "I was hoping to find you here. Shocking news about Bertram Delacorte."

Johnny looked up at me, trying to recall just who I was.

I pulled a chair over and sat down at the table with him. "It's Roth," I said. "I was in your father's regiment."

That seemed to penetrate through the fog of whiskey that apparently clouded his brain. "What do you know about Bertie?"

"I was hired to handle his case," I said.

Johnny started to blubber into his glass. "He was alive last night." He must have had a few before I got there, and he was well on his way to getting sloppy drunk. I just hoped I could get some sense out of him before he passed out.

"Were you with him?" I asked.

"We were together when he was arrested," Johnny said. "We were at Devil's Hole for the ratting. There was a black-and-tan feist, part terrier, part bulldog, must have put down a dozen rats in a minute. Bertie had just bet me a ten-spot that the dog would get another dozen and then the police grabbed him and took him away."

"Did they tell him what the charge was?" I asked. This would have been part of my defense, if the case had gone any farther. It's a constitutional right for a prisoner to know what he's being charged with, and if the police hadn't told Delacorte what the charge was, I could have moved for dismissal, even without Miss Peggy's confirmation of his alibi.

Johnny snuffled into his drink. "I think they said something like, 'We arrest you on the charge of murder,'" he said. "And they hauled

Bertie off in a Black Maria."

"Did you see them take him away?" I asked.

"I ran after them, when they were stuffing Bertie into the police carriage, and he yelled out, 'Tell my uncle what's happened.' I supposed he meant his Long uncle, since he'd been living with him for the last few months, and not the Delacorte clan. They'd be useless anyway, a high-nosed bunch who never cared much for Bertie or his mother."

"Bertie's mother was a Southerner, wasn't she?" I said. "Colonel Delacorte was right to send her North."

"I suppose so," Johnny said. "But that's not the point, is it? I had to sober up before I went to see Mr. Henry Ward Long, and by the time I'd gotten back to my lodgings, and put myself together and put on a better shirt and collar, it was nearly six o'clock, and I just caught him on his way out of his office and on his way uptown. And then I was nearly killed by that Plug-ugly brute he's taken on to keep the rest of the riff-raff off his new carriage, before I could get Bertie's message through."

"And how did Mr. Long take it?" I asked.

"That man is made of ice," Johnny said. "He heard me out, and then he said, 'It won't do the lad any harm to sit in a cell until morning. I'll see to him then.' And off he went, cool as a cucumber, with his coachman whipping up those grays of his, and the Plug-ugly glaring down at me like I was a cockroach."

I listened to this and started counting back. If Bertram Delacorte had been arrested in the afternoon, the word must have gotten to Mr. Long well before Johnny Ellison arrived. No one of Bertram Delacorte's standing would be allowed to pass into the Tombs unnoticed and unremarked. If nothing else, one of the police reporters would have been on Long's doorstep within the hour, asking if his nephew had, indeed, committed murder, and what did he have to say about it.

That being the case, it was starting to dawn on me that Mr. Henry Ward Long might have had some ulterior motive in hiring Uncle Ephraim Pettigrew to defend his nephew, and bringing me into the case with no preparation whatever. Why would he try to sabotage his nephew's case? It bore thinking about.

Johnny was blubbering into his drink again. "And I was the very first one Bertie came to when you got him off," he said. "He told me you weren't all that clever, but that fat girl from Pettigrew's office came in at the last minute, just like a play, with the information that he was at the Veteran's Ball when that wretched woman was killed, and so he couldn't have done it at all."

"When did you see him last?" I asked.

Johnny took another swig of the whiskey, to jog his memory. "Dinner time," he said. "We went to Rector's, and had a good dinner. Then we went to some places and had some drinks, and then we went to Madame Mag's, on Twenty-Fifth Street."

Madame Mag runs one of the most luxurious brothels on a street that specializes in expensive sin. The place is notorious for its "circus performances", in which young women cavort with the patrons in public displays of erotic behavior. I, of course, had never been inside the doors. I couldn't afford it even if I wanted to participate in such events, which, let me state for the record, I do not. There are certain matters that demand privacy. I shall say no more.

I wasn't surprised to learn that Broadway Bertie had been a patron of Madame Mag. It sounded like just the sort of thing he'd enjoy.

"Bertie had plans," Johnny said. "He was full of ideas. He told me he was going to settle things with his uncle, and we could go ahead with our theater."

"I heard about that," I said. "Something about building a theater up on Forty-second Street, behind the car-barns?"

Johnny leaned forward, nearly spilling his drink. "I happen to know that the elevated railway is going to go all the ways uptown," he said. "When it does, the horse-cars will not be needed, so the stables will be empty. We can get one of those stables for a song. Bertie was going to put up a stage, and have one of those dance-halls, like the ones he saw in Paris, where people dance, but there are also shows. He'd seen some girls doing the can-can, and he thought he'd bring it over here. It would be a sensation!"

It would surely be that, I thought to myself. I'd heard about this dance, where the girls kicked so high you could see their underpinnings. In fact, there were rumors that one of the specialty dancers at Madame Mag's left off the underdrawers altogether. If anything could get people north of Fourteenth Street, I suppose that would, but I couldn't imagine why Mr. Henry Ward Long would provide the money to back such a show.

"When did you leave Madame Mag's?" I asked Johnny.

"I stayed with one of the gals," Johnny said. "I didn't go home until very, very late."

"What about Bertie?" It was like pulling teeth, trying to get information out of this young sot.

"Oh, he was talking with some of the gals," Johnny said. "I went upstairs, and he was still in the parlor."

"So you don't know when he left," I said.

Johnny poured himself another drink. I saw that I would get nothing more out of him.

By this time the bar-room had filled up with the men on whom the business of New York, and by extension, the nation, depended. I caught a glimpse of Commondore Vanderbilt, tall and sprightly, even at seventy-six, yelling at his rival, Jim Fiske, who is shorter and louder, both in voice and dress. I made my way through the press of people, thinking to hear more about either Delacorte or his theatrical schemes, but my ear caught my name being shouted.

"Mr. Roth! Mr. Joshua Roth! Message for Mr. Roth!" The hotel page-boy's shrill voice cut through the babble.

"Yes, boy, what is it?" I answered the call.

"Message for you, sir, at the front door."

I saw a youth waiting for me, his oversized cast-off clothes marking him as one of those boys called Street Arabs who eked out a meager living running errands for pennies.

"Got a message for Mr. Roth," he gasped out, as if he'd been running, which indeed he had.

"I am he," I said.

"It's from Mr. Riley, sir. He says to come to the saloon behind the car-barns, and he's got some important information for ya about the man in the piksher." The boy stopped to take another breath. "He give me a dime and said you'd do the same."

Twenty cents would buy this lad a hot meal and a spot on the floor in a flop. I added another nickel to it, so that he could get a pallet in addition to the place on the floor.

THE GUILTY CLIENT

Then I looked up and down Twenty-Third Street. The damp mist had become a sort of drizzle, not quite rain, but not quite clear either. I wasn't about to walk the two miles uptown, but the street was full of private carriages. I stepped between two elegant equipages to flag down a cab, and ordered the driver to go to Forty-Second Street and Eighth Avenue.

I was preoccupied with what I had learned from Ellison, and forgot one of the rules that old Sergeant O'Hara tried to drum into me: a good soldier always knows what going on around him. I suppose this is why I was never a very good soldier, and why I caught the bullet that gave me my injury.

However, I was not thinking about anything but Bertram Delacorte and who hated him enough to kill him, and what, if anything, it had to do with the brutal murder of a colored woman passing herself off as White. The answers to those questions were yet to be answered, and some of those answers lay on Forty-Second Street. As for the result of my inattention, I will let Michael take up the narrative from here.

SECTION 5: MICHAEL

CHAPTER 16

When we split up, Joshua took a cab over to East Twenty-Third Street. I stayed on the West Side, working my way gradually uptown, from saloon to saloon.

My thinking was this: This fellow wore the Union uniform, and the markings on his cap showed he was from an Infantry regiment. He had one of the patches that General Kearny devised, to tell who was who, and that patch meant he was from a New York regiment, which was the Excelsior Brigade, set up by old Dan Sickles. Most of the New Yorkers in the Excelsior Brigades knew each other, one way or another, even though we were in different regiments. Like Joshua and me, in the Fifth New York, and the Eleventh New York, which was mostly the old firehouse Bowery B'hoys, we knew each other by sight, if not by name. So, thinks I, he's a New Yorker, but not one of the first lot. That probably meant he stayed home as long as he could, until the Draft caught up with him. He looked about twenty years old in the photograph, but there were plenty about who could pass for older or younger than their years.

Now, thinks I, going the next step, as Uncle Ephraim taught me, where do you find old soldiers, who can perhaps identify this fellow? A good many of the veterans came back to find their old jobs had been taken from them. Where did they go? They went to the Ward Boss, and he got them a job working for some contractor, who had a tie to the City. Plenty of those going, to be sure, what with tearing down this and rebuilding that, and putting up the new elevated railroad tracks, and laying down the pavement on the streets going

THE GUILTY CLIENT

uptown. And, thinks I, there was the horse-car lines, of which there were at least ten, and all of them would need drivers for the horses, and grooms to tend them, and stable-boys to muck them out.

And where would these old soldiers go for their evening's rest and relaxations, as the officers put it? To the corner saloons, of which New York has more than churches, much to the dismay of the good folks who preach Temperance.

So it was that I started walking uptown, while the cold damp drizzle worked its way into my coat and destroyed my new derby hat, and I wished that I had taken Joshua's advice and stopped at my boarding-house for my mackintosh raincoat and a bumpershoot.

I now state, since Miss Peggy is transcribing these notes, that I am not a drinking man. Whatever is said about the Irish, it does not apply to Michael Riley. I've seen too many good men destroyed through the drink to put myself into their company.

However, if a man goes into a saloon, he has to buy a drink. I had to visit a number of them, and in each one I ordered a shot of whiskey and put it to my lips, took a sip, and made a comment about the weather, which would lead into a discussion about the filthy stuff that we'd gone through in the camps, and that would lead to another discussion whereby I would learn who had gone where. In time I would produce my photograph and ask if anyone knew who this fellow was. If anyone asked why I wanted to know, I had my story ready. I said I was a lawyer and this man might be in the way of an inheritance if I could find him. In a way, this was true, only what he was going to inherit was a pack of trouble, if I could track him down.

I did not drink much at any one saloon, but I was getting a bit muzzy by the time I reached the car barns at Fifty-Second Street and Eighth Avenue. I had had far too many sips of whiskey, and had been told a lot of stories by old soldiers who may or may not have been at Gettysburg, Bull Run, Cold Harbor, or wherever, but none of them could tell who this fellow was.

It must have been near ten o'clock when I stumbled into the saloon behind the car barns. I wasn't even sure what it was called. All that I knew was that I had to get in out of the wet, and that I had better not drink another drop or I wouldn't remember anything anyone told me, true or not.

I found a bench along one wall, and collapsed down upon it, jostling the man next to me. He turned around, ready to fight, then yelled out, "By all that's holy, it's Lieutenant Riley!"

I turned around, and tried to make out who it was. The saloon was full of smoke from pipes and cigars, and not all that well lit to begin with, and truth to tell, I wasn't seeing too clearly by then, but the voice came back to me.

"Foghorn Mulligan!" I took a deep breath and wished I hadn't. The smoke was like to choke me.

"That's me!" It was indeed Mulligan, who was made a Corporal because he had the loudest voice in his squad and could relay the Captain's orders the best.

"Working on the cars, are you?" says I, which was the best I could come up with. Why else would Mulligan be in the saloon, behind the car barns, if he wasn't working on the cars?

"That I am," he says proudly. "I've come up in the world, Lieutenant. I'm chief driver on the Broadway Line these days, and a fine job it is, too. Steady work, a fat pay check, and even a nice turkey at Christmas from the Boss." He looked me over. "By golly, you look terrible, man. What's taken you out on a nasty night like this?"

I shook my head to clear it. "I've come up in the world, too," says I. "I'm at City Hall, working for the District Attorney."

That drew a yell from Mulligan. "Hey, boys, the Lieutenant's working for Tammany! Give him a drink!"

I held up a hand. "Now, boys," says I, "I'm not here for my pleasure, but on business." I took the photograph out of my breast pocket. It was getting a bit worse for wear, but the face was clear enough. "Do any of you know this fellow? He's got a New York badge on his shoulder, but he wasn't with the first of us, so he might have come in after I mustered out in '63."

"Now why'd you do that?" Mulligan says. "We was supposed to be mustered out, too, but instead we got sent up to Gettysburg. Hot fighting there, but we whupped them Rebs good and proper."

"And then that fool Meade let Lee get away!" That from someone in the crowd, who had joined Mulligan and me.

There followed a long discussion of the might-have-beens, and who should have done what, which I will omit in the interests of brevity. Also, because I was gradually sobering up, and didn't take much part in said discussion. Truth was, my enlistment was up, and as Joshua was in hospital, I stuck by him until he got orders West, and I could get back to Uncle Ephraim and my proper sphere, which was lawyering.

Finally I says, "Well, I guess General Butler thought he needed a good lawyer to help him keep order in New Orleans more than Meade needed a bad marksman in Pennsylvania. Not much choice there, I can tell you."

"I heard Captain Roth caught a minie ball," says Mulligan. "Damned bad luck."

"He did," says I. "He shoved me out of the way, and took the bullet that might have blown my brains out. Got the Purple Heart for it, too."

"A good man, Captain Roth," Mulligan says, and there was agreement amongst the rest of the men.

"None better," says I, and I mean it. You might think that Joshua and I are two men who would never be friends, being that we're different as chalk and cheese, like my Da used to say. He's on the Defense, and I'm on the Prosecution side of the courtroom. He votes Republican, I'm Democrat. He's a thoughtful, quiet sort, whereas I'm one for a good time and a good tale. I'm Irish and Catholic, and he's a Jew, which some may fault him for, but I don't worry a man about his religion, if he don't press it upon me. But the two of us worked well in the War, and now we're as good friends as any I've known.

So once again I showed the picture, and this time I laid it out straight. "This picture came out of a lady's belongings, and we think he's connected with a murder case."

"Did he do it?" Mulligan asks, and he takes a squint at the picture.

"We don't know. We won't know until we find him and ask him where he was on Appomattox Night," says I.

"I was at the Veteran's Ball with my missus," Mulligan says proudly. "I saw you with old Pettigrew's gal. You going to marry the boss's daughter?" He gives a knowing laugh and a wink. "She's a handful, I hear."

"Miss Peggy's a fine girl, don't get me wrong," says I, "but marrying her would be like marrying my sister. Let alone her Auntie Sarah would have ten conniption fits at her wedding a Catholic."

From the back of the crowd comes a shout. "Hey, that's Roaring Billy Kendall!"

This from a grubby-looking fellow with a straggling beard, who got shoved forward to talk to me. He was my age, but I could already tell the signs of a drunkard. His hand was shaking as he handed the picture back to me, and his eyes were bleary, and his nose was starting to go red. It wouldn't be long before he'd be having the DT's, thinks I, but it won't stop the horrors from coming at him in the night. I've known many a man who went that way, and I swore I wouldn't, nor would I let Joshua, no matter how bad the nightmares got.

"Kendall?" I says. "That's the name of the woman who was killed on Appomattox Night."

There was a sudden silence. Then the fellow who had recognized the picture speaks up: "Well, that there is Billy Kendall. I was there with him when we all went to have ourselves taken, before we went down to the ferry to join the troops. He had a gal with him, which he gave his picture to, and he was that taken with her, he was going to marry her when he got back, or so he said. We sort of ragged him about it in camp, but he wasn't a man of easy temper, so that stopped soon enough."

"Violent, was he?" says I. My head was starting to clear, and I felt that it was worth the headache I'd have in the morning to find out what I'd come for.

"There was some who said he ran with the Plug-Uglies, and was being paid to join up instead of some rich man's son," Mulligan says, taking another look at the photograph. "Now I remember him. He was one of the Bounty Boys, and a fat lot of good they were, mostly fighting amongst themselves. I told 'em to save it for the Rebs, and they gave a good accounting of themselves on the line. Only thing was, after it was all over, their old habits took over, and they'd go over the battlefield to pick up anything lying about."

"Did he happen to pick up a Bowie knife?" says I.

"Now, how did you know that?" says Mulligan.

I says, "Suzanna Kendall, the woman who had the photograph, was killed with a Bowie knife. This is not going to be in any of the newspapers, boys, because the police are keeping it quiet, but it's so. Now, tell me whatever you know about Billy Kendall."

The young drunk gulps a bit, then says, "Him and me used to run with the Plug-Uglies, sure enough, but we was kids, out on the game, you see. We didn't do nothing more than stand look-out, but Billy, he got more of the grub because he's bigger and good with his fists, so he'd get more than his share, and he give it to me. I'm called Shorty McGee," he says, by was of introduction. "Billy took care of me on the streets, and I watched his back for him."

That made sense. It's the way things were on the streets and in the gangs, when two lads would pal together, one of 'em big and tough, and the other small and smart. It's the way Joshua and I worked, except that both of us were pretty smart, and neither of us was much in the brawn department.

"Tell me what you know about Suzaanna," I says. I was beginning to see what Uncle Ephraim would call a pattern emerging.

"She was a maid in some rich guy's house," Shorty says, "and Billy met her when he and me was hired to watch over the house when the rich guy went away to Brooklyn for the summer, the year the war started. The rich guy paid us a ten-spot for the two months, just to stand outside his front door on Washington Square and not let anyone else in but the ladies and gents who came calling."

"Do you remember who the rich guy was?" I asked.

Shorty shrugged. "It was a while ago, and I don't recall too good. Billy said we should do it, make ten dollars doing nothing but stand around and look mean. Easy money! Trouble was, we couldn't do like the gang wanted, and let 'em in to pick the place apart, and when the riots started, we was stuck on Washington Square." He sort of ran down. Someone handed him a drink, and he gulped it down.

"And after the riots?"

"Oh, the rich guy paid Billy and me to go and sign up, because he didn't want his own kid to get shot at," Shorty said. "Or maybe it was his sister's kid. Whichever it was, Billy took the money and give it to the gal he was seeing, and told her he'd be back when it was over, and they'd be married."

"And your regiment went off and you saw the elephant," says I.

Shorty nods. "That we did. It was awful. I went one way, and Billy went another, and I didn't watch his back." He started to blubber. The other men had heard this before.

Mulligan shook his head. "Shorty's never got over what he did, Lieutenant. We keep him here to muck out the stables, and groom the horses. He's good with 'em, and the Plug-Uglies never get this far uptown. They're strictly downtown, never go above Houston Street, and so we tell Shorty that they won't come after him for letting Billy down."

By now my head was as clear as it was going to get without a night's sleep and a good breakfast. I looked around the room for someone who could get a message downtown to Joshua. There was a lad in one corner, and I beckoned over to him.

"Here's a dime," says I, "and there's another when you deliver this message. Go to the Fifth Avenue Hotel, and ask for Mr. Joshua Roth. He's a long, dark man, with a short beard, got one sleeve pinned up. You tell him I've got important information about the man in the picture and that he should meet me at this here saloon."

"Yes, sir!" The boy all but saluted. He took my dime and ran outside.

I started calculating. Give him half an hour to run all the ways downtown, then give Joshua the same to get back here. That gave me an hour to enjoy myself, and so I did, tucking into some vittles at the free lunch counter and indulging in one, and only one, mug of beer. The rest of the time was spent in soldiers' talk, which I will not waste time repeating here.

CHAPTER 17

IT TOOK LESS THAN AN HOUR for Joshua to get to the saloon, and I spent the time conversing with the old soldiers, swapping lies and telling jokes. More to the point, I had me a solid ham sandwich, to offset the garlic dinner that I'd had to eat at Uncle Ephraim's.

It was Mulligan recognized Joshua first. "Here's the Captain!" he sings out. "'Ten-hut!" And the talk stopped, dead.

"At ease, men," says Joshua, and there was a laugh. Then he looked about the place. "I see some faces I know," he says.

"Some of us made it to the end," Mulligan says.

"And you were one of them, Corporal," says Joshua, shaking his hand.

"I wound up a Sergeant," says Mulligan, puffing up his chest. "We heard you was wounded, Captain. Damned shame."

` Joshua says, "I'm no Captain, not any more. Just Mr. Roth, Attorney at Law." He looked about for me. "I got a message that Michael Riley was here."

At which, I made myself known, and the two of us sat down on the bench together, with the rest of the car-men huddled about.

I says, "According to Mulligan, here, the man in the photograph is one Billy Kendall, and it seems that Suzanna Kendall was his wife. Or as good as," I amended, not knowing if there had actually been marriage vows spoken between them.

"Indeed," says Joshua. "The people at the boarding-house where she stayed thought that she was a War widow, who might not have actually been legally wedded to a serving soldier."

Shorty McGee pushed himself to the front of the crowd. "He was nuts on her," he says. "And the boys ragged him about it. All you had to do to get him fighting mad was sing 'O Susannah'."

"That must have made things lively in camp," says Joshua. As well he should, being that 'O Susannah' was about the most popular song sung, after 'Lorena'.

"That's the truth," says Mulligan. "After he'd been in the stockade a couple times, I told him to save it for the Rebs. We give it to 'em hot and heavy and that's when he went down. I don't remember seeing him after that."

"That was another mess," says one of the other car-men, and most of them agreed with that, although not in exactly those words.

Joshua sums it up: "So, this fellow Kendall joined up in the Fall of '63, after the Draft Riots. He had his photograph taken and gave it to his girl, Suzanna, who was a maid in someone's home." He turned to Shorty. "Do you remember exactly where this house was that you were sent to guard?"

Shorty screwed up his face with the effort. "A ways uptown," he says. "Washington Square. A nice big house, only one family in it. Plenty of good stuff, too, but we wasn't let inside past the kitchen door."

"Do you remember whose house it was?" Joshua asks.

Shorty shook his head. "I'm trying to remember, but it was a long time ago, and I didn't really catch the name. Billy talked to the man. He was a tall man…that was it! It was something like High or Wide…"

"Was it Long?" Joshua asks, all of a sudden.

"That was it!" Shorty cries out. "Long! That was the name!"

Now Joshua starts thinking out loud, in a sort of sing-song style. "Let us suppose," he says, "that a very rich man decides that the best way to keep the gangs out of his house is to hire one of the younger gang boys to watch the house. And let us suppose that this boy sees one of the female servants in the house, and makes her acquaintance. And let us suppose that this acquaintance ripens into something more."

"But he don't know she's Colored," says I.

"No, he doesn't," says Joshua, "for the very good reason that she doesn't tell him. As has been noted, she is very fair-skinned. As far as Billy Kendall is concerned, she is a maid in the house, and as far as she is concerned, he is her ticket to freedom, at least, until Emancipation came along."

THE GUILTY CLIENT

Mulligan is following this. "But Captain," he says, "Billy Kendall died on the line."

"Did he?" Joshua asks. "Or did he fall down, and stay down, and wait until the battle was over, and then hook it out of there? Plenty of men went missing after battles, and not all of them were dead or wounded."

"Deserted, did he?" Mulligan says, and from the look on his face, I could tell that it would go hard on Billy Kendall if ever Sergeant Mulligan caught up with him, even after five years of peace.

"Missing in action," says Joshua. "And then he got back home, but it took a while, and by then the War was over. So, what does he do?"

"He goes back to the Plug-Uglies," says I. "But they aren't the same gang, and he's not the same kid."

"So, where to turn next?" says Joshua.

"Back to the man who hired him in the first place," says I. "Mr. Henry Ward Long."

"And we've seen him ourselves," Joshua says, looking down at the photograph again. "He's that bodyguard who rides up with the coachman."

I took another look at the photograph, and put my finger under the nose, to make a mustache. "So he is," says I. "And now we know where to find him."

I shook Mulligan's hand, and headed for the door, with Joshua behind me. I peeked out, to if the weather had cleared.

The rain had stopped. I could see glimmers of puddles on the cobblestones in the light from the lanterns that had been hung at the corners of the car-barns. Somewhere beyond the circle of the light there was something moving that made a ripple on the shining rain puddles between the cobblestones.

"There's someone out there," says I, softly, to Joshua. "Did you tell anyone to meet you here?"

"Not that I recall," Joshua says. "How many do you make out?"

"Two by the far barn,' says I. I could see them now, big fellows, one holding a short club, the other with a fist clenched in a way that meant knuckle-dusters. I didn't see any knives, but that didn't mean they weren't carrying any.

"Two more over there," says Joshua. He nodded to the right. My two were to the left. I could see them moving in, carefully stepping on the slippery cobbles, picking their way between the bits that the horses had left behind. I could hear the horses themselves whickering and stamping in the barns, as if they knew something was going to happen outside.

"For Gawd's sake!" one of them bawls out, "one's a half-pint and one's a cripple. We dassen't move on 'em. It ain't right!"

"We ain't being paid to be gentle," yells out the one nearest me. "Jest don't kill'em, that's all the boss wants. Teach 'em not to mix in where they ain't wanted."

"We'll see who learns from who," I says to myself, and I stepped into the circle of lantern-light, waiting for them to make the first move, while I sized up the opposition.

My two were big, burly bruisers, one with a broken nose, the other with a scar over one eye. Street fighters, I judged them, more used to shaking down storekeepers than handling someone who'd seen the elephant.

They came at me one at a time, which was their first mistake. I grew up fighting big bullies like them, and I knew how to take them down. Broke-nose was the bigger one, and he tried to throw a punch at me. I ducked, and gave him one in the bread-basket that knocked the wind out of him. Then Scar-face gave a swipe with his billy-club that fanned my cheek, but my head wasn't where it was supposed to be. Instead, I rocked back on my heels, and nearly went arse over teakettle on those slippery stones that the horses had covered with their muck. I staggered into Broke-nose and the two of us went down in the slop, with me kicking and punching anything I could get to, while Scar-face tried to find something to whack.

I landed a few on Broke-nose's ribs, and he got me a good one on the shoulder that had my arm tingling. I kicked out, to get Scar-Face down, and got him in the knees just as he was about to bring that billy-club down on my head. The club went wild, Broke-nose was cursing up a storm, and Scar-Face fell on top of the two of us. I wriggled out from under them, and kicked some more once I found my feet. I heard grunts and more curses, and left them down on the cobbles while I looked about me to see how Joshua was doing, and if he needed any help.

Joshua was doing better than the bruisers expected. His two were shorter than he was, which isn't surprising, since he's a long drink of water, with no fat on him at all. He was using his feet, kicking with a side-swipe to the ribs that left one of the bruisers retching under the lantern, while he hung onto the arm of the second man who was trying to use his club. Joshua hopped back, then kicked high and straight, and got the bruiser down with a one-two kick that would have floored anyone with less belly-fat. This one just gasped and staggered out of the way, while his pal took over. By then, the first man had caught his breath, and came back at Joshua, and got another kick for his pains.

"Do that again, and we'll get the other arm for ya," growls the second bruiser. "Then your fat gal friend will have to feed ya with a spoon!"

By this time the noise had brought the car-men onto the scene. They took a look at the battle and went after our attackers themselves. Joshua and I staggered into the lee of the car-barns and let Mulligan and his boys finish what we'd started.

"Where's the ring-leader?" Joshua asks, while I got rid of all the whiskey and the ham sandwich in the most direct way possible.

"Who?" says I, when I was finally able to speak.

"The one who knew who we were," says Joshua. "A Half-pint and a Cripple. That's you and me, not flattering, but accurate."

"We showed 'em," I says. "A Half-pint and a Cripple indeed!"

"We did," Joshua says, and he starts to laugh. "Michael," he says, " when you found me in New Orleans, do you remember what I told you I was going to do?"

"Something about going West," I says. "Dodge City needed a lawyer, you said, and you'd a mind to see the country."

"And do you know what you told me? Don't go West, you said. Come back to New York and rest for a bit. Nice, genteel, New York!" He starts to laugh like a loony.

"What do we do now?" says I, while he catches his breath.

"We follow Bertie's trail," says Joshua. "We go and visit Madame Mags, and we find out what he was doing on the night he was killed."

"And then?"

"We take what we learned back to Uncle Ephraim, and see what he makes of it," says Joshua. "I only hope we're uptown enough for West Twenty-Fifth. I hear they only cater to carriage trade."

"Maybe we'd do better to get back to our boarding-house and clean up before we enter those doors," says I. "That's another mark against whoever sent those bruisers. I paid twenty dollars for this suit. It'll never be the same again."

"We don't have the time," says Joshua. "We've got to find Billy Kendall before he kills again."

"And what makes you think he'll be heading for Madame Mags?" says I.

"Because that's the last place Bertram Delacorte went, and that's where he spoke to someone," Joshua says. He looked about to see if there was any transport, but there were no cabs on Long Acre Square at that time of night, and the cars were put away. It was going to be a very long walk back to Twenty-Fifth Street. I was ready to kill Billy Kendall myself for leading us such a dance. I only hoped whatever he had to tell us would be worth the trouble he had made.

CHAPTER 18

Joshua and me had had a night of it already, what with the drink and the fight, but we'd got our blood up. We were tramping our way downtown when we saw a late cab making its way down Broadway to the barns downtown. We grabbed it, and gave the cabbie instructions to take us to Twenty-Fifth Street and Eighth Avenue.

Then we sat back and took stock of where we'd got to. Joshua told me what he'd found out about Suzanna Kendall at Mrs. Smith's, and what he'd found out about Bertram Delacorte's theatrical aspirations from Colonel Ellison's boy, and I went over what we'd learned from the old soldiers.

"So," says Joshua, "we've got a good idea of what transpired on the night that Suzanna Kendall was killed."

"Do we?" asks I. I still didn't see any sense to the proceedings.

"I think it happened this way," says Joshua. "According to the boarders, everyone at Mrs. Smith's house was out and about, except the family and the servants, and Mrs. Kendall. The family was up on the top floor, the servants were all the ways in the kitchen, down in the basement. There would have been a floor between Kendall and anyone else either way.

"Billy Kendall gets into the house from the back alley…"

"And how does he do that?" I asks.

"He's an old Plug-ugly. He's learned how to get into and out of houses. He goes up the back stairs, and finds Suzanna."

"Why?" says I. "I mean, why does he go there at all?"

"To have it out with Suzanna," says Joshua. "For five years he's been stewing about the woman who betrayed him, took his money and left him. Now he's found her."

"Found her?" I says, like an echo.

"According to Mr. Lawton, the day he moved in at Mrs. Smith's, Delacorte had a fellow with him to carry his bag. Suzanna saw him and called him, 'Billy'. The man looked up and saw Suzanna. It must have been quite a shock to him seeing her after all that time."

"What did he think happened to her?" says I. "And why didn't he try to find her when he got back from the Army?"

"He may have tried," Joshua says. "We'll have to find him and get his side of the story."

"So," I says, summing it up, " Billy Kendall gets into Mrs. Smith's house and goes to have it out with Suzanna. What's he after?"

"He's a man of uncertain temper, and possibly drunk," Joshua says, thinking aloud, as is his way. "And they argue, and he kills her in a rage."

"That makes sense," says I. "But why drag poor little Bertie into this family spat?"

"That I cannot tell you," says Joshua. "But Bertram must have seen something or known something, to bring notice upon himself."

"Because, after a week of nothing to do, the police get an anonymous note telling them to look at the back of Mr. Delacorte's wardrobe, and there they find a coat covered with blood. And they go off and arrest Mr. Bertram Delacorte for the murder of Suzanna Kendall, on that evidence, and that alone. It's in the report that was handed to me, on Friday, at four in the afternoon, if you please, and I was told to be at the arraignment the following Monday. That's no time to prepare a case, Joshua, none at all, and I wasn't even given the proper police or medical reports."

"At that, you had more than I did," Joshua says. "At nine Monday morning I was summoned to Mr. Henry Ward Long's chambers and told to go down to the Tombs where Mr. Bertram Delacorte was about to be arraigned on a charge of murder in the first degree, and that was all I was told. Not even the evidence against him!" He gives a snort and a sniff, and adds, "And I had barely enough time to scribble a note to Miss Peggy to get down to the courthouse with her writing equipment, pad and pencil, and hoped that she would be able to get through the traffic to be there on time."

"And the arraignment was a farce," says I. "It was a put-up job, and no doubt about it. When Miss Peggy showed up, and gave

THE GUILTY CLIENT

her evidence, old Bacon was took aback, I could tell. He thought he'd be able to clear up the whole matter and get back to his own concerns."

"But if it was a put-up job, who did the putting?" says Joshua. "And why kill Bertie out of hand after he was turned loose?"

"Because they couldn't get the courts to do it for them," says I.

"But who is 'they'?" asks Joshua.

By that time we had reached Twenty-Fifth Street. West Twenty-Fifth Street is genteel enough from Fifth Avenue to Sixth. After that, the saloons and the gambling parlors start, and when you get past Seventh Avenue, most of the houses have a red lantern posted outside the door, a custom that started when they built the railroads, when they'd put a red lantern outside the tent where the soiled doves did their business.

There is a kind of ranking amongst the ladies of the night. The top of the trees are the ones who were kept by one man, like Miss Josie Mansfield, who has a house of her own, and servants, and a carriage, all paid for by Mr. Jim Fiske. Then there are the girls in the finer houses, who can pick and choose their customers, and down the line to the ones one the street, who have to take what they could get. There were plenty of those on parade that night, sauntering up and down in their gaudy gowns, calling out to the gents in their carriages, who were out to take advantage of having confessed all their sins on Easter Sunday, and were now out to commit a fresh lot.

Right away I could tell we would be in for a hard time of it if we tried to get past the doors of any of the establishments, dressed as we were and reeking of the muck we'd been rolling in during the fight at the car-barns. Most of the gents strolling up and down were in full evening dress, soup-and-fish, white tie and tails, hats and canes, not a plain suit in sight, nor a derby hat. Joshua's frock coat and stovepipe might pass muster, but my checked suit wouldn't get me past the kitchens of those places of sin, even if it wasn't stained with what was on the cobbles by the car-barns.

Joshua stiffened at the sight of all those girls peddling their wares. He's got a moral streak, though he don't interfere with anyone else's pleasures. As for me, Miss Peggy will forgive me if I admit to admiring the wares on offer, and I admit to accepting them on occasion. However, this was not the time or the place, and I had other business to attend to.

Madame Mag's was the largest house on the block, a new brownstone, with a high stoop that led up to the parlors on the first floor, and a little area-way that led to the kitchen-door under the stoop. The big bay windows of the front parlor had the curtains part-way opened to show the world some of the doings within. We could see the girls, dressed in their silk gowns, and the gents, in frock coats and cutaway tails, white shirt-fronts and fancy cuffs, all enjoying each others company. Outside the house were a few of the better sort of street gals, who tried to snag the gents who might not have enough coin or connections to get into Madame Mag's. There was a fellow at the front door who looked old enough to have been one of the original Bowery B'hoys, who acted as bouncer, and tried to shoo the street gals away. He'd look the gents over, and decide who would go in and who not, and as many were turned away as were let in.

"This won't do," says I, after seeing two or three top-hatted customers being given the gate. "We'll never get in as we are."

Joshua was about to agree, when we heard voices just inside the door to the kitchens in the area-way.

One was all too familiar: Captain Clubber Williams, staking out his claim. "I don't care what you paid before. It's ten percent now, every month, or I run the lot of yez in."

The other voice was female, and I thought I recognized it, although I hadn't heard it in a very long time. "Do you know who comes here, Captain? Do you really think they'll let you bleed me dry?"

"They won't lift a finger, and you know it," says Clubber. "Ten percent, and be glad it's not fifteen."

The two of us sink back into the shadows, and let Clubber pass, on to his next stop. Then I steps out and says, "Hello, Maggie, it's been a long time since we fought over a crust of bread."

She looks out the door, and sees me and gives a yelp. "Mickey?"

"It's Michael now, and not Mick or Mickey," says I, with dignity. "Joshua, this is a very old friend of mine, who used to go by Maggie the Mouth. Maggie, this is my good friend, Captain Joshua Roth, and we'd like a word concerning one of your best customers, Mr. Bertram Delacorte. Is that his wake you're having upstairs?"

Maggie looked around and drew us into the little pantry that led to her kitchen. She takes a gander at me, and says, "I heard you'd come up in the world, Mickey. What've you been up to?"

"It's a long story, and not for telling tonight," says I, and took a good look her. She's a good five years older than me, still red-headed, although I grant you some of it might have come out of the henna bottle, and well-shaped. She must have had the Devil's own luck, too, to have come this far, managing her own house instead of walking the streets or picking pockets, as she used to when we were kids, running wild on the West Side docks.

"Miss Mouth," Joshua begins, but she stops him.

"It's Madame Mags," she says, "and that's all it is now." She gives me another once-over. "I heard you won a medal," she says.

"The Rebs kept shooting at me," I says, modestly. "I had to shoot back." There was a lot more to it than that, and both of us knew it, but the family reunion would have to wait for another time, as Joshua reminded me with a sharp "Ahem!".

"You must have heard that Bertram Delacorte was killed last night," Joshua says.

"More like yesterday," says I. "It would have been around this time yesterday. We know he went here with Johnny Ellison. The question is, what did he do here, and did he talk with any of the girls?"

Maggie gave me a nasty grin. "Oh, he was here, all right. I won't deny it. And he talked with one of my best girls. Dutch Mitzi, they call her, but I think she's German or Russian or Polish or something else. She can talk some English, but that's not why they come here to see her."

"Just to see her?" says I. "She's not . . ."

"Hooker's Army," Joshua says, referring to those gals who were all over the troops when we were stationed in Washington.

"She's special," Maggie says, and makes a quick decision. "You're not fit to be seen in my parlor," she says, with a sniff, "but you can stand by the back-stairs door and watch the show."

"And then we want to talk with this Dutch Mitzi," says Joshua. "She might be able to tell us something that will lead us to his murderer."

"I don't know what she can tell you," says Maggie. "We had the usual crowd here last night, and Delacorte was celebrating what he called 'a release from durance vile'. Ha! He had one night in the Tombs, and that's nothing to what some of my gals tell me they got before they came here. I could tell you a tale or two…"

"I'm sure they could, and perhaps they are even true," Joshua says, stiff and solemn. "But at the moment, ma'am, what we need to know are the movements of Mr. Bertram Delacorte on the night of his death."

I could see Maggie was about to ask the main question, which is, "What's it to you?" I answered it for her. "We've connected Delacorte's death with that of a woman in a boarding-house on East Twenty-Third," I said. "It's not nice, a man who takes a Bowie knife to a woman."

Maggie gives a shudder. "If someone like that's on the loose, I'll help you find him, and welcome the chance," she says. "Come on up, and watch the circus!"

Joshua and I followed her up the back stairs, to where the two parlors had been thrown together to make one large room. Then the curtains were drawn down over the windows. No point in giving the passers-by outside a free show!

And quite a show it was, too! I'd heard about them, of course, and there were always stories in the newspapers that hinted at the goings-on at the better class of houses, but this was enough to make Mr. Casanova blush.

I will not describe everything that went on, because Miss Peggy is going to transcribe this report, but I will say that the girls' talents included certain feats of dexterity involving the lower portions of their anatomies, and that the audience was most appreciative, throwing down silver dollars which the girls were then to pick up without the use of their hands. There were songs, and the young woman who sang had a perfectly lovely voice, to match her completely exposed bosom, which she manipulated with muscles alone. Finally, there was an explosion of music from the piano player, and Dutch Mitzi, the star of the show, appeared, performing the latest sensation, the French Can-Can, which she did with great abandon, and much ruffling of petticoats, and no drawers at all. It was a most riveting sight, and I could see why young Delacorte might have thought that people would actually pay money to see her, even with the drawers on.

There was a round of applause when Mitzi finished, and more silver dollars were thrown at her. These got picked up by a hefty fellow in a dress-suit that didn't quite conceal his muscular build.

Mitzi sashayed around the room, accepting the applause like a prima donna at the Opera while the other girls paired off with their gents and headed up the front stairs to the bedrooms and whatever went on there. Maggie beckoned Mitzi over to us before she could be taken over by one of the gents. The big bruiser came along to stand behind her, like a big dog guarding its mistress.

"Mitzi, these two gentlemen are here to ask some questions about Bertram Delacorte," Maggie says. "Just tell them what happened last night."

"Notting happened," Mitzi says, giving us a look like we was cockroaches "Bertie comes, he sees me dance, he tells me he vill make me star of new theater. I am not to be *kurve*, I am to be dancer only. He vill pay me only to dance." Joshua gives her a hard look, but says nothing, leaving it to me to continue.

"We know he came here last night," I says. "You did your act." I pulled out my watch, and noted the time, which was nearly one in the morning. "Do you, um, perform at the same time every night?"

"Midnight show," says Maggie. "What did you think of it?" She gives a sly grin at Joshua, who doesn't answer. As for me, it wasn't the girls I felt disgust for, it was the men who paid to watch them.

"Most interesting," says Joshua. He turned to Mitzi. "Did Mr. Delacorte, ah, take you, ah, upstairs?"

"Bertie vas not like dat," Mitzi says. "He vas gentleman, alvays. He come to see me dance. I tell him I haf new dance, *le danse du ventre,* the vitch he haf never see before."

Joshua translates, "Dance of the stomach?"

Mitzi holds her hands over her head and gives us a demonstration, and quite a sight it was, too. She could move her midsection up and down and side to side, all without use of her hands. "I learn ven I vas in Odessa," she says.

"You seem to be a well-traveled young woman," Joshua says.

Before we could get any further, there's a bang at the front door and in marches Clubber Williams, with a squad of blue-coats at his back. He ignored the gents, all of whom started to pick up their hats to leave, but went straight for Mitzi's man.

"Heinz Guttenberg, I arrest you for the murder of Mr. Bertram Delacorte," Williams says, grabbing Heinz by the arm.

That was a mistake. Heinz wasn't about to be taken prisoner by anyone without a fight, and a fight there was, rampaging all over the parlor. Heinz used his fists, the coppers used their clubs, and the patrons used their feet to get out as fast as they could. Maggie stood there screaming while her fine parlor was smashed to smithereens and her customers were on their way out the door, all except the ones already upstairs.

Joshua and I had had our fill of fighting for the evening, so we stood back and let the blue-coats do their duty until they'd clubbed Heinz down. Mitzi was screeching, Maggie was cursing, and the gents were leaving, all at once.

By the time it was all over, Heinz was hauled up onto his feet by two blue-coats, and Joshua was ready to act.

He steps forward and pulls his calling card out of his vest pocket, and sticks into Heinz's hand. "I'm Joshua Roth, Attorney at Law," he announces. "Mr. Guttenberg, can you give me one of those silver dollars you've got in your pockets?"

Heinz nods and hands Joshua a cartwheel. Then Joshua says, "Captain Williams, this man is my client. Take him down to the Tombs and book him if you must, but I will be around in the morning to bail him out. He is totally innocent of this charge, and you know it. By tomorrow afternoon, I will prove it!"

Clubber just grunts, and shoves Heinz out the door and down the stairs. Maggie turns on Mitzi.

"You stupid little Sheeny bitch!" There was more, but I will spare Miss Peggy's ears. "Get the Hell out of here! I never should have taken you in, Bertie or no Bertie! Beat it!"

Mitzi was in tears. "Vere shall I go? Vat shall I do? Heinz is going to prison, and he did not do notting!"

"I don't care where you go," Maggie yells at her. "I won't have you here! Git upstairs, get your traps, and get out by daybreak!"

Mitzi starts wailing in several languages, one of which has Joshua picking up his ears. Then she heads up the stairs, and comes down about fifteen minutes later with a full carpet-bag, a fuzzy fur coat and a bonnet with a fur trim to match the coat.

"I go," she states grandly. "But I vill not be *kurve* and I vill dance again!" She swept out, like a theater star, but when we got outside she broke down.

"I hav no place to go," she says, between sniffles.

I knew of only one person who would take someone in at this hour of the night, which was by now very early morning.

"I only hope Aunt Sarah won't kill us for bringing her a guest," I says, and I led the way over to Bank Street.

SECTION 6: PEGGY

CHAPTER 19

After Michael and Joshua had left on their various errands I remained with Uncle Ephraim in his den, wondering what I should do next. Should I continue to transcribe the notes I had taken during the day? Should I attempt to decipher Michael's scrawled additions to those notes? Or should I do as most young ladies would do on a weekday evening, and join Aunt Sarah in the back parlor on the other side of the hall, where she would sit of an evening while I read to her from one of the new books, or from Harper's Weekly?

Uncle Ephraim sat staring into the small fire flickering in the fireplace, mumbling to himself, his hands propped up on his midsection, his thumbs revolving about each other.

"Facts," he muttered. "We don't have facts, we have suppositions, and we can't do a thing with suppositions and hearsay. They don't hold up in court. We have to have facts!"

"We have some facts," I said. "It is a fact that Bertram Delacorte was at the Veteran's Ball, and that he was seen there by several people besides me. It is also a fact that he was arrested two weeks later, on very little evidence, and that as soon as he was let go he went somewhere, changed his clothes, went somewhere else…"

"Too many somewheres. Where did he go? What did he do there?" Uncle Ephraim growled testily.

"I'm sure Michael and Joshua will find the answers to those

questions," I said, soothingly.

Aunt Sarah put her head in at the door to the den, "Ephraim, are you well? I thought I heard Michael leaving. Come and join me in the parlor."

"I'm still hungry," Uncle Ephraim grumbled. "Sarah, I don't like that cook."

"I'll see what I can do about it tomorrow," Aunt Sarah said.

"Shall I have Mandy make you some bread-and-milk?" I suggested. Mandy doesn't cook full meals, but they did teach her to make a few basic dishes at the Colored Orphans' Asylum, and the one that usually soothed Uncle Ephraim's indigestion was the bread-egg-milk concoction that some call French Toast. I didn't know if the fiery Italian cook would allow our frightened servant to approach the sacred stove, but something had to be done or Uncle Ephraim would be impossible to live with tomorrow.

The domestic scene was interrupted by a knock at the front door.

"Nine o'clock?" Aunt Sarah glanced at the clock over the mantel, next to Mr. Lincoln's shrine. "A little late for evening calls."

Mandy came in and announced, "Mr. Thomas Murphy, and his ma, Mrs. Murphy."

Tom Murphy is the Ward Heeler for Bank Street, a large, beefy sort, who had been a runner when his father had been with the local fire station before the War. He had fought valiantly against the mobs in the Draft Riots, and had earned his current position by bringing in more votes for the Democratic Party than there actually were voters in the district. He was shoved into the den by his diminutive mother, who glared at Aunt Sarah before facing Uncle Ephraim.

"We got something to say, Mr. Pettigrew," Mrs. Murphy began. "Tommy, say your piece." She gave her hulking son a buffet on the back that put him opposite Uncle Ephraim.

Mr. Murphy sighed before addressing Uncle Ephraim, as if to say, Don't blame me for what I have to say, I'm doing it to please my mother. "Good evening, Mr. Pettigrew," he said, "Mrs. Pettigrew, Miss Peggy." He nodded to all of us, then recalled that he was still wearing his derby hat. Once that had been doffed, he got another vicious shove from Ma.

"Good evening, Mr. Murphy," Uncle Ephraim said, matching politeness with politeness. "May I ask the reason for this late call?"

"Go on, Tommy, you tell him," Mrs. Murphy urged.

"Well, sir, it's like this." Murphy stopped again.

"Sit down, man, and spit it out. I don't like having to look up at you. Peggy, give Mr. Murphy a chair."

I moved the one that Michael had just vacated, and Mr. Murphy sat down. "I've been asked....that is, we've been somewhat discommoded ..." he stuttered.

"I've heard about the garlic problem," Uncle Ephraim said, with a bland smile. "Well, sir, that is going to be taken care of, and that right smartly. Right, Sarah?"

Aunt Sarah smiled weakly. She wasn't looking forward to the next attempt to converse with Maria Luisa, but clearly we could not continue to employ a cook whose food we could not eat, and who had made herself obnoxious to the neighborhood.

"Well, now, that's good to hear, sir." Mr. Murphy turned his hat over in his hands.

"Was there something else?" Uncle Ephraim prodded him, after a moment's silence. Both of them know that since Uncle Ephraim is an avowed and committed Republican, Tom Murphy has no political influence in this household, whatever else he may do or not do for the other tenants on Bank Street.

He blurted out, "It has come to my ears, sir, that you might intend to move away from this ward."

"Now, where did you hear that?" Uncle Ephraim said sharply.

"It's being spoken of," Mr. Murphy repeated.

"By whom?" Now Uncle Ephraim was getting annoyed.

Mr. Murphy shrugged and looked at his mother, who looked at Aunt Sarah, who looked back at Uncle Ephraim.

"'I may have said something to Margaret," Aunt Sarah said, in her own defense. "But I do not converse with Mrs. Murphy on any subject, and certainly not on the subject in question."

"Then let me remind you, Sarah, that I have no intention of removing myself from this house," Uncle Ephraim stated firmly. He turned to Murphy. "It was deeded to me by my illustrious father-in-law on my marriage to Mrs. Pettigrew, and when I go, if such is

THE GUILTY CLIENT

the will of the Almighty, I will leave it to my only living relation, my brother's daughter, Miss Margaret Pettigrew."

"What!" I burst out. "But what about Aunt Sarah? It's her house! Her father meant for her to have it, I'm sure of it."

"Don't you worry about your Aunt Sarah," Uncle Ephraim told me. "She's well provided for. As for this house, it's sitting on what may be the only bit of land on Manhattan Island not owned by Astor or one of his kin. As long as I'm in it, no one can try to claim this block for Eminent Domain, not even the high-and-mighty Boss Tweed!"

"Eminent Domain? What's that?" Mrs. Murphy asked, with a suspicious frown.

"It means, madam, that as long as I own this property, I can block any attempts to raze the buildings on or around it, should the City of New York decide to re-zone this district, to enhance the revenues to the City," Uncle Ephraim explained.

"That is, no one can knock down these houses to put up something else that will bring in more money." I simplified the matter.

"Knock down the houses?" Mrs. Murphy repeated.

"Once the elevated railroad goes up, this area can be used for commercial purposes," Uncle Ephraim went on. "Warehouses, horse-barns, offices."

"And what of the people living here?" Mrs. Murphy was quick to grasp the most important part of the issue.

"That, I fear, is of no concern to Astor and his crew," Uncle Ephraim said blandly. "It's the money they're after. They can make more of it by renting the land to commercial users, and they don't have to provide amenities such as sewerage, gas-lighting, and water for ware-houses or horse-barns. I have no doubt that there would be an outcry at the displacement of so many worthy citizens from their homes, but in the end, Mrs. Murphy, you and your family would be evicted, to make room for more lucrative tenants."

He had spoken the magic word. The one thing that any tenant on Bank Street feared was eviction, and the loss of that sanctuary, however small, that meant Home to the weary worker and his family.

Mrs. Murphy turned on her son. "You didn't tell me that we'd be evicted!" she screeched.

"No one said nothing to me about eviction!" Mr. Murphy protested. "It was put to me that if Mr. Pettigrew was to leave this ward, that his house might be up for sale, that's all."

"Then you may put all fears to rest, Mr. Murphy, Mrs. Murphy. I shall be taken from this residence feet first!" Uncle Ephraim smiled upon them benignly. "Bank Street will remain, first and foremost, a residential neighborhood, and I hope, madam, that we will remain good neighbors. Good evening, Mrs. Murphy, Mr. Murphy. My servant will show you out."

As soon as she heard the door close behind the Murphy mother and son, Aunt Sarah turned on Uncle Ephraim. "Ephraim! You can't mean to stay here! Once the elevated goes up, it will be impossible to live here! No one calls now, and no one will ever call again! How can Margaret find a beau if she doesn't pay calls, and if no one calls on her? How can I continue to keep up my acquaintance?"

"The way you do now, Sarah. You hire a cab, and you drive over to the East Side," Uncle Ephraim said. "As for Peggy, she's had her chance, and she's made her choice. She's better off in the office with me than she would be sitting in a parlor, drinking tea with the rest of those babbling geese, and you know it."

Aunt Sarah was close to tears. "But Ephraim," she wailed, "we can't just let her be an old maid."

I decided to make my own feelings known. "I am only twenty-five," I pointed out. "That is not especially old. And I find the work at Uncle Ephraim's office interesting."

"And where do you expect to find a husband?" Aunt Sarah challenged me. "Among the stevedores? Or the sea captains and mates? Don't think to marry one of them, my dear, for they all have wives in every port. And as for the men you'll meet in a courtroom, the lawyers won't even give you the time of day, especially if they think you're after their clients."

"I'm not looking for a husband anywhere," I shot back. "As long as I have my own money, and my own place to live, I don't need one."

"There is more to marriage than that, my dear," Uncle Ephraim said, smiling at Aunt Sarah. I suddenly got a glimpse of a world that I had ignored, a depth of feeling between these two people who had

THE GUILTY CLIENT

been the mainstay of my existence. I could not tell them that I had once had hopes of such a relationship for myself, and that those had been dashed when the object of my affections had returned from the War mangled in body and mind.

We had had this conversation many times in the five years since the War ended. Aunt Sarah was convinced that I ought to be married; I was just as certain that I would not marry anyone for whom I did not feel both affection and respect. There was only one person who had evoked those emotions in me, and I could not let him know it, particularly under the present circumstances.

"Well, dear, we will discuss this later," said Aunt Sarah, putting the unpleasantness aside, as if it had never happened. Now, let's see if Mandy can make your Uncle Ephraim a nice dish of bread-and-milk to soothe his digestion."

The kitchen had been cleared, although there was still a faint odor of garlic. Mandy did what she could, casting apprehensive glances at the door to the back stairs that led to the attic bedroom assigned to Maria Luisa, who had retired for the night.

The bread-and-milk was duly eaten. Uncle Ephraim and Aunt Sarah went to their chamber at the back of the house, overlooking the garden; I went up to mine, which faced the street, which was noisier and more prone to street odors.

There Mandy helped me remove my dress and corsets, and undid the crown of lank fair locks that was the best I could do for a coiffure. My hair is stubbornly straight, defying every effort to achieve the cascade of curls that Fashion and Aunt Sarah decree for young women of my station.

"We goin' to get a new cook?" Mandy asked, as she brushed out my hair and started to put it into a braid for the night.

"I suppose so," I said, with a sigh. I wasn't looking forward to trying to explain to Maria Luisa that her services were no longer required, and that she must leave Bank Street forthwith.

"Get some sleep, Mandy," I said, and stood in front of the fireplace in my bedroom for my evening ritual. Every night, since I was old enough to remember, I had faced these two ancient daguerreotypes: one showing a fleshy man in a figured vest and frock coat, his necktie artistically careless, one hand thrust into his trousers pocket, the other into his vest, the other showing a slender dark woman, her hair in side curls, in the bell-shaped crinoline dress of twenty years ago. These were my parents, and every night I had said the same prayers: "God Bless Papa and Mama, and keep them safe, wherever they are."

I wondered if they were safe, or even alive, but I said the prayer anyway. Then I crawled into my bed, and tried to compose myself for sleep, but sleep did not come very easily. I kept going over and over the events of the day, and could make no sense of anything that had been done or said.

I turned down the flame on the bedside lamp and tried to sleep. The noises from the street had never disturbed my repose, but the creaks and groans from the old attics still had the power to stir my imagination. When I was a child, I would hear strange scufflings and mutters, whispers and soft rappings, and I would shiver with fright, wondering if there were hobgoblins and other fanciful creatures living there. As I grew older, I realized that a house so near the river would attract vermin of various sorts, mice and the cats that dined upon them, and I told myself that my fancies were just that: nonsensical musings, that had no basis in fact. Still, it was hard to ignore the noises, and I found it hard to get to sleep. My brain was still working on the problems of the day.

It had been a very long day, and it was about to get longer.

CHAPTER 20

I FINALLY SETTLED INTO A KIND of fitful doze, half-asleep, half-awake. I was jolted into full wakefulness by a shrill whistle from the street below my bedroom window.

"Neighborhood louts," I said out loud, and punched my pillow into a more comfortable shape.

A louder whistle, and a rattle of pebbles jerked me awake. I grumbled and mumbled to myself as I went to the window and peered out into the street.

I could barely make out three people standing in the street under the lantern that custom and the City Council demanded every householder place in front of his door.

"Peggy! Open the door!" came a stifled cry.

"Michael? What are you doing down there?"

"Come down and open up, and we'll explain."

I threw my wrapper on over my nightgown, lit my kerosene lamp, and hurried downstairs to let them into the hall. Michael and Joshua were reeking of horse and worse, and between them was a young woman.

"What are you doing here, and who is this woman?" I demanded.

Joshua made the introductions. "Miss Peggy Pettigrew, this is Miss Dutch Mitzi," he said solemnly.

"Dot is vot dey call me," Miss Mitzi said, with great dignity. "I am *artiste de theatre*. I dance."

"I'm sure you do," I said. I drew Michael aside in the hall. "What can you be thinking of, bringing a woman like that here?" I hissed at him, hoping that Aunt Sarah and Uncle Ephraim would not be disturbed by this late-night call.

"I didn't know where else to take her," Michael said, with a scapegrace grin. "Her, um, employer has just kicked her out, and she's a material witness. She was the last person Bertram Delacorte talked to before he left, um, the place where she was."

"You mean she's a…" I couldn't say it.

"I am dancer!" Mitzi insisted loudly. "I am no *kurve*!"

"Yes, of course," Michael said, trying to quiet her. "Mitzi, Miss Pettigrew is going to let you stay here for the night, until we can take your testimony, and get Heinz out of the Tombs."

"And who is this Heinz?" I asked.

"Her, um, protector," Michael said. "Clubber Williams just arrested him for murdering Bertram Delacorte."

"Did he?" I looked at Joshua.

"Heinz don't kill anyone in America," Mitzi stated. "In Odessa he kill Turkish soldier. This is vy ve go to Paris."

Clearly Miss Mitzi had had an adventurous life. I brought the lamp closer so that I could inspect her. She was somewhat older than me, with fair hair that did not need the use of irons to attain the correct curls, and a trim figure clad in a somewhat moth-eaten fur-trimmed coat and pert fur hat, worn over a blue satin dress trimmed with white lace, cut lower in the front than Aunt Sarah would allow for one of my gowns.

I was now able to look Michael and Joshua over, and I was appalled. "What have you two been up to?" I said. "You're all bruised, and you smell like a stable."

"We have been looking for information, and we have found it," Joshua said, with much aplomb. "Some of the information concerns that photograph you found in Mrs. Kendall's trunk."

"You know who it is?"

"We think it is a man called Billy Kendall, who is now employed by Mr. Henry Ward Long as a bodyguard," Joshua told me.

"And where does this Heinz come in?" I wanted to know. "What connection does he have with Suzanna Kendall?"

"He doesn't," Joshua said. "But it's quite likely that he saw Bertram Delacorte in the company of Billy Kendall, after Delacorte left the establishment where Miss Mitzi works."

"And someone don't want the two murders connected," Michael added. "Clubber didn't say anything about the Kendall murder when

THE GUILTY CLIENT

he took Heinz Guttenberg in. Just Bertram Delacorte."

"On what evidence?" I asked.

"I've no idea," Michael said, with a shrug. "I've been out of the office most of the afternoon. My guess is that this is one they'll hand off to one of the other Assistant DA's, maybe even Bill Tweed Junior, to give him a little newspaper play. 'Boss's Son Nails Murderer!'" He quoted an imaginary newspaper headline.

"But Heinz did not do dis!" Mitzi protested. "He vas mit me all night, after Bertie vent out. I take vun gentleman upstairs, vich I haf to do, and did. Den Heinz and me, ve make plans."

"Is there anyone else who can verify this?" Joshua asked.

Mitzi shrugged, showing off more bosom. "De other girls, dey know Heinz. He is bouncer. If dere is trouble, he takes it out to street."

"Does he own a Bowie knife?" Joshua continued his questioning, as if he was in the office instead of in the hall at Bank Street at nearly two o'clock in the morning.

"*Nein*, vat he vant mit knife?" Mitzi said scornfully.

"That's my case, in a nutshell," Joshua said. He turned to me. "Miss Peggy, our client is now in the Tombs. We've got to be there tomorrow, early, with the bail money to get him out before he gets railroaded. I'll call for you here, at eight o'clock, tomorrow…" He stopped and consulted his pocket-watch. "No, it's now today. This morning. And this time, I'm not going to let a client get away to be murdered!" His voice rose, and I tried to hush him.

"Please! You'll wake Uncle Ephraim and Aunt Sarah!"

It was too late for that. "What's this about murders?" Between indigestion and indignation, Uncle Ephraim had clearly been as wakeful as I, and he now descended the stairs to confront the late-night visitors.

Uncle Ephraim in his night clothes is an awesome sight. His garment of choice is something called a 'caftan', one that was brought to him by one of his sea-faring clients, a vast cotton object that covers him from neck to ankles in stripes of various startling hues. It looked like one of Mr. Barnum's circus tents billowing about him as he reach the hall.

"Joshua, Michael." Uncle Ephraim greeted them. "You've been

in a fight, I see. Who won?"

"We did, but only with help," Michael admitted. "Uncle Ephraim, we've got a house guest for you. She's a material witness." He nodded towards Mitzi.

"We've got another client," Joshua added. "He's in the Tombs, charged with killing Bertram Delacorte."

"Another attempt to fob the murder charge off onto someone else," Uncle Ephraim said. He looked Miss Mitzi up and down, then said, "We can't stand around here, boys. Come into the den, and we'll sort all this out."

We crowded into Uncle Ephraim's sanctuary. I lit another lamp, and Uncle Ephraim settled into his chair. "Well, young woman, what have you to say for yourself?"

Mitzi looked around the room and tried to assess all that had happened in the course of a few minutes.

Joshua said something to her in a language that sounded almost like German, but wasn't quite. Mitzi's eyes opened wide and she responded similarly, volubly, and at great length.

Joshua translated. "Miss Mitzi's full name is Miriam Zelman. She's from Russia, originally, and has been across Europe with Heinz, dancing wherever she could find an audience. She is, as Michael and I can testify, not a prostitute as defined by law, but a performer of exotic dances. Heinz Guttenberg is her manager, not precisely a pimp. She attracted the attention of Bertram Delacorte last year, in Paris, and it was Delacorte who arranged for her to come to America. According to Mitzi, Delacorte also brought her to the attention of Madame Mags, who gave her employment as an exotic dancer. The ah, intimate functions of the house were distasteful to her, and she performed them only to re-imburse Delacorte for the money he advanced to get her here."

I wrote all this down, wondering just what Joshua was leaving out of Miss Mitzi's narrative.

Mitzi spoke up again, this time in English. "Ven Bertie comes last night, ve talk. He says he haf not money to build theater now, but vill haf very soon, and ven he make the theater, I vill be star dancer."

"Indeed." Uncle Ephraim looked at Michael and Joshua. "A theater?"

THE GUILTY CLIENT

"On Forty-Second Street, behind the Reservoir," Joshua explained. "I spoke with one of Bertram's cronies. He was of the opinion that Bertram had gone to one of his wealthy relations for the money, and was refused."

Uncle Ephraim frowned. "Old Mrs. Delacorte would never hand over money for such a frivolous undertaking as a theater, especially one that specialized in lewd dances."

"I don't think it was the Delacortes he meant," Joshua said slowly. "He wasn't living with the Delacortes, was he? He'd made his home with the Longs, not the Delacortes, since he came back from Europe. It would be Long he'd go to for money, just as he went to Long, and not Delacorte when his number came up in the Draft."

I made a noise. "He would! Just like that nasty boy to shirk his duty!"

Joshua said, "I think you may be doing him an injustice, Miss Peggy."

"Boys younger than he went," I said, stubbornly. And I felt my face redden, as I recalled the day that I bade Michael farewell, and saw his friend being harangued by a little man in a black coat and broad-brimmed hat. I had caught a few words: "Is this why I come here to America? To see my son go to get himself killed in a war about *schvartzes*? If you do this, then you are not my son! I will say Kaddish now, not later when you are killed in this war, that is not your business!"

"His father was dead," Michael pointed out. "His mother may have had a hand in keeping her baby out of the action."

"I've seen her," I put in. "She's very emotional."

"Hysterical, you mean," Michael said, unkindly.

"And it can't have been easy for a lad whose father had been a West Point man to sit back here in New York and not go," Joshua added. "Especially if it was because his Mama wouldn't let him."

"A case of fox and grapes," Michael said. "You know, the fox said the grapes he couldn't get at were sour. Bertram Delacorte said he didn't want to go, because he couldn't go. Mama and Uncle Henry Long wouldn't have it."

"The point is," Joshua said, bringing us back to the present, "that if Bertram Delacorte wanted money, he wouldn't go to his father's relations, but to his uncle-by-marriage, Henry Ward Long."

"And Long wouldn't back a show like that either," Uncle Ephraim said firmly. "He's a stickler for propriety is Henry Ward Long."

"So," I said, "Bertram asks for money. Uncle Henry refuses. They quarrel, and Uncle Henry throws Bertram out of the house."

"And he goes to Mrs. Smith's boarding-house," Michael finished for me. "Why there?"

"Because that's where he could stay that's only a block or two away from the nice, new brownstone that Mr. Long just moved into," I said slowly. "And because he didn't have enough money to pay for the Astor House or the Fifth Avenue Hotel, and everyone in those places would know it."

"So," Uncle Ephraim said. "Bertram moves into Mrs. Smiths . . when?"

"Ve talk at beginning of April," Mitzi said. "Vas before *Pesach*."

"Just before Easter," Joshua explained.

"A week before Appomattox Night," I said.

"He is at Mrs. Smith's for a week, and in that time he sees Mrs. Kendall," Uncle Ephraim went on.

"And she sees him," Joshua said. "According to one of the boarders, the sight of Bertram was enough to send her into a fit of terror. Although," he added after a moment's thought, "it might have been the other man. The one who brought Bertram's baggage in when he arrived. Billy Kendall."

"And who, exactly, is Billy Kendall?" Uncle Ephraim asked.

"Billy Kendall is the man in the photograph that Miss Peggy found in Mrs. Kendall's trunk," Michael explained. "And according to my informants, Billy Kendall, who was once a member of the Plug-Ugly Gang, was hired by Mr. Long during the War to stand guard over his Washington Square residence while the family was away, enjoying the sea breezes in Brooklyn. I strongly suspect that Billy Kendall is the man who was paid $300 to serve instead of Bertram Delacorte."

"Then it would seem that we should talk with Mr. Billy Kendall, right soon," said Uncle Ephraim.

"Not now, though," Michael said, with a mighty yawn. "I don't know what Mrs. Baumgarten will think when the pair of us come reeling in at this hour."

"You could stay here, in your old room," Uncle Ephraim offered.

"No, I've got to get my other suit, and get this one cleaned," Michael said, looking at the ruin of his clothes. He tried to brush off some of the dried grime, and felt a crackle in his breast-pocket. "Mother of Mercy, I'd clean forgot about that!" He took out the paper that he'd found in the bottom of Bertram Delacorte's wardrobe. "What have we here? 'To Suzanna'."

"A letter?" Uncle Ephraim held out a hand for it.

"A poem, by the look of it," Michael said, and passed it over to Uncle Ephraim, who passed it over to me.

"Read that, Peggy," he said. "I left my specs upstairs."

I squinted at the spiky handwriting. " 'Had we but world enough and time, this coyness, lady, were no crime'," I read. "That sounds familiar."

Joshua nodded. "It's 'To His Coy Mistress', by Andrew Marvell. A poem, written over two hundred years ago."

"Well, Bertie Delacorte certainly didn't send this to Mrs. Kendall," I said, reading on. "This is an older man writing to a young girl, telling her to give in to him because he might die soon, and then they'd regret not having done it."

"Dirty old man!" Mitzi sniffed.

"But that's not Bertie," Uncle Ephraim said. "Give me that, Peggy. I want to take a better look at it, in the daylight. Meanwhile, you boys need your rest, and we've got to get Miss Mitzi, here, settled for the night."

"And I have to be in the Tombs tomorrow, to get Heinz out on bail," Joshua added.

Mitzi looked at us. "Vat I do now?" she wanted to know. "I vill not go back to dat house."

"Certainly not," came from the door to the den. There was Aunt Sarah, her night-cap bristling with curl-papers, her ample form covered in her silk wrapper from Japan. "You're staying here. Come along, girl, and we'll get that muck off your face."

"I do apologize for bringing this woman here," Joshua began.

"Nonsense, Mr. Roth. It's not the first time a fugitive has found a sanctuary in this house," Aunt Sarah said. She took Mitzi by the hand and I watched in some astonishment as Aunt Sarah led Mitzi through the hall and up the back stairs to what I had always assumed was the attic where the old trunks and furniture were stored.

"Go back to bed, Peggy," Uncle Ephraim ordered. "We've got a lot to do in the morning. Michael, you'd better start acting like a Prosecutor, or you won't have a job, Tammany or no Tammany protection. Joshua, you're going to have to find more evidence before we can move against this Kendall. As for Miss Mitzi," Uncle Ephraim said, "no one is going to bother her in this house."

A thought occurred to me. "Miss Mitzi," I called up the stairs, "can you cook?"

She stopped half-way. "I can make kasha," she said.

"What's that?" Michael wanted to know.

Joshua chuckled to himself. "I supposed you'd call it a kind of porridge, made from coarse wheat or barley," he said. "My mother used to cook it." He said no more. He rarely spoke of his family, and when he did, it was with bitterness and sorrow.

I thought back to my childhood, and the furtive sounds that had terrified me in the night. I had never dared to question anything then, fearing that I would be abandoned, like the children I saw in the streets, if I displeased my aunt and uncle. Could it be that Aunt Sarah and Uncle Ephraim had been harboring escaping Negroes? It would explain a great deal of what had gone on in the house.

However, all that was in the past. The present meant that Joshua and Michael must get back to their own lodgings, Mitzi must go up to the attics, and I must get some sleep, and be prepared for another eventful day.

SECTION 7: JOSHUA

CHAPTER 21

Michael and I board at Mrs. Baumgarten's on West Fouth Street. We managed to get in without too much trouble, and I gratefully found repose on the iron bed-stead furnished by that redoubtable widow.

Army life accustoms a man to early rising, and I was able to grab myself eggs and sausage, coffee and bread, while Michael was still snoring in his own room. One of the advantages of growing out a beard is that I don't have to shave, which cuts down on the time needed to make a reasonable appearance in court.

Peggy was up, dressed, and ready for me when I walked over to Bank Street, and the early cabbies were eager for a fare, so we made good time getting to the New York City Hall of Justice, popularly known as The Tombs. It's well named, for it was built along the lines of the Great Pyramid in Egypt, with its top cut off, a massive stone structure built to strike terror into the heart of anyone who has to enter it, on either side of the Law.

It was barely eight-thirty in the morning, and already the place was crowded and noisy, what with the police going on and off duty; the prisoners' families, clamoring for attention; and the lawyers looking for clients. I was saved that last indignity by virtue of my association with Mr. Pettigrew. I, at least, had a legitimate client.

I made my way through the crowd to the desk where a police sergeant sat, ignoring the Public, and swilling at a bottle of beer.

"I'm here to see my client," I told him. "Heinz Guttenberg. Brought in last night, on a charge of murder."

The sergeant looked me over, and took in my injury. Miss Pettigrew smiled demurely at him.

"Come on, Sergeant," she said. "You know me. This is Uncle Ephraim Pettigrew's new partner, Mr. Roth."

This seemed to mollify the sergeant. He consulted his ledger, and bawled out to someone behind him "Take the counselor to the Interview Room."

The Interview Room turned out to be a barren dungeon, with no other furnishings than a single chair. Heinz was led in by a guard, who regarded him warily and kept one hand on his baton at all times, even though the prisoner wore handcuffs.

Heinz was in a sorry condition. He'd had an eye blackened, and there were bruises on his hands; his dapper dress suit was torn at the shoulders and there were marks on his trouser-legs where he had been struck with clubs. I did not know how many bruises lurked under the coat and trousers, but by his swaggering attitude, and by the respectful distance kept by the guard, I imagined that Heinz Guttenberg had given as good as he got before being hauled off to this vile place.

"Good morning, Mr. Guttenberg," I said. "I want to get your statement before we go to court."

Heinz glared at me fiercely. "I tell you what I tell the policemans. I know nothing of what happened to Bertie Delacorte. I hear about it yesterday, when someone comes to the house to tell us that he is found in the river."

I motioned for Miss Peggy to sit in the sole chair. "Take this down, Miss Pettigrew," I said. Then I turned back to Heinz.

"What, exactly, transpired between you and Bertram Delacorte on the night of April 26th?" I asked.

"Eh?"

"What happened when you saw Delacorte?" Peggy translated for me.

Heinz thought it over. "He comes with Johnny Ellison," he said. "They are both drunk, but Bertie is not so drunk as Johnny. He sits with me, and says that he doesn't have the money he needs yet, but he has a way to get it."

"I see," I said. I was getting a glimpse into the mind of Bertram Delacorte, and a nasty mind it was. He had the poem, which had been written and sent to Suzanna Kendall, by an older man, who would be vulnerable to blackmail.

"I tell him, Mitzi has had offers from other men," Heinz went on. "He tells me, do not take these offers until he can settle his affairs. I also tell him that I need money for citizen papers, because Mitzi and me, we are not citizens, and if we are not citizens, we get sent back to Russia, and this would not be good for me or for Mitzi."

He meant one of those citizenship-mills, run by Tammany lawyers, to expedite citizenship requests, thus bringing up the voting rolls. It meant more votes for Tammany, and although many good folk were granted citizenship quickly and easily, so were a number of people who were not so welcome amongst the population of New York City and the United States of America. I didn't know whether Mitzi and Heinz would be considered among the first group or the second.

"You're not a citizen?" I said. I might be able to get the case dismissed on the grounds that he was being illegally detained.

"But I want to be," he protested. "I cannot go back to Russia. I am wanted there."

"Mitzi said that you'd killed a man in Odessa," Miss Peggy put in.

"A Turkish soldier. He was drunk, and he was trying to rape Mitzi," Heinz explained. "It is how we met."

"I see," I said, and oddly enough, I did. Mitzi danced, he provided protection, and the two of them were able to get across Europe without too much difficulty in these times of strained relations between nations.

"So," I said, getting back to the business that had brought us here, "tell me what happened after you talked with Mr. Delacorte about the money, and the citizenship papers."

Heinz shrugged. "Then came the performances, as you have seen, and Mitzi did the can-can dance, and one of the other men took her before Bertie had the chance, and she went upstairs." He stopped, red-faced, and glanced at Miss Peggy.

"And then what?" I prodded him.

"And then he looked out the window, and made a noise, like, 'What?'" Heinz said. "And he took his hat, and he ran outside, to the stoop, and he looked in the street."

"How do you know what he did?"

"I followed him," Heinz admitted. "I thought he was trying to run away, without giving me any money for Mitzi or my citizenship papers. But he was not running away, because he said, 'Wait here, Heinz, I just saw someone I have to talk to'. And he ran down the street, after a carriage."

"He chased a carriage?" I repeated.

"The carriages, they drive slow," Heinz reminded me. I'd seen it myself, the carriages with the gentlemen making their choices of the wares offered by the women of West Twenty-Fifth Street, and the way the women beckoned and flirted with the occupants of those carriages.

"Did you recognize the carriage?" I asked.

"It's dark," Heinz said. "But I think it was a funny color. Not black, like most carriages. The kind with a seat for a groom behind, and two men up top, a driver and another man."

"A Stanhope," Miss Peggy said. "With a groom, a coachman, and a bodyguard."

"My, my, my," I said to myself. We'd seen just such a rig yesterday, and we knew to whom it belonged.

Heinz frowned, trying to remember everything he could about that encounter. "He yelled after the carriage, he called out, 'Billy!'".

"Billy Kendall," Miss Peggy said.

"Who is that?" Heinze asked.

"A man who seems to disappear whenever we try to find him," I said slowly. "Mr. Guttenberg, I am going to move for dismissal of your case, on the grounds that there is absolutely no evidence that you have any reason to kill Mr. Delacorte, you do not own a Bowie knife, and you were in the company of several women in the house of Madame Mags most of the evening. Miss Pettigrew and I will see you in court."

I let the guards take Heinz away. Then I turned to Miss Peggy. "I don't like the way this is going," I said. "The deeper we get into it, the worse it looks. We've got to find this Billy Kendall, and soon. He's what we used to call a loose cannon, too dangerous to haul and likely to go off at any moment."

"It shouldn't be too hard to catch up with him, if he's Mr. Long's bodyguard," Miss Peggy said, in her matter-of-fact way.

"Unless someone warns him that we're after him," I said, as we went through the screaming horde in the anteroom and headed across the street to the Criminal Court building. "What worries me is that he might decide to make a run for it, and go back to his pals in the Plug-Uglies. We'll never find him then."

"Let's get Mr. Guttenberg released first," said Miss Peggy. "Then we can take care of Mr. Kendall."

Down the front stairs we went, heading towards the half-finished building that faced Chambers Street. As we looked for an opening in the traffic, we were accosted by a bearded gentleman, some inches shorter than myself, sober black frock coat and vest, topped with a broad-brimmed felt hat.

"*Landsman!*" he greeted me.

I stopped, reasonably sure of who I was facing. I do not usually make my religion known, and to be named by a fellow-Jew meant that someone had done some digging into my past.

"Mr. Hummel, I preseume?"

"Of Hummel and Howe. That's me, Abe Hummel, at your service." He made an brief bow in the direction of Miss Peggy, and handed me his visiting card with a flourish.

"What can I do for you, Mr. Hummel?" I said, aware that this man represented one of the most notorious and most sought-after firms of defense lawyers in New York, and that all eyes would be upon the two of us.

"Ah, Mr. Roth, it's what I can do for you," Hummel said, with a knowing grin. He took me by the arm and led me a few steps away from Miss Peggy. "It's come to our attention that you're a comer, Mr. Roth. A rising star in our municipal legal firmament. A War Hero, wounded gallantly in our Nation's defense, now coming to the rescue of the innocent, trapped in the toils of the Justice System."

"I have been hired to defend my clients," I admitted.

"And a fine job you've done, too, in a very short time," Hummel said. "Finding an alibi for Bertram Delacorte, and now I hear you're defending this Guttenberg, who's accused of killing him."

"Word certainly gets out quickly," I said. "You might very well have a grape-vine telegraph direct to Mulberry Street," meaning Police Headquarters.

Hummel edged me farther away from Miss Peggy. "Now, my partner and I, that is, Mr. Howe, realize that young fellows like yourself may not always know where their best interests lie. They may tie themselves to unworkable partnerships."

"Such as?" I wanted to see just how far this would go. Hummel and Howe are reputed to be the most prestigious and the most skillful defense attorneys in New York, but they are known to have the most brazen of criminals on their client list, beginning with Madame Restell, the abortionist, and going down the line to run-or-the-mill burglars and bashers of storekeepers.

"Ephraim Pettigrew is a gentleman of some standing in our legal community," Hummel said, "but his day is past. His practice is not profitable. He spends his time staring at the ships on the docks, writing contracts and bailing sailors out of the city jail. Hardly a lively practice for a young man like yourself, sir."

"Have you another offer in mind?" I asked.

Hummel looked around, then said softly, "We could take you into our firm, not as a full partner, you understand, but as an associate. You would benefit materially, sir, and we would have the advantage of your considerable talents."

I gave this offer all the consideration it was due, which was approximately one minute. Then I said, "Mr. Hummel, this is a very generous offer, but I feel that at this time I cannot accept it."

Hummel frowned. "If it's your cut. . ." he began.

I cut him off. "Mr. Hummel, I would not become a part of your firm for any share of your proceeds. I have already given my support to Mr. Pettigrew. As for the practice being too quiet, well, sir, I must confess that I had a difficult time after my injury. First in Washington, then in New Orleans, working with the military tribunal, I found myself in certain difficulties, due to the stressful nature of the work I was being asked to do. However, my doctors tell me that I am very much improved since I started sitting by the river, watching the ships on the docks with Mr. Pettigrew. It is very soothing to the nerves."

I could see Hummel getting more and more nervous as I spoke, probably wondering if I was going to go off into a raving fit right there on the steps of the Tombs.

"So you see," I went on, "It would really be for the best if I continue as I am. I thank you for your offer, Mr. Hummel. It has given me something to think about."

It certainly did. I have only been in New York City since 1868, when I resumed my studies at the Columbia College School of Law. I passed the New York State Bar in December of 1869. I joined Mr. Pettigrew a month ago, and *People vs. Delacorte* was the first case of any note that I had pleaded before a judge in this city. Why, then should I receive an offer to join Hummel and Howe, a well-established legal firm, who certainly did not need a fledgling attorney as an associate? Someone really must want me off this case, I thought, and therefore I will stay with it until the end.

Miss Peggy had been watching the by-play between Hummel and me. "What did he want?" she asked.

"To get me off this case," I said. "And that is why I think we shall go forward."

Which is exactly what we did.

SECTION 8: MICHAEL

CHAPTER 22

After all the ructions of the day and night before, it's no wonder that I nearly missed the call to breakfast at Mrs. Baumgarten's.

I took stock of myself. I had a few black and blue marks over the ribs, and a bruise on my cheek where I'd hit the cobbles, but I didn't look too bad. My fine new suit was a nasty sight, all covered with the muck of the fight by the horse-barns, so I had to put on the second suit, not as natty or as cheerful. My hand was shaking, so I decided to skip the shave for the day, and wait until I could get to the barber down the street. I've considered letting the whiskers grow out, like Joshua, but mine comes in red, in patches, and I wind up looking like a hayseed. Not the sort of thing needed to make a good impression on the Court and the Jury!

Joshua was already gone by the time I got downstairs, and so was most of the breakfast ham and eggs. I got the leavings, a cup of coffee, and a slab of bread, and ate as fast as I could, while going over the doings of the day and night before.

It was easier to walk down to Chambers Street than to try and get a cab, so I didn't reach the court-house until well after nine o'clock. I knew I was in trouble when I saw young Bill Tweed coming down the grand staircase just as I was going up.

Young Tweed is taller and thinner than his famous Pa, and he sports a grand mustache instead of a shaggy beard, but there's no doubt that he's a chip off the old block. Let no one think that this youngster is riding on the Boss's coattails; he's out to make a name for himself. Still, I couldn't help but twit him a bit, me being the one

THE GUILTY CLIENT

who's usually saddled with his case-work.

"Well, well," says I, "you're up early this morning." Young Tweed don't usually put in an appearance until noon, if then.

"I'm due in court," says he, trying to sound important.

"Indeed," says I, trying to brush past him.

"They're arraigning the fellow who knifed Bertram Delacorte," says Young Tweed, "and I've caught the case. My father's seen to it that there'll be plenty of Press coverage."

"You're handling Heinz Guttenberg?" I says. I had hoped to catch that one myself, being that I could tie it into the Kendall murder.

"What do you know about that?" says Young Tweed.

"I was there when Clubber Williams made the arrest," says I.

"Then you'd have had to recuse yourself in any case," says he, smugly.

"How did you catch this one?" I asks.

"If you'd have stayed in your office, instead of gallivanting about with your Sheeny pal, you'd have known that Clubber Williams wasn't going to let the grass grow under his feet. He had his men out as soon as Delacorte was identified, tracing his movements. They found some drunk who saw Delacorte coming out of Madame Mags with this Heinz, and once Clubber had that, he got himself a warrant and arrested Guttenberg. You should leave the police work to the police, Riley."

And he taps me on the shoulder and off he goes, leaving me seething.

Now, what I should have done was go to my own office and let Young Tweed handle the case. This I could not do. I knew that Heinz had been framed, and I was as sure as a man can be that Billy Kendall was the one who had killed both Suzanna Kendall and Bertram Delacorte, although I could not for the life of me think why.

So I trailed after Young Tweed, and slipped into the back of the courtroom, behind the line of reporters who had been tipped off by Boss Tweed's men that the Delacorte case was coming, and that there would be fireworks galrore.

I wasn't the only one. The New York County Court is as good a free show as the general public can get, and word had got out that there was a murderer going to be arraigned, and that Young Tweed was up for the Prosecution. I found myself wedged in between a hefty old-timer in the Plug-Ugly striped vest and plug hat, and a young woman with a very low neck to her dress. I squeezed through the crowd, and got over to the Bar with wallet and watch still on my person, not for lack of someone trying to nip both.

Pickpockets have a grand time when there's a good court case going.

I felt someone else breathing down my neck. There was Davy Jonas, ears pricked up, pencil and pad handy, taking down every word. He'd get his scoop for the *Sun*, and be out before anyone could catch him.

Joshua and his client were at the Defense side. Heinz had been roughed up in the Tombs, but I'd bet anything you like that no one would get a confession out of him, with or without persuasion. Joshua was ready to proceed, and Miss Peggy was sitting right next to him, paper and pencil before her.

The bailiff bellows out, "All Rise!"

In comes old Judge Bacon, a skinny old gink with white hair all on end, who's been sitting on the New York Bench since Fernando Woods put him there, and no one can get him off it.

He looks at Joshua, and points his finger at Miss Peggy. "Mr. Roth, why is that female still here?"

Joshua stands up and says, "Your Honor, as you see, I have a slight disability. Miss Pettigrew is here to serve as my clerk, to take accurate notes of what is said, and to provide assistance should I need it."

"There are plenty of men who can do that," Judge Bacon says.

Joshua says, "Your Honor, my senior partner, Mr. Ephraim Pettigrew, has trained Miss Pettigrew in her position, and it at his request that she continues in it. I must defer to his wishes on this point."

Old Bacon gives him a nasty look, and slams his gavel down. "Proceed!" he orders. "First case?"

"People versus Guttenberg," says the bailiff.

Heinz stands up.

"What is the charge?" Bacon asks.

THE GUILTY CLIENT

"Murder in the second degree," says Young Tweed. "In that Heinz Guttenberge did deliberately kill Bertram Delacorte on the night of April 26, 1870."

Great sensation in the crowd, much muttering about Germans and how tough they was.

"Fast work, catching him the next day," says Judge Bacon. "How do you plead?"

"Not guilty," says Joshua firmly. "Heinz Guttenberg did not kill Bertram Delacorte."

"You sound very certain, sir," says Judge Bacon.

"It is our contention that Mr. Guttenberg is accused of a crime he did not commit, and we intend to prove it."

"Oh, really?" Judge Bacon says, nastily. "Have you another alibi up your sleeve, Mr. Roth? Was Mr. Guttenberg dancing with Miss Pettigrew at the time that Mr. Delacorte met his untimely end?"

Joshua bites back whatever he was about to say. "At this time, we ask that the prisoner be dismissed."

"On what grounds?" says Young Tweed.

"On the grounds that there is no evidence to connect Mr. Guttenberg with any crime whatsoever, and certainly not this one," Joshua shoots back at him.

Young Tweed strokes his mustache. "The People will prove that Heinz Guttenberg has a connection with the deceased," says he. "There is a witness who will attest that he saw the prisoner in conversation with the deceased just before the time of the murder."

"Have the police found the murder weapon?" says Joshua.

"No, but…"

"Have they found a motive?" says Joshua.

Young Tweed makes a nasty face. "The deceased, Bertram Delacorte, had a, hum, relationship, with a young woman who is a known companion of the prisoner," he says.

"That is hardly a reason to kill a man," says Joshua. "If you will not dismiss, then I move that bail be set."

"This is a capital offense," says Young Tweed. "Absent any evidence to the contrary, the People insist that Guttenberg be held for trial."

"Have you any evidence at this time?" Judge Bacon asks again.

"Not at this time," Joshua has to admit.

"Then bail is denied. The prisoner Guttenberg is remanded to the custody of the Court until such time as he is brought to trial." The judge whacks down his gavel, and Heinz is led off by a squad of blue-coats.

Davy Jonas can't wait to get out to his paper. I grab him and drag him aside.

"Do you really think that Dutch bruiser would bother to take a knife to a silly fellow like Delacorte?" I says.

"It don't matter what I think," Davy says. "The Delacortes are Old Money, and Broadway Bertie was connected with the Longs as well. Nothing like a juicy scandal to sell papers!" And he was off and running, like they say at the race-track.

The crowd thinned once the next case was called, some poor shopkeeper who'd objected to some rowdies who demanded protection money, and had taken a broom to them. I knew what would happen; the rowdies would be let go, the shopkeeper would get a fine for throwing them into the street, and next time he'd pay like everyone else. It wasn't one of my cases, and I was just as glad.

Joshua and Miss Peggy pushed their way through the crowd and met me in the corridor outside the courtroom.

Joshua was so angry I could almost see steam rising from his ears. "Guttenberg is going to hang, if we don't find Billy Kendall," he says, once he can control his feelings.

"That shouldn't be too difficult," says Miss Peggy. "He's been seen on Mr. Long's carriage often enough. He's not in hiding, is he?"

"No, he's not," says Joshua. "But we have no direct evidence to connect him with either crime."

"Of course we do," says Miss Peggy. "We found the photograph in Mrs. Kendall's trunk. We have to ask him why she had it, how she got it, and whether or not he had given it to her."

"And do you really think that Mr. Henry Ward Long will allow one of his servants to be questioned?" I says.

"It's not up to Mr. Long," says Joshua. "It's up to the police to find Billy Kendall, and bring him in for questioning."

THE GUILTY CLIENT

"On what grounds?" says I again. "That we found a photograph in a dead woman's possessions?"

"It'll do for a start," says Joshua.

"If Clubber thinks he's already got his man," says I, " you won't find him ready to let him go, especially not if he's been given a very good reason not to look further."

From the look on her face, I could tell that Miss Peggy agreed with me, and didn't like it any more than Joshua did.

"We have to find this Kendall person," she says firmly. "Talk to him, and hear what he has to say."

"And see if he has a Bowie knife," says Joshua. "Right now, the only evidence against Guttenberg is the word of one witness who saw him arguing with Delacorte. According to Heinz, that argument had to do with getting Mitzi out of Madame Mags establishment and onto a stage, where her talents could really be appreciated by an adoring public."

I glanced at Miss Peggy, who was trying to look innocent. I don't know how much she knows or guesses about places like Madame Mags and what goes on in them, but I suspect she has a good idea of it. And she's met Miss Mitzi, and for all I know, gotten a sample of the sort of dancing she does.

"I'll have a word with Williams," I says, but I know it won't do much good if we don't find Kendall and get him to talk.

"But where to start?" Joshua wonders aloud. "New York's a big city."

I says, "We start with the Plug-Uglies. That's where Kendall got his start, and that's where he'd go, if he was on the run."

"Is he running?" Miss Peggy says. "After all, he was sitting on the carriage, right next to the coachman, when Mr. Long came calling on Uncle Ephraim. He was practically flaunting himself in our faces!"

"Then let's go ask Mr. Henry Ward Long about his bodyguard," says Joshua.

"He don't have to see you," I says.

"Then I'll remind him," says Joshua. "He's still our client, isn't he? He wanted us to find Bertram's killer. Now Clubber Williams is claiming the reward, instead of Pettigrew and Roth, and we have every reason to suspect that this is a fraud. I think Mr. Long will see me under those conditions. Come on, Miss Pettigrew, we've got some calls to make."

"Are you sure you want me along?" says Miss Peggy. "Mr. Long will not be pleased."

Joshua gets that determined look again. "Miss Pettigrew, I am getting very tired of Mr. Long and his affairs," he says. "This has gone on long enough. Two people are dead, by the same hand, and we have evidence that links these deaths with someone in the employ of Mr. Henry Ward Long. Therefore, we will call on Mr. Long and find out what, if anything, he can tell us about Mr. Billy Kendall, particularly, why Mr. Kendall should want to take a knife to his estranged wife, and then attack the relative of his employer!"

With this, Joshua marches out of the courthouse, with Miss Peggy at his heels. I was torn between my duty to the City and my curiosity as to what was going to happen next. In this case, as always, compromise won out. I scrawled a note for Uncle Ephraim, and found a runner to take it to the West Street offices; then I headed up to my own office and a pile of papers that waited for me there. There were still plenty of rogues and vagabonds in the Tombs, and the People of the City of New York were paying me to see they stayed there.

SECTION 9: PEGGY

CHAPTER 23

ONCE JOSHUA AND I MANAGED to get through the crowd and onto the court house steps, we took shelter behind one of the grandiose pillars that adorned the façade, and took stock of our situation. The weather had turned, as it usually does in New York, from the balmy breeze of yesterday to a cutting wind that sent hats bowling down the street and threatened to lift my skirts to impolite heights.

Joshua scratched at his chin whiskers, as is his habit when thinking. Then he said, "I am taking you back to the office, Miss Pettigrew. Things are about to get very dangerous. I would not have you hurt."

"That's very kind of you," I said, "but I am not going to be shoved aside any longer while you and Michael go chasing after that murderer Kendall."

"Alleged murderer," Joshua amended. "Right now we don't know that he killed anyone, not even on the battlefield. He might have jumped bounty, and he might have deserted under fire, but none of this is proven, and until it is, he's not guilty of anything."

I made a noise of disgust. "Nevertheless, you are pursuing him, and I will not be left out of it."

Joshua finally looked me full in the face. "I am trying to protect you, Miss Pettigrew," he said.

"And what makes you think I need protection?" I countered. "I assure you, Mr. Roth, I have faced enemy fire just as you have. While you were on the Western line safe behind your bunker, I was right here in New York, with a howling mob in the streets calling for blood. Aunt Sarah and I sat for three days in the kitchen, armed with iron pans and kitchen knives, waiting for the worst, while Uncle Ephraim organized the defense of the docks, so that the rioters should not get the arms and ammunition meant for the troops. Our maid barely escaped from the Colored Orphan's Asylum with her life. They were hunting them down in the streets, Mr. Roth! Little girls!"

I let more of my anger escape than I usually do. The experiences of the Draft Riots were such that I prefer to bury them deep, and not bring them out of my memory.

However, Joshua's bland assumption that because I was here in New York I did not understand the horrors of the War set me afire. I should not have been so vehement, I suppose. It definitely took him by surprise.

He stepped back, as if to avoid enemy fire. Then he said, "I had heard about it, Miss Pettigrew. I didn't realize how bad it was."

I calmed myself, and said, "It was very bad. For three days, there was pure anarchy, until the Federal troops got here from Pennsylvania. Uncle Ephraim's longshoremen had to use force to hold the ferry landings clear, so that the troops could get ashore and establish order."

Joshua took all this in, then said, "I still think it's a bad idea for you to continue to search for Billy Kendall with me, when you might be more use with Mr. Pettigrew, acting as Signals Officer, co-ordinating our efforts."

"How do you mean?"

"Someone has to know what everyone is doing, so that we don't cross each other up. Captain Williams didn't tell anyone what he was doing, so Michael and I spent an evening chasing our tails and getting into a fight that we didn't have to get into, and we all arrived at the same place at the same time. This shouldn't happen, Miss Pettigrew. I only wish there was some way to get messages across this town faster than feet can carry them."

"Telegraph?" I said.

"Unwieldy for small distances," he said.

"Semaphore?" I ventured.

"Too much traffic, too many buildings."

"Very well," I said, most reluctantly. "I concede you the corn, Mr. Roth. Take me back to Uncle Ephraim, and I will act as your Signals Officer. You can tell me your part of this case, and I can put it all together for the files."

"Wait," Joshua said. "Look there!" He pointed to the bottle-green Stanhope carriage in the street in front of us.

"That's Mr. Long's turn-out," I said.

"With or without Mr. Long in it?" Joshua asked, following my pointing finger with his eyes.

"I don't know," I said, "but there are two men on the box, and one up behind."

Joshua swore under his breath. "The *chutzpah* of the man!"

"What do you mean?"

"He's flaunting Kendall in our faces," Joshua said grimly. "Well, this time he won't get away with it. We are going to beard Mr. Long in his lair, Miss Peggy. Like it or not, he is going to answer some questions, and he will not escape this time!"

We followed the green Stanhope on foot as the matched grays trotted sedately through New York's oldest streets, which had been laid out when the colony was called Nieuw Amsterdam and Pieter Stuyvesant had tried to govern it. The carriage stopped in front of one of the smaller brick buildings, and Mr. Long emerged, exquisitely dressed and completely imperturbable.

Joshua's long legs had kept pace with the carriage. My shorter ones had had more difficulty staying with him, especially when hampered by hoops and petticoats. Nevertheless, the two of us accosted Mr. Long on the sidewalk, breathless, but determined.

"Good morning, Mr. Long," Joshua said. "We have news for you concerning the death of your nephew, Bertram Delacorte.

Mr. Long tried to look down his nose at Joshua. He couldn't do it, since Joshua was just as tall as he, and held himself with military erectness.

"I have already been informed that the murderer has been apprehended. I will reward Captain Williams suitably for his diligence. There is nothing more to say." One of the Long flunkies had the door open to receive the senior partner of Long and Delacorte. Joshua stepped in front of Mr. Long.

"Heinz Guttenberg did not kill your nephew, Mr. Long. He is being framed, just as Bertram was framed for the murder of Suzanna Kendall. In fact, Mr. Long, we would like a word with the man sitting on the box of your carriage, Billy Kendall."

Mr. Long looked up at his bodyguard. "I don't know anyone by that name. The man who you see is called Will Kennedy."

"That may be what he's called now," Joshua said, "but ten years ago he was Billy Kendall, and he was one of the gang kids who was hired to watch your house while you were away for the summer."

"Nonsense!" Long snorted at us. "Kennedy! Come down and tell these people who you are!"

The man on the box took a look at us, and declined the invitation. Instead, he joggled the arm of the coachman, who looked down at Long, who stared back at the two of them.

"Gee-up!" Kendall shouted.

The nervous horses threw their heads up and down, prancing in place.

"Kendall!" Joshua shouted. "The game's up! Come down and talk to us!"

"Gotta git me first!" Kendall reached behind him, under his coat, and drew out a large-bladed knife. "Spring'em, Jack!"

The coachman took one look at the knife, another at Mr. Long, and a third at the traffic.

"I can't go fast in this mess, Will," he said, with a despairing look at us, as if to say, I'm doing the best I can to calm this lunatic. "The hosses won't stand for it."

"I won't be took!" Kendall cried out, and jabbed the coachman with the point of the knife.

The coachman let out a yell, the horses jumped forward, and the carriage started to move.

"He's running away with my horses!" Long cried out. "Stop that carriage!"

Joshua and I trotted after the rig, threading our way around cabs and wagons, keeping the green Stanhope in sight.

"This won't do," Joshua said, as much to himself as to me. He waved at the nearest cab, a sagging wreck pulled by an aged horse that might have been the offspring of the famous yellow steed of M. Dumas's D'Artagnan. "Hey, there, can you follow that green carriage? There's five bucks if you can catch it."

"What's the beef?" the cabbie wanted to know.

I shouted, "There's a man in it who's trying to run off with my sister!"

"Don't waste time jabbering, girl! Get in the cab!" Joshua shoved me into the vehicle, shut the door, and clambered up onto the box with the driver.

"Where'd he go?" I tried to see out the window, but my hat got in the way.

"I see 'em!" The cabbie pointed his whip at the green Stanhope, turning into Broadway.

"Can you catch up with them?" Joshua asked.

"Old Buttercup, here, used to race at Saratoga," bragged the cabbie. "She's not the prettiest nag, but she can still take the shine out of the other fillies when she's a mind to."

"Then let's hope she has a mind to," Joshua commented.

We began to pick up speed, as we made our way up Broadway. The traffic slowed the Stanhope, even as it allowed the smaller cab to shorten the distance between us. I leaned out the window, to see what was going on.

"Stay inside!" Joshua yelled down at me, as the wind nearly took my hat off.

"What's happening?" I shouted back.

"We're gaining on them!"

The traffic thinned as we reached the theatrical district near Canal Street. At that hour of the morning there would be no crowds of spectators, no eager audiences. The green Stanhope saw an opening, and dodged into it. Our cabbie clicked his tongue. Old Buttercup seemed to sense that there was something interesting afoot, and that she would be a part of it. She pricked up her ears, and picked up her feet, as if to say, I may have a few years on me, but I can still keep up with the best of them.

We jogged past the theaters, past the Peale Museum, past the shops that catered to the wealthy. We were nearly at Washington Square, when a large wagon loaded with house-furniture pulled in front of us. Someone had decided to move before the First-of-May, and we were stuck!

Our cabbie cursed, the furniture-wagon driver answered, while I poked my head out the cab window and saw the green Stanhope disappearing into the general ruck of wagons, carts, and carriages.

"We've lost them!" I wailed.

"No we ain't!" Our cabbie had taken the chase as a personal challenge, spurred on by the promise of a week's pay for one ride. Old Buttercup and our cab slid past the furniture-wagon with inches to spare on either side. The green Stanhope was barely visible, heading around the park at Washington Square.

"Where's he going?" I wondered aloud. "Shouldn't he be going to the Points?"

"He's heading for Harlem," Joshua shouted at the cabbie. "He can lose us amongst the shanties and shacks, and get to the High Bridge. Once there, he can get off Manhattan, and we'll never find him again."

"He's got a ways to go," the cabbie said grimly. "Come on, old gal! Show 'em what won the cup at Saratoga!"

We picked up speed as we trotted around Washington Square and into Fifth Avenue. The green Stanhope was now clearly visible, well ahead of us.

"He thinks he's clear," Joshua said. "The Stanhope's slowing down."

"It's the hosses," our cabbie told him. "Them grays isn't made for this kind of work. They're for show, not for speed. Now we'll get 'em!"

He didn't even have to use the whip. As soon as Old Buttercup saw the broad paved road ahead of her, she picked up her four feet and started to move with a speed that had me bouncing around the cab like a hot pea on a griddle. All I could do was grab the strap and hang on, wishing all the while that I was up on the box with Joshua and the cabbie so that I could see the race for myself.

Fifth Avenue has been deliberately made broad, so that the sporting gentlemen may race their rigs of a Sunday. However, this was a Thursday, and I saw the outrage on the uniformed policeman standing on the corner of Twenty-Ninth Street as we hurtled past him.

THE GUILTY CLIENT

He took action at once. He pounded his night-stick on the pavement to signal his fellow-officers that there was something wicked afoot, and that he needed assistance. Then he started to run after us, shouting "Stop that, you fools!" (Although 'fools' was not the exact word he used.)

Fifth Avenue past Thirtieth Street is being taken over by ever larger houses, some close to being palaces, and traffic is limited to those vehicles that are required to serve the exalted beings who inhabit them. There was no obstruction as the green Stanhope and its grays headed North. However, the stamina of the horses limited the distance they could travel, and Old Buttercup gained slowly but steadily as the gray horses lost their wind and started to stumble.

The green Stanhope came to a dead stop at the corner of Fifty-Ninth Street and Fifth Avenue, just before the grand entrance to the Central Park. Old Buttercup pranced past, her head high, as if to say, Young people have nothing on us old folks! We've got the staying power, we do! We pulled in ahead of the green Stanhope, and Joshua slid down from the cab to let me out.

Coachman Jack was berating Kendall, comforting his horses, and apologizing to Joshua all at once. Our cabbie was waiting for his promised five-spot. A second cab drew up, with Mr. Henry Ward Long inside. A third vehicle joined the group, carrying a squad of uniformed policemen.

I sat in the cab, waiting for someone to help me down. That's when I saw the object of the chase clambering down from the Stanhope, thinking to make his get-away before the whole imbroglio was sorted out. He stepped into the street, right in front of the outside door to the cab.

I opened the door, fast, jostling him so that he dropped the Bowie knife. Then I whacked him again with the cab door, and followed it with a sharp rap on his head with the paper-case I was still carrying, which dented Kendall's soft plug hat, but only slowed him down a little.

With a final yell of defiance, I hopped down from the cab, thinking to lay hold of Kendall. Instead, I slipped off the step, and the two of us went down in a tangle of hoops and petticoats. Kendall and I rolled over and over, with me yelling and him cursing, both of us kicking and whacking anything that came near a fist or a foot. I realized that I was affording the population of Fifth Avenue a view of my stockings and petticoats, but propriety had to give way to necessity. I must stop Billy Kendall from escaping Justice yet again!

I wound up on top, and firmly sat on my captive until Joshua picked me up, and handed Kendall over to the nearest representative of New York's Finest, as they like to be called.

"What's going on around here!" The police officer bellowed, his voice, cutting over Joshua's commands, Billy's curses, my wails, and Mr. Long's orders.

"Arrest that man," Joshua said, pointing at Kendall. "He's a murderer. He killed Bertram Delacorte and Suzanna Kendall."

"I didn't mean to," Kendall whined.

"He's ruined my horses!" Long added, more infuriated by the damage to his livestock than to his kinsman.

Coachman Jack turned to his employer. "He's got a big knife, Mr. Long. I didn't want to do it! Look at them! They'll never be the same again! You bastard!" He turned to Kendall. "Making me ruin good horses!"

"What about that murder? Doesn't that matter to you?" Joshua shouted at Long.

"I know nothing about that. What I do know is that this man nearly killed my horses!"

"This ain't a Sunday, and it ain't a racing-day," the officer said, latching onto the one certainty in this affair. "I'm sorry, Mr. Long, but you should know better than to run your horses of a Thursday. I'll have to write you up and fine you."

"I will pay the fine," said Mr. Long, with great aplomb. "It seems that this man, who is no longer in my employ, is accused of committing a crime. Perhaps you should call for assistance in apprehending him."

"No need for that," I said. "I've got him."

Indeed I did. I had him by the arm, and I wasn't going to let him go until we had his story out of him.

"Where to now, Mister?" Our cabbie was still waiting for his money. Old Buttercup snorted and kicked her feet, as if to say, Come on, boys, let's do it again!

THE GUILTY CLIENT

"West Street," Joshua decided. "We'll take this fellow to Uncle Ephraim Pettigrew, and let him question him before we take him on as our next client. I think he may need a good defense attorney."

CHAPTER 24

It took some time to organize our procession back to the West Street offices.

First there was the jurisdictional dispute to settle. Billy Kendall, or Will Kennedy, had killed two people, one on the East Side in Captain Walling's precinct, the other on the West Side, where Captain Williams held sway. Which murder took precedence, and which police department was to hold him? After much negotiation, it was decided that since the Kendall murder occurred before the Delacorte murder, it was Walling who should have the honor of the arrest.

Then there was the small question of identity. Mr. Long insisted that the man before us was Will Kennedy, a veteran of the War, whom he had hired as bodyguard because he wanted to help a distressed soldier, although he disapproved of giving charity to beggars. Joshua said that he could provide witnesses to identify the man before them as Billy Kendall, one-time member of the Plug-Ugly Gang, who had been promised a bounty if he went into the Union Army in place of Bertram Delacorte, whose number had been drawn in the Draft Lottery.

Kendall himself ended the wrangling by admitting that he was both. "I had to do it," was his constant refrain. "I didn't mean to, but I had to do it."

Joshua took charge, as if leading his men into the battle-line. "Cabbie, you will convey me, Miss Pettigrew, and this man to the offices of Mr. Ephraim Pettigrew, on West Street, near the docks. Officer, you may call both Captain Walling and Captain Williams to meet us there. As for you, Mr. Long, you may accompany us or not, as you prefer, but I am sure you will want to consult with Mr. Pettigrew before tomorrow night. The case will be concluded by then."

As always, a crowd had gathered, drawn at first by the unorthodox Thursday race, and then by the sensational arrest of the murderer, Kendall. I spotted Davy Jonas working his way through the crowd.

"Joshua," I said, "this is going to be in the newspapers by tomorrow morning." I nodded towards Davy. "We'd better get out of here, before he can ask for a statement."

Once again, Joshua showed why he had been made a Captain. He shoved Billy back into the cab, handed me in after him, and swung himself on top, next to the cabbie. Old Buttercup pricked up her ears, as if to ask if she could run another race, then shook her head, and settled back into the dull routine of threading her way through the New York traffic.

"West Street!" Joshua ordered, and off we went, leaving them all to sort it out for themselves: the policemen of two belligerently opposed forces, Mr. Henry Ward Long and his aggrieved coachman, and Mr. Davy Jonas, scribbling madly on his note-pad.

It was well into the afternoon when we finally got back to the offices of Pettigrew and Roth, and I was becoming more and more aware that I had not eaten anything since breakfast. Mitzi's kasha had turned out to be a loathsome-looking blob of boiled grain, and Maria Luisa's idea of a morning meal was very strong coffee and sweetened biscuits. None of this had been very filling or nourishing. I was starting to become dizzy.

Joshua seemed to be impervious to hunger or thirst. He would not stop until we reached our destination. I would have to wait until we reached the docks, where Uncle Ephraim was waiting for us. There I was able to refresh myself with a sweet potato and a cup of root-beer, both from the street vendors doing a brisk trade among the seamen and stevedores on the docks. It was not what Aunt Sarah would have liked, but it did keep me from fainting until the matter of Billy Kendall could be sorted out.

Uncle Ephraim had already received a note from Michael, informing him of the morning's events. Now he sat back in his chair and regarded Billy Kendall thoughtfully.

Billy looked battered and chagrined. On closer inspection, he was the man in Mrs. Kendall's photograph, some twenty pounds heavier and ten years older, his face filled out and adorned with a magnificent drooping mustache, with an interesting scar that ran from the corner of his left eyebrow into his hair, under his hat.

"Sit down, my boy," said Uncle Ephraim, nodding towards Billy. "I prefer to sit, and I prefer to see the people I speak with."

Billy looked around. I placed the wooden chair reserved for clients in front of Uncle Ephraim, and retreated back to my own desk, where I could write down every word that was said, and embellish the note-pad with my sketches.

Joshua said, "Mr. Pettigrew, this is Mr. Billy Kendall, who now goes by the name of Will Kennedy. I am not too sure how that came about."

"It was the War," Billy said. "I was in the War, and I got shot, and I was lying there, and there was another feller next to me on the dead-wagon, and he had a paper on him said his name was Will Kennedy. I'd got a paper said my name, and I thought, I don't want to do this no more, but if I run, they'll bring me back. So I put my paper on the dead man, and I took his."

"And Billy Kendall was listed as killed in action," Uncle Ephraim concluded. "I see. Very clever, Mr. Kendall."

"It wasn't supposed to be that way," Billy said.

"Indeed?" Uncle Ephraim leaned back in his chair, his hands propped across his midsection. "How was it supposed to be?"

Billy leaned forward, eager to explain himself to a sympathetic listener. "I was supposed to go in the army, and get the money," he explained.

"For Suzanna," Uncle Ephraim said.

"That's right!" Billy exclaimed. "That's just right! See, she was just the prettiest thing I ever did see, and she told me how it was, and that she was bound to those people."

"To Mrs. Delacorte, that is," Uncle Ephraim said. "She was a servant, wasn't she? But to people like Mrs. Delacorte, who was brought up in the South, that wasn't exactly right, was it? Because here in New York, if a servant don't like her position, she can leave it, can't she? And she gets wages, don't she? But Suzanna couldn't do that, because she wasn't just a servant, she was a slave, wasn't she?"

"That's right!" Billy nodded. "See, me and my pal…"

"Shorty McGee," Joshua put in.

"That's right! Me and Shorty, we ran with the gang…"

"The Plug-Uglies," Joshua told Uncle Ephraim.

"Hey, whose story is this?" Billy asked, irritated at being interrupted. "Like I said, me and Shorty was running with the Plug-Uglies, learning how things was done. He was good at nipping, but me, I couldn't get close enough because I was a big fellow, even when I was a kid. So when there was a job, he'd be took along to do the upstairs, and I'd be left outside to keep watch, and take care of any rowdy-dow."

"Apprentice burglary," Uncle Ephraim summed it up. "How did you come to leave this lucrative profession?"

"Huh?" Billy looked puzzled.

"When did you start guarding a house instead of robbing it?" Joshua interpreted.

Billy said, "That was Shorty's idea. See, he went up to one of the houses on Washington Square, where they was getting ready to go away from the city, which he said he could tell because they had all the wagons ready with furnishings and stuff, and he worked it out with the top servant that if we got the job of guarding the house, we'd see that no one came near it, because we was Plug-Uglies, and the other gangs wouldn't touch a place that we wanted. He figured it out, that we'd get more for not lifting stuff than we would for lifting it and fencing it."

"A variation on the protection racket," Joshua said, with a snort of disgust.

"But we come through for them," Billy said earnestly. "Shorty and me stood there all summer, and no one else would mess with that house, nor any other on that row, because we was Plug-Uglies, and they didn't want no trouble with them."

"And that was when you became acquainted with Suzanna," Uncle Ephraim said.

Billy sighed. "Yep. She was so pretty, and so fine. She wasn't with the ladies, she'd been left behind to stay in the house. She didn't tell me why."

"I can guess," said Uncle Ephraim.

I had an idea myself, but I did not wish to disillusion neither my uncle nor our potential client as to the extent of my worldly knowledge. When the ladies of the family left for Brooklyn or the mountains, the gentlemen would be able to do what they liked with the female household staff. It was common knowledge, but never discussed.

"When did she tell you her true situation?" Joshua asked.

"Huh?" Once again, Billy Kendall's verbal deficiencies were revealed.

"When did she tell you she was a slave?" Uncle Ephraim did the translating this time.

Billy thought, then said, "See, the War was going on, and there was talk about freeing the slaves, and I said that some folks said it weren't such a good thing, because then all the free niggers would come up here and take away jobs from white men, but Suzanna said that weren't so, because most of the niggers in the South was on farms, and couldn't do the jobs we did anyways, except for the ones like her, which was house niggers. That's the first time I ever thought about that, but she looked almost white, you couldn't tell what she was, and by that time, I was so in love of her, it didn't matter nohow. So I says that if we get married, she'd be free, because I'm free. But she says that's not so, because there was some feller who was up North, and he lived free, and he got took down South anyways, because he was a nigger, and that's the way it was, and the big judge said it was so."

Uncle Ephraim's affable smile disappeared during this recitation. "That damnable Taney!" he snarled. "That damnable decision!"

"Dred Scott," I said, recalling the dinner-table discussions of my youth.

"That was the feller!" Billy cried out. "That was the name of him, the nigger that was took! Suzanna knew about it, and she told me that so long as she was in that house, she belonged to Mrs. Delacorte's family. So I said, she could buy herself free, and then we could be married."

"Marriage?" Uncle Ephraim said. "You were how old? Nineteen? Twenty?"

Billy shrugged. "I don't know how old I am exactly. My ma didn't exactly keep count, and I don't know who my pa was. But I had a job, guarding the house, and a place with the Plug-Uglies, should they need someone to do some bashing, so I figured I could keep a wife, but I didn't have no money to buy her out. And there she was, with the Master after her, and I was getting crazier and crazier, and then Shorty, he comes up with the answer. Shorty always knew the answers. I should of stuck by Shorty, but it didn't happen that way. I hope he got through the War."

"He's alive, but he thinks it's his fault you got killed," Joshua told him.

"But I didn't get killed," Billy protested. "See, when the Draft Lottery was announced, there was a big rowdy-dow, and then there was a bounty announced. If a man took on another man's place, he'd get three hundred dollars. So Shorty says, if I go to the army, I'll get the money. I can give it to Suzanna, she can buy herself free, and we can be married."

"A good plan," Uncle Ephraim said. "But it went wrong, you said."

Billy hitched his chair forward. "See, some of the fellers had gone to the Army right away when the War started, because they thought it would be an easy way to get money for fighting, which is what they done anyways, and some went with the Zouaves, because the fire companies did, but they weren't good for the Army, and they got sent back home. Dishonorable discharge, they called it. For fighting each other instead of Rebs, and for running away after the fighting at Bull Run. So Shorty and me, we figured, we'll be bad soldiers, like them, and get sent home."

"So the two of you joined, and received the bounty," Uncle Ephraim said.

"That's right!" Billy was amazed at Uncle Ephraim's sagacity. "I got me a uniform, and me and Shorty and some of the boys went and got our pictures took, and then me and Suzanna went and got the license, and I said that when I come home, I'd finish the job and do it proper, but that this would do for now. And that she could call herself Kendall, like a proper lady, because she told me she didn't have no name but the name of the people that owned her. So she could be Suzanna Kendall, and I had the judge write it down so's we could copy it, so we wouldn't have to make our marks."

"Because neither of you could read or write your own names," I whispered.

Billy shrugged. "I never got the schooling, and she told me she wanted to learn, but slaves wasn't allowed to." He took another breath, and went on, "And so Shorty and me went away, and I tried to be a bad soldier and got into a lot of fights, because the other fellers ragged me about Suzanna."

"So your sergeant told us," Joshua said.

Billy stared at him. "Old Sergeant Muldoon? Did he get through?"

"He did." Joshua said. "He told me that by the time you got to the Wilderness, every hand was needed, even the bad ones. I was in New Orleans by then, but we heard it was bad."

"It was awful!" Billy shuddered at the memory. "I'd done plenty of fighting on the streets, but this was all woods and Rebs shooting at us, and then we couldn't see what was coming at us, and there was things in the bushes and trees, snakes and bugs and other stuff. And me and Shorty got separated in all the smoke and the noise, and I got creased in the head, and I didn't know where I was for a while, until I was in a wagon next to the Kennedy feller," Billy said.

"I see," Uncle Ephraim said. "So, Mr. Kendall. . . or shall I call you Kennedy?"

"You can call me Billy, if you like, or Will," said Billy. "I answer to either one."

"So," Uncle Ephraim went on. "You went into hospital, and then were given a medical discharge."

"By then the War was almost over, and I was made a hospital orderly," Billy said. "And then I had to get home, but I had a time doing it."

"And when you got back to New York, things had changed," Joshua said, as one who had been through much the same experience.

Billy nodded in agreement. "So, I went to the house where I'd been hired, but Suzanna wasn't there no more. The feller who'd took me on was gone, too. But there was Mr. Long, and he looked me over, and said he needed someone to sit on his carriage and look tough, so's no one would mess with his horses. And he'd pay me to do it. So I took the job."

THE GUILTY CLIENT

"As simple as that," murmured Joshua.

"But what about Suzanna?" Uncle Ephraim pressed him. "Didn't you try to find her?"

"I asked Mr. Long," Billy said. "And he told me he would look for her, but he told me she had disappeared, no one knew where she'd gone. Once the slaves was freed, they could leave, and Suzanna had left the house on Washington Square."

There was a silence. I contemplated the villainy of a man who would lie to such a simple soul as Billy Kendall. Mr. Long must have known where Suzanna had gone; he must have arranged for her to get the pension that would come to the widow of Billy Kendall.

"Tell me about Bertram," Uncle Ephraim said, after Billy had composed himself.

"Nothing to tell," Billy said. "He was a kid when I went to Army. He'd been called up, and I went in his place. When I come back, he was away, traveling in foreign parts."

"Then he came home," Joshua prompted him. He turned to Uncle Ephraim. "It seems Mr. Bertram Delacorte had become enamored of Miss Mitzi Zalman and her artistic interpretations of the French cancan and the Turkish *danse du ventre*. It was his notion to present this exotic entertainment in a theater of his own."

"I don't suppose Mr. Long cared for that idea," Uncle Ephraim said dryly.

"He didn't like it," Billy said. "And he and Mr. Bertram had a big fight. I could hear them yelling at each other all the ways down in the kitchen."

"Down?" Uncle Ephraim asked.

"The new brownstones have the kitchens in the cellars," I reminded him. "By this time Mr. Long had removed to the new house on Thirty-Second Street."

"That's right," Billy said. "We wasn't in Washington Square no more. We was Uptown! It wasn't like the old house, no stores nearby, nothing but houses and gardens, and I got a room in the stables, with Jack Coachman. Not bad, but too much like camp for me. I like streets and people around me."

"So," Uncle Ephraim picked up the thread of the narrative. "Mr. Bertram comes home from Europe, Mr. Bertram's uncle and he quarrel, Mr. Bertram leaves."

"And he don't know where to go, but Jack Coachman says there's a boarding-house he knows of, where Mr. Long sometimes sends his relatives when he don't want them visiting him. So off we go, to Mrs. Smith's."

"Where you look up, and there is your long-lost love, Suzanna." Uncle Ephraim declaimed, with a theatrical gesture worthy of Mr. Booth at his most dramatic.

"I saw her, and she saw me, and right then I knew that I'd been had, done over, lied to, and I wanted to have it out with her, but I couldn't do it then, because there was some feller standing there behind her." Billy said.

"Mr. Lawton," Joshua explained to Uncle Ephraim.

"So you bided your time," Uncle Ephraim said to Billy.

"That's right," Billy said, with a nod. "Like I learned, you never crack a house without you check it first. I'd go over there, when Mr. Long had come home, and the horses were stabled, and I'd look at who went in and out, and when."

"Very clever," Uncle Ephraim said.

"Mr. Long said so, too," Billy said.

"Indeed?"

"Well, he saw me going out, after dinner, and he asked where I was going, and I told him about how I'd found Suzanna, and I wanted to have it out with her, about how I was alive, and how things were with us. And he said that Bertram had been after her, too, the way men are with women, and that made me mad, because Suzanna had said that someone in the house had been after her, and that Bertram was just about the age to chase the gals in the house. So, I told him that if Bertram was the one, he'd wish he hadn't touched Suzanna, because I'd make sure he never took on another gal again!"

Billy stopped to take a breath.

"So then Mr. Long said he'd help me out. He said he'd make sure I had time to talk with Suzanna," Billy said.

"And he provided Mr. Delacorte with the tickets to the Veterans' Ball," Joshua said slowly.

Billy continued his narrative. "So when I saw the house was clear, and the lights was on in the kitchen and the top floor, but off except for Suzanna's room, I snuck in the back alleys and up the privy stairs, which wasn't used no more, and I talked with Suzanna."

"And what did she have to say for herself?" asked Uncle Ephraim.

"She was scared," Billy said. "She said she'd heard that I was dead, and she'd claimed my pension, and that and what she made from sewing was all she had to live on. She wouldn't say nothing else, even though I showed her my Bowie knife, what I took off a dead Reb in the Wilderness, but I knew she couldn't live in a place like that without someone else paying, and I asked her who it was, only she wouldn't tell me, and I asked her again and again, only she wouldn't say…"

Billy broke down, burying his head in his hands. "And then she was dead, and I had blood all over my coat, and I had to get back to Mr. Long's, so I went over the back fence, and back to the stables on Thirty-Third."

"With your coat," Joshua said.

"I took it off when I got back to my room, and I hid it in the stable," Billy said.

"And then I washed up at the pump, and went to bed."

"And did you tell Mr. Long what had happened?" Joshua asked.

"He didn't ask me," Billy said. "I did my job, like I always do. It was just before the Easter holiday, and there's a big to-do at Grace Church, where everyone puts on their best duds, and shows off their rigs, and I got a new outfit, like everyone else, but Jack Coachman's got to wear this green livery, but mine was a good new suit. And along comes Bertram, like a fool, in a fancy frock coat and high hat, waving a piece of paper under his uncle's nose, telling him that he'd pay for it."

"The poem," I said. "In Mr. Long's handwriting."

"And then I heard that Bertram was taken up for Suzanna's murder. I knew he didn't do it, but I couldn't say nothing, because then I'd be charged, and I don't want to swing for something that I didn't mean to do."

Uncle Ephraim nodded. "Let me guess what happened next. Mr. Long had sent his carriage to pick Bertram up at the court-house, but he wasn't there. Then you went back to Mrs. Smith's and he wasn't there either. He'd gone to the house on Thirty-Second Street. He bathed and changed into his evening dress, and then he went out."

"That's right!" Billy said, astonished. "That's exactly what that bastard did! He went out and ate and got drunk and went to the places on West Twenty-Fifth Street!"

"Which is where you found him, arguing with Heinz Guttenberg," Joshua said.

"He was with this big Dutchman, and they were jawing, and then he saw me, and he knew who I was, and he ran after me, and we went down the street, to where it was quiet, by the warehouses near the river," Billy said.

"And you had it out with him," Uncle Ephraim said.

"I didn't mean to do it," Billy explained. "But he wouldn't say if he'd messed with Suzanna or not. He kept saying it wasn't him, but he knew who it was, but he couldn't tell me right then, he had to do something else, so I got out my Bowie knife and sort of tried to persuade him, but we backed up and up and then he was in the river, and I couldn't see him no more."

"What about the bloody coat?" I asked.

"I don't know nothing about that," Billy said. "I couldn't keep the coat in the stables, the horses get spooked by blood, so I threw it away. I don't know how that got into Mr. Bertram's rooms, and that's the honest truth. I told you all I know, so what happens to me now?"

Before we could answer that question, both Captain Walling and Captain Williams arrived, with their respective warrants, and the full majesty of the Criminal Justice System descended upon Billy Kendall, alias Will Kennedy.

"Will Kennedy, I arrest you for the murder of Bertram Delacorte," Clubber Williams announced.

"Billy Kendally, you are under arrest for the murder of Suzanna Kendall," stated Captain Waller.

"Give me a dollar, Billy," Uncle Ephraim asked.

Billy complied, looking bewildered.

"This man is now my client. I claim the right of confidentiality. You may take him to the Municipal Prison. We will make all our evidence available to the District Attorney's Office at the proper time."

Billy looked at Uncle Ephraim. "You're my lawyers?" he asked.

"A cripple," Joshua said. "And the half-pint's the prosecutor. You shouldn't have tried to intimidate either of us, Kendall, but I'll do my best to get you off, just as Riley will do his best to hang you. That's our job, and we both do it as best we can."

Billy was taken by squads of police, all arguing as to who should have the honor of booking him.

Davy Jonas poked his head into the office. "I followed the police carriages," he said. "Any statement for the Press?"

"Only that the man they arrested was the killer of both Suzanna Kendall and Bertram Delacorte," Uncle Ephraim said. "That much is clear, Jonas. Go off, now, and do your job, and let us do ours."

Davy loped down the docks, and Uncle Ephraim frowned at Joshua and me. "There are still some questions I want answered," he said. "Billy Kendall may have been the killer, but there was someone behind him, using him, poor fellow. Someone with a nasty, sneaking mind. I have to think this over. Peggy, get on home, and see whether there's going to be anything edible on the table, or if I'll have to have something brought in."

Joshua sighed heavily. "I'd better get back to the Tombs and get Heinz out before he finds himself being charged with assaulting a police officer."

"And I'll get on home, and tell Mitzi that he's being released," I said, putting on my hat and picking up my sketch pad and pencil.

Uncle Ephraim stopped me before I could leave. "Peggy, you've been taking down everything that was said, haven't you?"

"Of course I have," I said. "I always do."

"Then leave that pad of yours with me," Uncle Ephraim said. "Someone said something, and I have a point to consider."

I handed him my notes, and once again Joshua and I parted company, he to negotiate for Heinz Guttenberg's release, and I to deal with the growing tension on Bank Street.

CHAPTER 25

Bank Street was in a total turmoil as I approached our house. With the First of May on a Sunday this year, the moving frenzy had already begun. Some of the tenants were moving out, seeking new pastures for their endeavors or trying to escape the noise of the new elevated railroad construction. More tenants were moving in, having achieved enough success to remove themselves from the more noisome tenements downtown.

The babble of tongues was intense, with German and Irish accents predominating.

Mr. Tom Murphy stood at the doorway of his residence, beaming expansively at each new arrival, tipping his hat to the ladies, and shaking the hand of each man, reminding them that this block was made more desirable by the presence of the Tammany Ward Leader in their midst.

"I'm here for you," he'd call out. "The Democratic Party's on your side, sir!"

"Good afternoon," I greeted him.

"Miss Pettigrew!" He hurried over to me. "I was hoping to speak with you."

"It won't do you much good," I said. "Uncle Ephraim is a Stalwart Republican, and you know better than anyone else that women don't have the vote."

Murphy sighed. "D'ya know, Miss Pettigrew, there's times I wish they did vote. If they was all like Ma, they'd be a powerful force for the Party. But that's not what I've got to say. It's about that cook of yours."

I sniffed the air. The garlic odor was not quite so penetrating, probably because of the stiff wind blowing off the river, but it was certainly noticeable.

"I have tried to communicate with Maria Luisa," I told Murphy. "It doesn't seem to work very well."

Murphy strutted a little. "Miss Pettigrew, as Ward Leader it's my duty to provide for my constituents, whoever they may be. Mr. Tweed says that it's up to us to make folks vote for us, by showing 'em that we're for 'em."

"And you're doing quite well at it, Mr. Murphy," I said, with some asperity. I wanted to go inside, where I could have a cup of tea and loosen my corsets. I was bruised from my encounter with Billy Kendall, and hungry enough to eat one of Maria Luisa's garlic messes. I knew my dress must be stained from the various substances on the street. Even Fifth Avenue is not immune to the effluvia left by horses. Mr. Murphy didn't seem to notice either my disarray or my disagreeable tone of voice.

Instead, he said, "Well, Miss Pettigrew, it's this way. If, in the course of conversation, I hear that a certain property is up for sale, or that a certain railroad is going to be built in a certain place, as I see it, I should use that knowledge to buy into that property, or to invest a little of my own money in that railroad's stock. And if I can help my family to a better life, what's the harm in that?"

I could have read him a lecture on ethics, but this was neither the time nor the place. Instead, I said, "Did you stop me to read me a tract on Tammany politics, Mr. Murphy?"

"I just wanted to explain what I was up to, so's you wouldn't think I was interfering with your domestic arrangements."

"I beg your pardon?" I could see someone just behind Mr. Murphy, waiting to be introduced.

"Here's the answer to both our problems, Miss Pettigrew." Mr. Murphy stepped aside, to reveal a stout gentleman in a frock coat worn over a stained white apron and checkered trousers. "Miss Pettigrew, this is Mr. Luigi Sillipigni. Mr. Sillipigni wants to open a restaurant around the corner on Greenwich Street."

Mr. Sillipigni bowed. "Good day, *signorina*," he said, carefully pronouncing each English word. "I am pleas-ed to meet you." He looked at Murphy, as if to gain approval for his efforts.

I returned the bow. "I am not sure I understand, Mr. Murphy."

Murphy explained. "You see, Mr. Sillipigni here's got a problem. He wants to open a place that sells food, only his cook up and left him. Something about wages, I think. You've got a problem. You've got a cook who cooks food that you don't like, and that stinks up my Ma's back yard. I'm the man who solves problems, Miss Pettigrew. If Mr. Sillipigni likes your cook's cooking, then he'll take her on and the cooking will be over on Greenwich Street, where Ma can't smell it."

I regarded Mr. Murphy with a new respect. "That makes perfectly good sense, Mr. Murphy. If you and Mr. Sillipigni will just step this way, maybe we can sort all this out to everyones' satisfaction."

I led the two men around, through the side alley, to the kitchen door. Clashing pans, screams and imprecations, and the ever-growing odor of garlic were evidence of Maria Luisa's culinary efforts, and Mandy and Mitzi's attempts to deal with them.

Mr. Sillipigni sniffed the air. "Aaah!" His worried air changed to a smile.

Mr. Murphy and I were not so appreciative.

"She's at it again," I muttered to myself, as I entered the arena.

Maria Luisa had acquired some meat, and was pounding it into submission with a large wooden roller. She already had one of her spicy sauces simmering on the stove, and the ingredients for another were assembled on the kitchen table in front of her.

Mitzi had been suborned into acting as second chef, protesting loudly that she was a dancer, not a cook. Mandy was scrubbing away at a long green object that might have been a cucumber, except for its thinness and excessive length. A purple vegetable had been sliced open, ready for some kind of operation. I had no idea what any of this meant, but it betokened something to Mr. Sillipigni, who began speaking as soon as he stepped into the kitchen.

He bowed to Maria Luisa, and announced who he was. He then did the unthinkable: he dipped a spoon into the sauce and presumed to taste it.

The result was volcanic. Maria Luisa called down imprecations upon the creature who had dared to intrude himself into her kitchen.

Mr. Sillipigni informed her that her sauce was delectable, but that if she intended to cook for *Americani* she would have to moderate

THE GUILTY CLIENT

some of her spices.

There was a heated debate, conducted *fortissimo, molto agitato*, in Italian.

I could not follow all of the discussion. There was some confusion, due to a mixture of regional Italian accents. It seems Mr. Sillipigni hailed from Genoa, whereas Maria Luisa's native town was Naples, and there is as much vocal difference between them as can be heard between Americans from Boston and from New Orleans.

However, by the time the metaphoric dust had settled, Mr. Sillipigni was able to announce that he had come to an agreement with Maria Luisa da Napoli.

"This is a good cook," Mr. Sillipigni stated. "She is making veal scallopini, that is, a small piece of veal, with a good sauce. I have spoken to her about the use of garlic with Americans. They destroy their sensations of taste with too much hot coffee."

Maria Luisa stood with folded arms. "I cook," she said. She uttered more in Italian, apparently derogatory.

Mr. Sillipigni cleared his throat before he translated. "Signora da Napoli is grateful that you could give her work, but I think she will do better with me," he said, obviously editing as he went. "She was not contented with the ingredients in this house. Also, she says that the *puta* is not a cook." He glanced at Mitzi, who glared back.

"Miss Mitzi is a dancer," I explained. "She was only in the kitchen to do us a favor, in return for helping her with a problem of her own."

Mitzi said, "I am not *kurve*, I am not *puta*. I am not whore! I am a dancer, and I will not cook here any more!" She removed her apron, threw it to the ground, and stalked out of the kitchen, leaving Mandy to deal with the rest of the food preparation.

I turned to Mr. Sillipigni. "Will you please explain to Maria Luisa that she can finish out the week, and we will pay her what is owed. Then she can take your position, and we'll all be satisfied."

This was conveyed to Maria Luisa, who accepted the news with a characteristic toss of the head and another spate of Italian, ending on an interrogatory note.

"Signora da Napoli will cook until Sunday," Mr. Sillipigni said. "She was worried, because here she has a room, but she does not know where to stay. I tell her of a woman on Mulberry Street, a widow who has a place where she can sleep, near my restaurant."

A thought occurred to me. "Won't your wife object to a woman working in your kitchen?" I asked. I know there are some restaurants where women cooks are unwelcome, although there are many where the cook is the matriarch of a large family, all of whom work in the place.

"Alas, I do not 'ave wife," Mr. Sillipigni said with a dramatic sigh. "I 'ave *fidanzata* in Genoa."

Maria Luisa raised her head at this news, and looked Mr. Sillipigni over carefully. I could see her weighing the possibilities in her mind. Here was a man, not too old, single, with a flourishing business (after all, he could hire a cook!), and an American citizen to boot. Something in her attitude made me wonder whether that *fidanzata* in Genoa would ever see the United States as the bride of Mr. Luigi Sillipigni.

"I cook for 'eem." She pointed to Mr. Sillipigni. That settled the matter.

"Thank you so much, Mr. Sillipigni," I said. "*Grazie*."

Tom Murphy beamed at the two cooks as they continued to converse in Italian.

"Now, Mr. Sillipigni," he said, "you mind who helped you out, and you vote Democrat in the next elections."

"You bet!" Mr. Sillipigni bowed to Maria Luisa and to me, shook Murphy's hand, and strutted out of the kitchen, clearly pleased with himself.

Mandy edged towards me. "Does this mean we gotta get another cook?" she asked.

I realized that it did. "I'd better notify the agency myself," I said. "This time I'll make sure that whoever comes can speak English."

I escorted Mr. Murphy back outside through the garden and the alley, to his post in front of his own house.

"Thank you very much for you help," I said, and meant it. "I may have misjudged you, Mr. Murphy."

"I'm glad to hear you say that, Miss Pettigrew," Murphy said. He glanced at the front parlor window, where his mother stood, arms folded, glaring at him.

"I really must go in now," I said.

"One moment." Murphy took a deep breath. "You know, Miss Pettigrew, we've lived in this house next door to yours for five years. We've been neighbors, so to speak, since the War ended."

"I am aware of that, Mr. Murphy," I said.

"I know that right after we moved in, a lot of the people what was here moved out, but Mr. Pettigrew stayed."

"You heard his reasons," I said, wondering where this was leading.

"Now, I know there are differences between us, Miss Pettigrew. And I know that your Aunt Sarah is from Old New York people, and you go to Grace Church of a Sunday."

"Where we pray for the souls of you Papists," I said dryly. "As I am sure you pray for us heretical Protestants. Did you have something to ask me, Mr. Murphy?"

He took the plunge. "Miss Pettigrew, there is to be a concert on Sunday afternoon, in the Central Park. As Ward Leader of this district, I have been given tickets of admission. May I ask, Miss Pettigrew, if you would accompany me to that concert?"

I had not expected this at all. I certainly remembered how Aunt Sarah had reacted when our neighbors had decamped, renting their house to the Murphy clan while they found better housing on the East Side. Mrs. Murphy had been a thorn in Aunt Sarah's side ever since. I had no particular animus against Tom Murphy as a man, only as a representative of a party that Uncle Ephraim despised.

"I should ask Aunt Sarah," I demurred.

"It's not a big thing, Miss Pettigrew. It's a walk in the park, and a chance to hear some lively music."

What he did not say was, You are well over the Age of Consent, you don't have any other prospects, and what's the harm in it?

"I owe my aunt and uncle the courtesy of informing them," I said. "But if the weather is fair, Mr. Murphy, I think I would enjoy a walk and a concert in the Central Park on Sunday, after church. Our service ends at noon."

Murphy grinned at me, nodded to his mother, and let me pass back into the house.

I found Aunt Sarah fussing in the back parlor. "Margaret, where have you been? You were supposed to have a fitting today. Miss Pinkney left in a huff, because you weren't there." She looked me over. "Whatever have you been doing? You look a sight!"

"I've been busy chasing a murderer," I said. "New dresses can wait. And I think we will have to be more polite to Mr. Murphy and his mother next door. He's solved our problem with Maria Luisa." I explained how our Ward Leader had matched the restauranteur in need of a cook with the cook in need of a more receptive audience.

Aunt Sarah sighed. "I suppose it's just as well," she said. "Ephraim really didn't enjoy her cooking. Only now we'll have to make do until I can find someone else."

"I think this time, I'll go to an agency," I said firmly. "There's no point in hiring a cheap cook. The results aren't worth it."

"I suppose you're right, dear," Aunt Sarah said. "Well, we'll eat what's put before us tonight, and see what tomorrow brings."

And with that hopeful remark, she went back to her correspondence. Aunt Sarah may not be able to make too many social calls, but she can always write letters.

"And Mr. Murphy has asked me to accompany him to a concert in the Central Park on Sunday," I added.

Aunt Sarah stopped writing. "Oh dear, now I've made a blot."

"And I said I'd go," I concluded.

"You can't be seen in Society with a Tammany Ward Heeler!" Aunt Sarah exclaimed.

"It's not a Society function," I said. "It's a public concert, in a public park. I think my reputation will hold up under scrutiny. Besides," I said bitterly, "I don't see any suitors on the horizon. Mr. Murphy has done us a service, and I am simply being, well, neighborly."

"We haven't been neighborly with the Murphy clan for five years," Aunt Sarah said. "We do not have to start now."

"If Uncle Ephraim won't move, perhaps we should," I said.

"We'll see what your uncle has to say when he gets home," Aunt Sarah said. I had a sudden shiver, recalling past occasions when I had done something that Aunt Sarah disliked. Then I had been worried that I might be cast away, thrown into the street like Michael Riley and the other vagabond children.

I reminded myself that I was no longer that woebegone child. I could, if necessary, support myself by selling my sketches to Davy Jonas and the *Sun*. I had the money that had been left to me by the sales of "Belle of New York". I could be an Independent Woman, like Mrs. Woodhull or Miss Claflin.

"What do you think I should wear on Sunday?" I asked Aunt Sarah.

She sighed, and reached for the latest Harpers' Weekly Magazine, and turned to the pages devoted to fashion. If I was going to destroy my reputation by being escorted in the Central Park by a Democrat, at least I would do it in style.

SECTION 10: JOSHUA

CHAPTER 26

ONCE BILLY KENDALL HAD BEEN TAKEN into custody, I hurried down to the Tombs to get Heinz out before he did too much damage to either himself or the men who had to guard him. I armed myself with a supply of greenbacks from the office safe. Mr. Pettigrew, who was a realist about such matters, explained that a small donation would grease the wheels of Justice.

I arrived at Centre Street at the same time as the police carriages. Billy Kendall was paraded through the crowd by Walling and Williams, a large man between two larger ones.

"Who's that?" came the cry.

"That's Billy Kendall, the killer of Suzanna Kendall and Bertram Delacorte," Williams stated.

I stepped forward. "Alleged killer," I said.

"Confessed killer," Williams corrected me.

"Confession?" There was Davy Jonas, pencil in hand, scavenging news for the *Sun*.

"This is neither the time nor the place for an interview," I said, with as much dignity as I could muster. "Speak to Mr. Pettigrew if you want more information. I am acting in Kendall's defense."

Off went Jonas, and I followed the police squad into the Tombs, where Billy Kendall was duly signed in.

"I want to interview him before your men get to him," I told Williams. "A copy of his confession will be sent to you as soon as

THE GUILTY CLIENT

Miss Pettigrew can write it out."

"We have to hear it ourselves," Willams said, and Walling nodded in agreement.

"You'll have it," I said. "I just want a word with my client, and I want it now."

I was shown to the same grim dungeon room in which I had spoken with Heinz earlier that day. Billy was shackled, and a guard stood over him, tapping his baton in one hand, as if daring the prisoner to try to escape so that he could be beaten into submission.

"Billy," I greeted him. "You've been arrested, on the charge of murder in the second degree, that is, premeditated murder. You've confessed, you have to plead Guilty." He started to speak, but I held up my hand to stop him. "Now, Billy, murder's a capital offense, which means you hang. However, I can try and get you a lighter sentence, a prison term, if you can plead to Diminished Capacity."

"What's that mean?" Billy asked.

"You told us you didn't mean to kill either Suzanna or Bertram Delacorte. You just got really, really angry, and that head wound of yours acted up, and you didn't know what you were doing." I had already rehearsed how I would present this to a jury, should the case come to trial. My hope was that I would never have to face a jury, and that both Billy and the District Attorney's Office would accept the plea of Manslaughter due to Diminished Capacity.

Billy considered this for a moment. Then he said, "You mean, I'm either dumb or nuts?"

"I wouldn't put it that way," I said.

"I would," Billy said. "Mr. Roth, I may not know how to read and write, but I'm not dumb. And I sometimes get mad and do things I shouldn't, but I'm not nuts, and I won't go to the bug-house. I killed Suzanna, and I'm going to swing for it. You let those coppers in now, and I'll sign whatever they want me to. I've been in Hell for three weeks, Mr. Roth. Let's end it now."

There was nothing I could do with him. He would meet his end like the Plug-Ugly gang kid he had always been, and that was that. I shook his hand, and turned to the jailers.

"He's ready to confess," I said. "Now let's get Heinz Guttenberg out of here. He's innocent of the crime for which he was arrested.

Billy Kendall just confessed to it."

The guard shrugged.

"Let him go," Williams ordered..

"On whose say-so?" The desk sergeant was being a stickler.

"On mine," Walling snapped out, unused to having his authority questioned.

"And mine," Williams added.

The desk sergeant went off, shaking his head at the vagaries of his superiors. I didn't know whether to be grateful for the opportunity to get my client away from the horrors of The Tombs, or to be appalled at the flagrant abuse of power shown by the two police Captains.

It took more time for Heinz to be released than it did for Billy to be taken, but I was persuasive, and if a few greenbacks changed hands, that was the price of Justice in New York City.

Clubber Williams had the grace to look Heinz in the eye and say, "I was only doing my duty, Guttenberg. But I tell you what I'll do for you. You go to a man called Harry Hill, and tell him Clubber sent you. He's got a place over on West Houston, just off Broadway, where he puts on shows. I think he'd go for your gal's act, and he's always got room for another big man like yourself to keep order."

"That's very good of you," said Heinz, shaking the hand that was offered. "I go now, and tell Mitzi." He started to straighten his cravat, and ran his fingers through his hair, in an attempt to make himself more presentable to his public.

"Only one thing," Williams said, before Heinz could escape. "When you go to Harry Hill's dive, there's a small favor you can do me."

"Ah?" Heinz knew what was coming.

"People like to talk in places like that. They celebrate, they get drunk, and they sometimes let fall a word or two about something that the police should know about. Get my drift?" Williams eyed Heinz.

"I understand, Captain Williams. I am not a police spy," Heinz said, with some dignity.

"I ain't asking you to be a spy. I'm asking you to do what any good citizen would do. You're going to be an American citizen, right?"

THE GUILTY CLIENT

Heinz nodded. "I am getting papers, ya."

"Well then." Williams turned to me. "This here's your lawyer, right? You ask him if it's not the duty of every American citizen to tell the police if there's something going on that they should know about."

I had to admit that this was so. "Mr. Guttenberg, Captain Williams is quite right. If you know of a crime that is being planned, or one that was committed, and you do not inform the police of it, you are as guilty as the criminals."

"There you are, Guttenberg," Williams said, triumphantly.

"And what do I get for this information?" Heinz asked, shrewdly.

"You get my protection, and knowing that you won't get rousted every time your little Mitzi wiggles her keester too hard," Williams said.

"Mitzi! I must go to her! Where is she? Is she all right?" Heinz forgot the moral exigencies of turning informer in his passion for Mitzi.

"She's at Mr. Pettigrew's house on Bank Street," I told him, and gave him instructions on how to get there.

With Heinz and Mitzi settled, my next call would have to be on the District Attorney's office. I had to find out who would be assigned to prosecute Billy Kendall.

I crossed Centre Street, and headed for the new court-house. Once more I was accosted by Abe Hummel.

"Mr. Roth," he said. "I hear you have yet another client. You seem to be picking them up at quite a rate for a young man in a slow office."

"It's been a busy day," I admitted. "And there have been some surprising developments in the Delacorte case. I'm sure you'll read about them in tomorrow morning's *Sun*." I started down the steps,

"I still think you would do better with us than with Pettigrew, but that's not what I wanted to tell you. It's about your father."

I turned back to him. "You know my father?"

"Best tailor in New York," Hummel said. "He altered this coat so it fits like a dream." He smoothed the fabric over his arms. "He's in *shul* on Friday nights, for the *Shabbes* service. You should go."

"I'm not religious," I said. What I meant was, I wanted no part of a God that would permit the horrors of war, and the devastations of the peace that I'd seen in the South.

"You don't have to be," Hummel said. "You put on a yarmulke and a tallis, you say a *brocha* or two, what's the harm?"

"Jews aren't popular in New York," I reminded him.

He shrugged. "We're not popular anywhere. I'm starting to hear things, *landsman*. We gotta stick together. Come to the *shul*, over on Broadway." He patted my shoulder and walked away.

I had not attended services since I left New York with my regiment. I had eaten *tref*, because that's what was being served, and if pork was in the pot, that's what I ate. If an order came to fight, it didn't matter what day it was, I fought. I didn't observe holidays, I didn't observe *Shabbes*, I didn't want to be a Jew, but that is what I was born, and that mark was forever on me. I thought it over as I made my way over to the court-house, to file the papers and find out when Billy Kendall was to be arraigned, and before whom.

Michael was just emerging from his hideaway as I came up the stairs to the Assistant District Attorneys' territory.

"Captain!" he greeted me. "I see you've joined the cavalry!" He waved the evening edition of the *Sun* at me.

Davy Jonas had managed to get his scoop in, just in time for the delectation of his readers. There it was, a highly-colored version of the illegal Thursday afternoon race up Fifth Avenue, between a pair of blooded grays, and a knocked-out old trotter, who had run the fine horses ragged and still had enough in her to take one more trip across town.

The illustration showed the cab and the Stanhope neck and neck, with a one-armed man (myself!) hanging onto the reins of one, and the killer Kendall, lashing his way north, on the other. It was totally inaccurate, and it would undoubtedly sell papers. What it would do to my reputation as a lawyer I did not dare to think.

"It didn't happen quite that way," I said.

"Did it happen at all?" Michael asked, with a grin.

"Oh, it happened," I said. "But the cabbie held the reins, and Kendall had a knife on the coachman. And what Jonas didn't put in was that in the end, it was Miss Pettigrew who actually caught

Kendall, and sat on him until the police came to arrest him."

"And now what?" Michael asked.

"And now, we have yet another client," I said. "I'm defending Billy Kendall. Who's prosecuting?"

Michael sighed ruefully. "It's me again, Joshua. And this time, I'm going to make the charge stick."

"You'll have to, I suppose," I said. "But be warned, I'm going to plead Diminished Capacity."

"The man's not crazy," Michael said. "He's not an idiot, either."

"No," I said slowly, "he's a man who's being used, but I can't for the life of me tell you why or by whom. When I left him, Mr. Pettigrew was mulling over that one."

"Well then," Michael said, "we'll leave it to Uncle Ephraim to sort it all out. We owe ourselves a good dinner, Captain, and this time, no garlic!"

SECTION 11: PEGGY

CHAPTER 27

TWO WEEKS PASSED IN RELATIVE QUIET. Various events took place, both trivial and momentous, in the lives of Pettigrew and Roth, and the City of New York.

Maria Luisa finished her week's employment, and took up a new position with Ristorante Luigi, where her pasta and red sauce was much praised by the Italian workers who were constructing the elevated railroad. Any odors of garlic were drowned in the general effluvium of Greenwich Street.

I visited an employment agency, that sent over Miss Eliza Pringle, a recent graduate of Mrs. Farmer's Culinary Institute (or so she informed me). Miss Pringle spoke English, with a decided New England broad a, and was an enthusiastic follower of the regimen prescribed by Dr. Slyvester Graham, who advised against the use of fried foods, hot breads and red meat, and was in favor of whole grain flour, fresh fruits and vegetables at every meal, and vigorous outdoor exercise. It was not a particularly tasty diet, but I found my skirt somewhat looser around the waist after two weeks of it. I was certain that Uncle Ephraim would not put up with it much longer. Aunt Sarah was already starting to talk about going to Castle Garden to see if she could find someone more amenable to our unhealthy way of living.

Joshua came in to the office a quarter of an hour late one morning, and confessed that he and Michael had spent some time at Harry

Hill's concert salon, where the latest attraction was billed as "French Mitzi, the Toast of Paree". Mitzi had found her audience, and very appreciative they were, too, throwing coins on the stage, and calling for encores. As for Heinz, he was lurking in the crowd, making sure that no one got too rowdy, and that any knifing or bludgeoning was done outside the premises. I would have liked to have accompanied them, but, alas, I was reminded that ladies did not go to places like Harry Hill's.

I did accompany Tom Murphy to the concert in the Central Park, much to his friends' astonishment. Uncle Ephraim was not pleased to see me associating with a Tammany man, and Aunt Sarah was in despair, crying that we would be ruined socially if it were known that I was being escorted to a public event by an Irish politician. I smiled at both of them, reminded them that I was of full age, and went off, determined to enjoy myself. Oddly enough, I did enjoy myself. I ignored the sly digs and barbed comments of the other women, at least one of whom might have wanted such a tempting prize as a bachelor in the Tammany Organization for herself. I listened to the music, smiled at anyone who greeted Tom, and tried to speak only about the fine day and the nice music, and how wonderful it was to have a Central Park, where the common folk like us could enjoy them.

Aunt Sarah's fears about my reputation being ruined by association with Tom Murphy were not totally unfounded, as we discovered when we attended the Divine Service at Grace Church the following Sunday. I was the subject of covert looks, and at least one cut direct, but Aunt Sarah took her usual pew, her head held high. Nothing would stop her from claiming her rightful place as one of the last of the Old Families. Judge Willson's youngest daughter might have married a poor man, she might live on the unfashionable West Side, in the shadow of the elevated railroad, but she was still a lady, and she would not show by one look or tear that she had been snubbed.

Together we went back to East Twenty-Third Street, only to find that Mrs. Smith's boarding-house was now under new management. A very brief letter explained that Mrs. Smith had decided that the air of New England would be better for her during the summer months, and that she had taken herself and her family to Newport.

Whether she would return in the Fall was, at this time, unknown. She thanked Aunt Sarah for her many kindnesses, and left no forwarding address.

Billy Kendall's impending demise was trumpeted in the pages of the New York *Sun*, and largely ignored by the other newspapers in favor of more fascinating topics, such as the increasing influence of Mrs. Woodhull and Miss Claflin on the ageing Commodore Vanderbilt, and the new city charter proposed by Senator Tweed and his luncheon partners. Then the news of the war between France and Prussia came through the cable, and that pushed Billy Kendall's fate further onto the back pages of the newspapers.

Joshua visited the Tombs daily, trying to convince Billy to stand trial and take his chances with the jury. Billy refused to take advantage of the loopholes of the Law. He would not plead Diminished Capacity, and he would not go to a mental asylum. He was resigned to his fate.

Davy Jonas' articles depicted Billy as a relic of the past, an old gang member who upheld an out-dated code of honor, as opposed to the modern crew of hooligans plaguing the streets of New York, who feared neither God nor Man, and certainly not the Police. Suzanna's racial ambiguity was ignored; she was the unwitting cause of Billy's downfall, the pretty servant, debauched by her employer, who had sought refuge with the young man who was willing to die for his country in order to provide her with an honorable name. Their love story became something out of Sir Walter Scott, with a few melodramatic flourishes from M. Dumas: separated by War, rejoined by Chance, and parted only by Death. According to the *Sun*, Billy had killed his true love in a fit of rage when he found out that she had betrayed him with Delacorte, then tracked down Delacorte and forced him into the river, causing his death.

Now Billy would hang, unrepentant, a Plug-Ugly to the last. So said Davy Jonas, and Billy insisted that it was so. Nothing that Joshua could say or do would convince him otherwise.

On the day before Billy Kendall was to hang, Joshua sat at his desk, in the back of the office, where the pawnbroker once had his sanctum. I was at my usual desk, carefully copying the documents of the Kendall case.

THE GUILTY CLIENT

"What's that idiot Jonas got to say today?" Uncle Ephraim demanded.

I handed him the newspaper. Uncle Ephraim read each article carefully, and had me insert the *Sun* into the growing file marked People vs. Kendall.

Then he sat, staring out the window, his hands laced across his middle, his thumbs revolving, as he went over all that had been done and said, as I had reported in my notes, with Michael and Joshua's additions.

Then he said, " Joshua, I want you to go down to Wall Street, and find that fellow from Mrs. Smith's."

"Which one?" Joshua asked.

"The one who said he sold stocks," Uncle Ephraim told him. "And if you can't find him here, find out where he is."

"What's he got to do with anything?" I asked.

"He's a loose end," Uncle Ephraim said. "I don't like loose ends."

"How loose an end can he be?" I asked. "He wasn't there when the Kendall murder was committed, and he certainly wasn't there when Delacorte was killed. He didn't even know Bertram, until they met in the boarding-house."

"So he says," Uncle Ephraim said. "I want to see him for myself. Find him, Joshua."

Off went Joshua, and I said, "I don't understand, Uncle. The case is closed. Billy Kendall is going to hang tomorrow. We can't re-open the case now."

"The case ain't closed until I say it is," Uncle Ephraim said. "And there are some points I don't like about this one."

"Oh?" I didn't know what to say to that.

"For instance, why did Bertram Delacorte stay in that boarding-house? Who put the coat in his wardrobe, and who informed the police that it was there? Why did Henry Ward Long wait a whole day before getting Bertram legal counsel, and most of all, Peggy, most of all, why me? That's what's bothering me, Peggy, and the case ain't closed until I figure it all out."

And he continued to stare out the window at the ships and the docks and the setting sun, until Joshua came back with the news that

Jerome Donovan had disappeared.

"There's a rumor that he's been sent to open a branch office in San Francisco," Joshua said. "But no one can tell me which office is opening a branch anywhere west of Chicago."

"Indeed," said Uncle Ephraim. "Peggy, I want you to send some telegrams. Joshua, get back to the Tombs. Get Michael on your side. Do anything, but don't let that young fool commit legal suicide! He may think he killed that gal, but he didn't. I only wish I could prove it!"

"He'll hang for Delacorte, if not for Suzanna," Joshua said.

"Damn him!" Uncle Ephraim swore, under his breath.

"I'm afraid his fate is sealed. Billy Kendall will hang tomorrow at high noon," Joshua said.

Uncle Ephraim shook his head. "Maybe so," he said, "but there's still more to this business. Peggy, write a letter, and see it gets delivered, by hand, tomorrow morning. We've got one more client to satisfy before I can close this case."

CHAPTER 28

BILLY KENDALL, ALSO KNOWN AS WILL KENNEDY, was hanged at high noon on Friday, May 13, 1870. Not even a last-minute telegram to Governor Seymour could save him from his own determination to die for the killings of Suzanna Kendall and Bertram Delacorte.

The event was not considered worthy of the front page of any of the New York City newspapers, being eclipsed by more spectacular doings abroad, and their repercussions on the American markets. Only Davy Jonas in the *Sun* felt it necessary to remind his readers that the last of the old-time Plug-Uglies had met his end in a fitting manner, defiant to the core.

Uncle Ephraim and I read the late editions, hot off the press, in an Extra Edition of the *Sun*. He said nothing as he went through Davy Jonas's turgid description of the ghastly scene.

"Don't go home yet," he told me, as I prepared to take my leave at three o'clock. "There's more to come. I'll need you here."

Sure enough, the bottle-green Stanhope carriage drew up on West Street, this time pulled by a pair of chestnut horses. It was rumored that the grays, having been found unworthy, had been sold to the same cab company that owned Old Buttercup.

Mr. Henry Ward Long emerged from his carriage, accompanied by both Joshua and Michael. He did not look happy.

"Why have you sent for me?" Mr. Long demanded, not even offering the most perfunctory of greetings. "What right have these two…" he struggled with the word, "gentlemen to insist that I accompany them here? Our business was finished when young Kendall was arrested."

"Good afternoon, Henry," Uncle Ephraim said, with his usual affability. "Take a chair. Michael, give Mr. Ward a place to sit down."

"I do not have to sit down and listen to you, Pettigrew," Mr. Ward said testily. "We have nothing to say to each other."

"Maybe you don't have anything to say to me," Uncle Ephraim told him, "but I have something to say to you. And you are going to hear it."

Michael and Joshua stood by the door, blocking Mr. Ward's way, one tall and gaunt, in his black coat and hat, the other short and natty, in a new checked suit and brown derby hat. Both had identical expressions of grim determination.

Mr. Ward sat down reluctantly in the wooden chair used by our clients. "Say your piece," he said.

"Some three weeks ago, you asked me to do you a favor," Uncle Ephraim began. "You asked me to defend your nephew, Bertram Delacorte, on a charge of murder. As it turned out, I didn't have to do anything; Bertram had a cast-iron alibi for the time of the killing of Suzanna Kendall. The following day, young Bertram was found dead, and you came to me once again, and asked me to find the killer.

"And I had to ask myself, Why me? I am not known as an expert in criminal law, far from it. We are not particular friends; I don't think we've spoken more than a few words, and those barely polite, since our last meeting, and that was at the obsequies for our late martyred President. So why, I had to ask myself, did you come to me, instead of someone like Howe and Hummel?

"Then there were the circumstances of the crime, and the subsequent police actions. My partner undertook the investigation, which had been so neglected by the proper authorities, and found out quite a bit about the late Mrs. Kendall, and more about young Delacorte, and none of it made any sense. According to the common theory, young Bertram had become enamored of Mrs. Kendall, she had rebuffed him, and he had killed her in a fit of rage. He, then, went off on a spree and was killed by a common ruffian in a brawl."

"And this did not satisfy you," Ward said.

"It did not." Uncle Ephraim stopped for breath.

"What was really interesting was that every time we got closer to the truth, someone tried to stop us," Joshua said. "First, I got a very forceful warning to stay away from the case. Mr. Riley, here, can testify to that. The next day, I was approached by Mr. Abe Hummel, of the well-known firm of Hummel and Howe, with a very lucrative offer of a place in their office. Which, by the way, I did not care to take," he added, with a nod to Uncle Ephraim.

Michael grinned nastily at Mr. Ward. "And what's more, sir, my office did not receive the usual notification that accompanies the arrest of a young man of good family, such as Mr. Delacorte. I don't say that it's right, but it's the custom for such a notification to be sent to the prosecutor of such a young man."

"So," Uncle Ephraim said, having caught his wind, "I had to ask myself what was really happening here. And I came up with a rather interesting theory."

"A theory?" Mr. Ward repeated.

"Just a theory, mind. You might call it, a drama. Even a melo-drama," Uncle Ephraim said. "Peggy, you take this down."

I drew up my ever-present sketch pad and pencil, and prepared to write.

"Where shall I start? With the War? Or with the marriage of Miss Juliet Patterson and Lieutenant Andrew Delacorte? The Delacortes weren't too pleased with their son's choice, but the girl was pretty, the young man was amorous, and the match wasn't a bad one, socially speaking. And so they were married, and lived in Washington City, where Mrs. Delacorte, who had been brought up in a slave-holding state, had a so-called servant, named Suzanna, in her domestic entourage. And when the War started, then Major, later Colonel Delacorte showed his true mettle by returning to New York and siding with the Union, as opposed to so many of the West Pointers who deserted their country and went to the other side.

"And so, Mrs. Delacorte came North, bringing her household staff with her, and that included the beautiful Suzanna, didn't she? Of course, no one knew she was a quadroon. None of the Northern servants would stay if they found out she was part Negro. She certainly didn't look Negro; she carried herself well and she spoke well enough, in the Southern style. As far as the rest of the Delacorte servants knew, Suzanna was Mrs. Juliet Delacorte's personal maid. Am I right, so far?"

Mr. Ward nodded briefly.

"Those were bad years for everyone. The War was going badly for the North, we had yellow fever and cholera in the city, and most everyone who could get away for the summer did so. In the second year of the War, Mrs. Delacorte and your wife, Mrs. Long, went to Brooklyn, didn't they? But there was the problem of the empty houses on Washington Square, and the gangs that might rob them, so someone in your household came up with a clever scheme. You'd hire one of the gang boys to guard the house, on the theory that he would keep the rest of the mobs away."

Ward smiled bitterly. "Set a thief to catch a thief. It worked, too. None of the houses on that side of Washington Square were touched, all through the War. We paid, and it was money well spent, in my opinion."

Uncle Ephraim nodded. "But there was one after-effect that you had not counted on. The youngster that you hired, Billy Kendall, saw the beautiful Suzanna, and fell madly in love with her. As for Suzanna, I can only guess at her motives. From what Billy said, she had been approached by someone in the house, and it is possible that she saw young Billy as a possible protector. When she revealed her servile status, he didn't seem to care, and he offered her the one thing she craved: Freedom!

"Then came the announcement of the Draft, and the Riots. I need not remind you of the chaos, and the horror of those days. At the end of it, the Draft bounties were announced, and Billy and Suzanna decided that he would accept the bounty, give the money to Suzanna, and they would then be able to live together as man and wife.

"Only, of course, that did not happen. Billy went to The Wilderness, and was wounded. He exchanged identity papers with a dead soldier, with the intention of deserting, but the wound was too severe, and he served his time, and was given a proper discharge.

"Meanwhile, here in New York, Suzanna Kendall, as she now was called, was informed that her husband, Billy Kendall, was dead, and that she was now entitled to a widow's pension. Was that when she came to you, Henry?"

Mr. Ward swallowed hard. "She came to me when she got the

telegram," he said at last. "She couldn't read it, of course. I was in the house when the telegram came. I was shocked to learn that she had been married at all, even though the ceremony had been of the briefest kind. She was…grateful for my assistance." He glanced at me, not knowing how much to reveal of Suzanna's gratitude.

"And she continued to be grateful after the War was over, didn't she?" Uncle Ephraim said. "Henry, you must have thought all was right with the world, as the poet said. You had everything a man could want. You had a fine position in Society, a wife who upheld that position, and an unblemished reputation in the business world. You had Mrs. Kendall…where did you have her, by the way?"

"I provided her with funds, from time to time, but she could support herself with her fine sewing and the pension I acquired for her," Ward said. "She resided in various boarding-houses. We could not meet in public, but I saw her from time to time in certain places on West Twenty-Fifth Street." He turned red with embarrassment.

"Most of all, Henry, you didn't have to worry about any interference from your wife's sister, because when the War was over, she'd decamped for Europe, like so many other Southerners, taking young Bertram with her, just when he was of an age to become a rival. And then…disaster! Mrs. Juliet decides to come home!"

Ward sighed. "It was old Delacorte's Will that did it," he said. "The old man died, and Juliet's income went with him. She'd had an allowance, just enough to keep her and young Bertram going, but word must have reached them about Bertram's loose living in Paris, and Juliet's friendships with the sort of people you meet at watering-places like Baden-Baden. When the Will was read, there was a paragraph that cut Juliet and Bertram off with a dollar each. Juliet had to come back to New York, and she had to make her home with Nerissa and me. She had no where else to turn."

"And that was the beginning of the end, wasn't it?" Uncle Ephraim continued, relentlessly. "Because young Bertram had spent his time in France picking up the worst part of French culture, hanging about in cafes and listening to rude singers and watching the cancan dancers, especially one named Mitzi. He came to New York, discovered that there were no places like the French dance halls, where polite people could come, but only dives like Harry

Hill's. Bertram decided that he could make himself a fortune if he could built one of the French-style café-concert halls, not on the Bowery, but uptown, where the respectable people were. The only thing he needed was money, am I right?"

Mr. Ward nodded. "Oh, yes. He came to me with his scheme, and he asked for money, and I told him that he had no idea what was involved in such a plan, how many palms he'd have to grease, how much he'd have to spend in promoting his theater, and what sort of people would oppose it. He would not listen to a word I said. He was enamored of some trollop called Mitzi, a so-called dancer he'd met in Paris. He installed her in one of the establishments on Twenty-Fifth Street." Mr. Ward sputtered indignantly.

"And there he saw you with Suzanna Kendall, didn't he?" Uncle Ephraim guessed.

"He dared to twit me with what he had seen! He said that he would tell his Aunt Nerissa, and if that didn't do it, he'd see that everyone knew that I had a Negro mistress. He knew about Suzanna, of course; she'd been his mother's slave, after all. And we quarreled, and he left the house in a huff, and where should he go but the one place I did not wish him to be! Of all places, Jack Coachman took him to Mrs. Smith's!"

"Where did Billy Kendall fit into all this?" I asked.

Mr. Ward had forgotten that I was there. Now he looked up, startled.

"Oh, he'd come around looking for a handout, and I felt sorry for the poor chap," he said. "I had no idea he was the same boy who'd taken Suzanna down to the City Hall back in '63. He'd put on muscle and grown two or three inches, and there was the scar and the mustache. He went by the name of Will Kennedy, and he said he was a bounty man, and he needed a job. I told him that all he had to do was sit on the box of my carriage and guard my back, and when I was home, he would stay in the stables and guard the horses and their tack. He did what he was told, and gave no trouble."

"But wouldn't he have seen you with Suzanna?" I blurted out.

Mr. Long reddened some more. "I would not take my carriage on those occasions," he mumbled.

"Very discreet of you," Michael said, with another grin.

"And then, another disaster," Uncle Ephraim said. "Bertram saw Suzanna, and Suzanna saw Billy. Everyone that you were trying to keep apart suddenly came together, and you had to do something, or your whole carefully planned life would come down, like a house of cards."

Mr. Ward sat up straight in his chair. "I did not want Suzanna to die," he said. "I wanted Bertram out of the way!"

"So you sent him the tickets to the Veteran's Ball to get him out of the house, on a night when your confederate in the house had told you that the other boarders would also be out. Your confederate set the clock back, to give himself an alibi, then went to see Suzanna, and discovered that someone else had been there before him. What was the plan? To abduct the woman?"

"Something like that," Mr. Ward said.

"But Billy Kendall had got there first, hadn't he? And so your confederate simply finished what he had started, let out a yell, took the back stairs, and came into the house with the rest of the pack when the alarm was given.

"Walling came around, decided that Suzanna had died because of a botched robbery, and that was that. Horrible crime, gangs are blamed, and life goes on, didn't it? And Bertram continued to live at Mrs. Smith's boarding-house, didn't he? And now he wanted more money, because he'd found something in Suzanna's room, something that definitely linked her to you."

Uncle Ephraim nodded to me. I extracted the hand-written poem from the file-box and handed it to him.

" 'To his coy mistress'. Not the sort of thing a love-sick youngster sends to the girl of his dreams, is it? Bertram wouldn't send any thing like this. I don't think he'd got past 'roses are red, violets are blue'. But you, Mr. Henry Ward Long, this is something you might have written for your gal, even if she couldn't read it. And she must have had some feelings for you, sir, because she kept it by her, didn't she?"

Mr. Ward stared at the paper. "How did you get that?"

"It was at the bottom of the wardrobe in Bertram's room," Joshua said. "Your man must have missed it when he put the coat there."

"That was a mistake," Uncle Ephraim said. "You should have left well enough alone, but you had to implicate your nephew. You found the bloody coat, you had your confederate put in into the wardrobe, and then he placed an information with the police. Bertram was arrested, he sent to you for help, and you came to me. And once again, I ask myself, why me? Why go to Ephraim Pettigrew, a man you have publicly chastised, a man who cut you out with the girl you might have married?

"And then Joshua told us a terrible tale," Uncle Ephraim said. His voice took on an edge, and he no longer looked so affable. "During his time in New Orleans, he was given a case to defend, a case that he was expected to lose. He won it, and the result was not what he thought it would be. So I ask myself, is someone trying to pull the same thing on young Bertram? Give him a lawyer that's expected to lose the case, so that Bertram will hang for a crime he didn't commit? Get the State of New York to do the dirty work for you, wasn't that the idea, Henry?"

"Chance!" Mr. Ward cried out. "How was I to know that your niece was at that ball, and that the fool, McAllister, would shove her into the arms of my worthless nephew, thus providing him with the one thing I was trying to deprive him of, an alibi? No one would have believed him if he had said that he was at the Veteran's Ball. No one would recognize him there, no one would believe that a young man who had accepted a substitute would be found there! He decided to go, perversely, and your Miss Peggy saw him and danced with him at the very moment when he should have been unaccounted for!"

"It must have come as quite a shock, then, when you came to me the next day," Uncle Ephraim said. "You would have to congratulate me on winning the case you thought my partner would lose, am I right?"

"He left New Orleans under a cloud," Ward said, glaring at Joshua. "I heard from my friends in the military that he had taken to laudanum, that he was known for going off into ranting fits of anger. He may have passed the New York Bar, but he had the reputation of being a madman. He should not have won that case!"

"But he did, didn't he," Uncle Ephraim said. "And then… reprieve! Bertram's dead, and you're home free, as they say in the base-ball games."

THE GUILTY CLIENT

"And Billy Kendall is still sitting on the box of your carriage," Joshua said slowly. "Until we find him, and he confesses to killing Suzanna. He says that Bertram wouldn't tell him who Suzanna's lover was, and that's probably true, Mr. Long. Bertram was still hoping to get the money for his theatrical enterprise from you. It was pure accident that he slipped and fell into the water."

"Poor Billy," Michael said. "He was convinced he'd killed the love of his life, and he was willing to be hanged for that. Delacorte's death could have been ruled manslaughter, and he'd serve a term in prison for it, but he'd be alive. You're a lucky man, Mr. Ward."

"Lucky indeed," Uncle Ephraim said. "You see, Henry, there's not a shred of actual evidence of any of this, other than this here poem, which will remain in my files.

As far as the Law is concerned, the case is closed. You didn't kill anyone yourself, and you didn't give any direct orders to anyone."

"Not even my supposed confederate at Mrs. Smith's?" Mr. Long sneered.

"Not directly," Joshua said. "It was Mr. Jerome Donovan, and he's proving to be a hard man to find. No one on Wall Street seems to know exactly who he was, or who employed him, or what stocks he was supposed to be moving. He's rumored to be in San Francisco, or maybe Chicago. He's just disappeared, and that's the truth."

"Of course, people disappear in New York all the time," Michael said, with a shrug. "Men come and go, and the streets are dangerous, and you never know what's going to happen to you. Jerome Donovan may turn up yet. People do."

Mr. Ward looked at the pair of them, then at Uncle Ephraim. "What do you want of me, Pettigrew?"

"I want what you promised, when this folderol started," Uncle Ephraim said. "I want my niece to be able to take the New York Bar Examinations."

"And I told you, that is impossible," Mr. Ward sputtered. "My colleagues will never agree. No woman has ever passed the Bar!"

"I beg your pardon, Mr. Long," I said, sweetly, "but I must disagree with you. I have a newspaper clipping that clearly states that a Miss Arabella Mansfield passed the Bar Examinations in the State of Iowa last year."

"Iowa!" Mr. Long snorted his disdain. "A desolate prairie, in which the dearth of qualified legal practitioners has lead to the necessity for allowing a female to enter the profession."

"Iowa may be frontier country, but it is still a state of our Union," Uncle Ephraim said. "If a woman can practice law in Iowa, she should be able to do so in New York. Peggy takes the Bar Examinations, and none of what has been said here will ever be revealed."

"She may apply," Mr. Long said. "She may even take the examination. That does not mean that she will pass the Bar, nor that she may practice Law."

"In that case," Uncle Ephraim said, "there is one other possibility. My partner, here, has an injury that makes it necessary for him to have someone in court to take notes for him. Miss Peggy has been refused entry to the witness tables, on the grounds that she has not passed the Bar. She's not practicing Law; she's acting as Mr. Roth's right hand, so to speak. Can you arrange that much, Henry?"

Mr. Long collected himself and stood up. "I can try," he said.

"Do better than that," Uncle Ephraim said. "Or I give the whole story to Davy Jonas."

Mr. Long glared once more at all of us, and departed, fairly exuding steam.

"Will he do it?" I asked. "Will I be allowed to take the Bar Examinations?"

"He won't get past George Templeton Strong," Uncle Ephraim said. "You won't be allowed to take the examination, Peggy, but you'll get a Law Clerk Certificate. That'll have to do for now."

"And now what?" Michael asked Uncle Ephraim.

"And now I think I will take Miss Peggy and Aunt Sarah to Rector's for a decent dinner," Uncle Ephraim said. "I have eaten as much healthy food as I can stomach. Peggy, Monday morning, you get another cook!"

CHAPTER 29

Dining at Rector's was not something to be taken lightly. There were certain preparations to be made. Aunt Sarah had to be notified, so that she could tell Miss Pringle that we would be dining out. The restaurant had to be notified, and a private room booked. A menu had to be decided, one that would satisfy the tastes of all diners concerned.

Joshua added to the difficulties by saying, "Perhaps we could postpone the celebrations for one more day, sir. I have an engagement tonight."

I shot him a glance, and wondered if this had anything to do with his conversations with Mr. Hummel that I had seen. Joshua was reticent about his personal life, but as far as I knew, he was not involved with any young woman. Where, then, did he go on Friday nights? I could not ask without seeming to pry, and Michael would not tell me.

So it was on Saturday night that we gathered at Rector's Restaurant on Fourteenth Street off Fifth Avenue, dressed in our finest. Aunt Sarah insisted that I must get one more wearing out of the pink ball gown that had been seen at the Veteran's Ball, while she was magnificent in mauve, draped in pale gray lace, wearing her amethyst set, the last of the jewels her father had left to her. Uncle Ephraim put on a stiff shirt for the occasion. Michael wore a tail coat, whereas Joshua's frock coat had to serve, as he refused to rent and did not care to buy a suit that he would rarely wear. In short, we were all ready for a repast fit for kings, and that we had.

By the time we had gone through the soup, the fish, the fricassee of chicken, the roast beef, and the platters of vegetables that went with them, I, for one, was quite replete. The waiters removed the empty plates, and set a decanter before Uncle Ephraim.

This was the signal for the ladies, Aunt Sarah and myself, to remove ourselves from the private dining room, and go to the small salon where ladies would gather after a meal, to allow their gentlemen friends the opportunity to smoke and drink brandy. Aunt Sarah nodded at me, and gatherer up her skirts, ready to do what Custom demanded, but Uncle Ephraim held up his hand.

"Now, Sarah," he said, "these boys have been waiting all evening to ask me something. I think you and Peggy deserve to hear it, too."

"Ephraim, you know that Margaret and I must leave you gentlemen alone," Aunt Sarah demurred.

"Sarah, this time I have to insist. It'll save me the trouble of telling the same story twice. I know Peggy here is just brimming with curiosity, same as Joshua and Michael." Uncle Ephraim beamed at each of us in turn.

"I don't have my sketch pad with me, Uncle Ephraim," I warned him.

"This is private," Uncle Ephraim said. "You can remember it, but don't take this down, Peggy."

Michael spoke up. "All right, sir, I'll ask. How did you figure it all out? Most of all, how did you know there was someone in the Smith boarding-house being paid by Long?"

Uncle Ephraim leaned back in his chair. "It was all there in Miss Peggy's reports," he said. "Between you three, you all had the pieces of the puzzle. It was just a matter of putting the pieces together in the right way, like one of those little toy maps they give to children to teach them their geography.

"To begin with, there was the botched investigation of the Kendall murder, and the framing of Bertram Delacorte. There didn't seem to be any reason behind her murder, and even less reason for Bertram to have done it. The evidence against him was purely circumstantial. According to Walling's report, the police searched the place and didn't find a murder weapon. If the coat had been there then, they'd have found it then. So, the coat had been put there afterwards, to frame Bertram. And don't forget that pistol. Bertram didn't have it with him when he was arrested, did he? If it had been there when Suzanna was killed, Walling's men would certainly have found it, and

THE GUILTY CLIENT

if it had been there when the coat was found, they'd have found it.. It must have been put there afterwards, between the time that Bertram was taken and the time we got there."

"But why fix on Donovan as the man?" Joshua asked.

"That was in your report, Joshua," Uncle Ephraim said. "When you interviewed him, Donovan indicated that he knew a lot more about Suzanna Kendall than he should have. He knew, for instance, that she was a Negro passing as White, something that very few people could tell merely by looking at her. He said that he made his living selling, but he didn't say precisely what it was he sold. Young Lawton, on the other hand, was open about himself. Anyone could check whether or not he worked at Stewart's, and he was willing to tell you about the young lady he's courting."

Joshua shook his head. "I didn't think anything of it at the time," he said ruefully.

"And then there was that attack on you and Michael," Uncle Ephraim went on. "You say in your report, Michael, that you heard one of the bullies warn Joshua to get off the case, and he specifically mentioned Miss Peggy."

"He did," Michael said. I felt my face grow red. He had tried to ease the blow, but the words 'your fat gal friend' still stung.

"You thought that Billy Kendall was behind that," Uncle Ephraim said. "But Billy didn't know anything about Miss Peggy, and he may have seen you about, Joshua, but he was outside when Mr. Long went into our office, so he wouldn't know whether Miss Margaret Pettigrew was slender or stout. A personal comment like that meant that someone had connected the two of you, and the only ones who had seen Peggy and Joshua together were the people at Mrs. Smith's."

"I see," Joshua said. "You could eliminate the two school-teachers; they certainly weren't at the Fifth Avenue Hotel when I received the message to join Michael at the car-barns. What about young Lawton?"

"He provided us with his whereabouts on the night of the Kendall murder," Michael reminded him. "It would be easy enough for us to check and see if he was where he said he was, and the girl might lie for him, but not her whole family."

"And what about Mr. Smith?" I put in. "He was in the house on that night."

Uncle Ephraim coughed, and looked over at Aunt Sarah. "I think we can tell her now," he said.

"Tell me what?" I asked.

"You see, Peggy, I can eliminate Mr. Smith from any communication with Mr. Henry Ward Long because Mr. And Mrs. Smith and your Aunt Sarah and I were once part of a very perilous enterprise, and Mr. Long was our most vicious enemy at that time."

"Perilous enterprise?" I echoed. "Do you mean the Underground Railroad?" I had read about this chain of houses and farms run by fervent Abolitionists, who assisted slaves in their desperate flight Northwards to freedom. At the time I had no idea that my aunt and uncle had been involved in it, but now I realized that many of my childhood fears were tied up in the strange noises, the secretive comings and goings, and the constant changes of household staff that were a feature of my early years.

"We didn't do much," Aunt Sarah said. "Only provided a place to rest for a few days, while your uncle could find safe passage for those poor souls."

"Seaman's papers for a lone man," Uncle Ephraim explained. "Or stowing a family, women and children, on a steamer bound for Albany, and from there on a canal-boat to Buffalo, where they could cross over to Canada. Not half as dangerous as what Smith was doing, down in Virginia, where he ran the risk of hanging for every soul he sent on to us in the North."

"And you knew!" I glared at Michael, accusingly.

He had the grace to shrug. "I ran errands," he said. "I could carry a message where no one else could. No one looks at the street kids."

"And I was not told!"

"You were far too young," Aunt Sarah said. "It had to be kept a secret, you see, and your childish prattle might have put those Negroes in terrible danger, especially after that dreadful Fugitive Slave Act went into effect, and we were actually breaking the law doing what we knew was the right thing to do."

"I see." There wasn't much more I could say. I had heard and seen things that I could not tell anyone, ghostly figures creeping in and out of the cellar doors, and I had held my tongue, for fear that I would be cast out, like Michael and the other ragged children on the streets.

"You could have told me later," I added.

"Well, dear, by then the War was on, and then, after the War, there was no particular need for the Underground, so we disbanded," Aunt Sarah said. "Of course, Mrs. Smith and her family could not possibly stay where they were, so they came here to New York, where I helped them as best I could."

And that explains the odd friendship between my Aunt Sarah and Mrs. Smith, I thought to myself.

Joshua brought the conversation back to the main topic. "All right, I understand how you came to light on Donovan, but Billy confessed to killing Suzanna. He said it himself: he was trained as a burglar, he got into the house, he threatened her with his knife, slashed and killed her."

"Oh, he did all that," Uncle Ephraim said. "But he wasn't an expert with that knife. He didn't know how to use it very well. Look at the nasty mess he made of Bertram! He slashed at Suzanna, cut her, and left her to bleed, horrified. Donovan had left the house with Lawton, as he told you, but before he did, he changed the clock on the stairs. Then he came back into the house and waited for a suitable time to remove Suzanna. Billy Kendall's entry into the plan was unexpected. Joshua, you play Poker, don't you?"

"I do," said Joshua. "It's one of the few games a man can play with one hand."

"I don't indulge in gambling, but I've heard that there's something called a Wild Card," Uncle Ephraim said.

"There is," Joshua said, with a grimace of disgust. "Sometimes the dealer will announce that one of the cards in the deck can be used for something else, like an ace, if it will improve the hand you're dealt. Good players don't like that; it changes the odds."

"Billy Kendall changed the odds for Henry Long," Uncle Ephraim said. "He was the Wild Card, the random factor that throws the game into confusion."

"You know, I don't think that Suzanna was supposed to be

stabbed at all. Donovan came into Suzanna's room to shoot her with that pistol. Then he'd have put it into Bertram's room and made sure the police saw it there. Bertram would have been arrested, and that would be that. Long would be in the clear, so would Donovan.

"But Billy Kendall got there first and stabbed Suzanna, then ran away. Donovan saw her bleeding, and left her there instead of summoning help. He didn't kill her; he just didn't save her."

"Death by neglect," Joshua stated. "Depraved Indifference to Human Life."

"But not murder, not under the Law," Michael reminded him. He turned back to Uncle Ephraim. "So, Donovan reports back to Long, and Long waits for the wheels of Justice to turn, but they don't turn fast enough, and Bertram is still there, threatening to expose his uncle as a hypocrite and a lecher with a Negro mistress. What's more, he's got proof, which he didn't have before. He's got the poem, in Long's handwriting."

"At which point, Donovan puts Billy Kendall's bloody coat into Bertram's wardrobe and sends a note to Walling that Bertram Delacorte is the murderer of Suzanna Kendall."

"And that drags us into it, and the rest spins out at you have see," Uncle Ephraim said. "Donovan was right behind you when you left Mrs. Smith's to do to the Fifth Avenue Hotel, Joshua. He'd have the time to round up a few bullies to take you down. Billy Kendall couldn't have done that; he was with Long, sitting on the carriage with Jack Coachman."

"Poor Billy," I said. "He was as much a victim as Bertram and Suzanna."

Joshua frowned down at the brandy-glass in front of him. "I don't like the thought of Donovan on the loose," he said. "We don't know where he is, or what he'd doing."

"But we do know that he's a dangerous man," Michael added. "Mother of Mercy, I wish there was some way to link up with people in a few other places. He might be anywhere by now!"

"He might be," Uncle Ephraim said, slowly. "San Francisco or Chicago, Boston or Philadelphia. I've sent telegrams to people I know in all those places, warning them that a man of this description may be heading their way, and to watch out for him if he turns up.

THE GUILTY CLIENT

But I think he'll lay low for a while. The only thing that has me worried is whether Long will tell him that we're onto him."

"That assumes that Mr. Long knows where this Donovan is," I said. "And I don't think Mr. Donovan is going to tell Mr. Long where he is."

"Until he needs money," Joshua said gloomily. "Then he'll be back in New York."

"And we'll be waiting for him," Michael said, with a confident grin.

"Until then, boys, I'm going to go home and get a decent night's rest," Uncle Ephraim said. "Sarah, on Monday I want you to go out and get us a new cook. Someone who'll give me a decent meal, with plenty of fried potatoes and a good round of roast beef!"

And that, as they say in the play, should have been the end of it. But, as in the theater, there was the Epilogue.

CHAPTER 30

As the mildness of May gave way to the heat of June, with its foreshadowing of the furnaces of July and August yet to come, the firm of Pettigrew and Roth found its client list enlarged, but not in the way that Mr. Roth would have predicted.

Joshua's prowess in defending first Bertram Delacorte, then Heinz Guttenberg, and finally Billy Kendall, all in the space of a week, for the same crimes, was the subject of rumor and debate amongst a certain element of Society. Apparently, Joshua Roth was now being spoken of with the same respect as Abe Hummel, although by a lower class of felons. The result was that a stream of shabbily-dressed people found their way to the brick building on West Street, asking for the assistance of Mr. Joshua Roth in defending their brothers, husbands, wives and sweethearts on charges that ranged from Assault and Battery to Fraud to Armed Robbery. Most of the cases were so obviously trivial that Joshua referred them back to their local Ward Heeler, whose business it was to deal with petty crime, but one or two of them were more serious, and Joshua did his best for them. He even managed to get two suspected burglars and a would-be arsonist off with lighter sentences, which gave him even more prestige amongst the gangs.

I was now officially recognized as a Law Clerk, and as such, I was permitted to sit at the Defense Table, taking notes, but not speaking aloud. As Michael put it, it wasn't what we wanted, but it was better than a poke in the eye with a sharp stick.

Aunt Sarah's culinary woes continued. Miss Pringle departed, deeply disgusted at Uncle Ephraim's insistence on fried foods and sweet desserts, to be replaced by Mrs. Fenster's second cousin, fresh from Bavaria, who plied us with German sour soups. She was replaced, in turn, by Lacey, Mrs. Smith's cook, who had not gone with the Smith's to Newport, and who turned up at the kitchen door needing work. We hoped that Lacey would last longer than anyone else. At least she got along well with Mandy, and could speak English, more or less.

It was a hot afternoon, nearing Midsummer's Day. I was copying yet another deposition when the bell over the door rang, and a skinny shadow fell over my desk.

"Hallo, Miss Peggy! How hot d'ya think it's going to get today?"

I looked up. "Mr. Jonas! Good afternoon. I have no idea how hot it's going to get today, but I wish we could go to Newport with the rest of Society. New York is no place to be in summer." I looked him over. He was no longer in his usual garb of well-worn frock coat and top hat, but had put on his summer coloration: white duster coat, striped shirt, straw boater hat. "What brings you here on a day like this? There's no news from France, except that the Prussians are moving in on Paris, and the Emperor is supposed to abdicate."

"I'm not on the International Desk," Davy reminded me. "And there's no Society News, neither. Everyone's gone to Newport. Except for Mrs. Long and Mrs. Delacorte; word is that they just sailed for Europe."

"A little dangerous right now, isn't it?" I commented.

"Only in France," Davy said, with a shrug. "The boat they're on is heading for Italy."

"As I understand it, Italy's not much better," I said, carefully looking over my copy, and wondering just what Davy had come around for. He wasn't the sort of person to waste time hanging about making conversation when there might be something more exciting happening around the next corner.

"I've got something for you," he said. "Remember Billy Kendall?"

"All his gang friends have decided that since they can't afford the services of Hummel and Howe, they'll take Pettigrew and Roth as an acceptable substitute," I said sourly.

"Can't complain that business is down, then?" Davy looked around him. Uncle Ephraim had already left to sample the new cook's attempts at a luncheon; Joshua had not come in from his duties at the court-house; I was left to keep the office by myself.

"No, I can't complain," I said. "Mr. Jonas, what do you want?"

"I came to drop off something you might like to read," he said, producing a paper-backed book from his coat pocket.

I looked it over. The cover showed a picture of a youngster in a striped shirt and plug hat waving a Bowie knife in one hand, and holding a purse in the other.

" 'Billy the Gang Kid'." I read the title aloud. "Mr. Jonas, is this supposed to be the story of Billy Kendall?"

He grinned at me. "Mr. Buntline read my pieces in the *Sun*," he said proudly. "He's been writing all those great tales about the Wild West, and he thought I could do something like that for the Wild East, right here in New York City. There's plenty of rubes in the sticks who like to read about all the sinful ways of the Big City, and even more folks here in town who enjoy a good story with lots of action. There's even a romantic element to it."

I flipped my way through the book. "This is ridiculous," I said. "You've got Billy Kendall as a hero! The poor fellow wasn't anything of the sort, and you know it!"

"Dramatic license," Davy said.

"Dramatic fiddlesticks!" I echoed. "You've made the gang kids sound like a bunch of rowdy schoolboys, when they were really thieves and hooligans, causing panic wherever they went, stealing from carts and shops, chasing down Negroes and Chinamen if they saw them, just acting dreadfully. And the Beautiful Susan! A maid in a fine house, who falls in love with Billy the Gang Kid on sight, impressed by his fine physical appearance and good manners. Billy Kendall had no manners at all, and you know it!"

"Now, Peggy," Davy said. "No one's going to know the difference. Billy Kendall in life was a sorry youngster, growing up on the streets, being taken advantage of at every turn. Everything he did turned out wrong. He even got hanged for the wrong murder, as I hear it. But in my stories…"

"Stories!" I was aghast. "Do you mean there are going to more of these books?"

"I just signed for five more," Davy said proudly. "And, I might add, I would never have done it if it wasn't for you, so I thought I'd let you know."

THE GUILTY CLIENT

Davy Jonas as anything but a nuisance, hanging about any crowd that formed on the streets in search of scandal and mayhem.

I picked up the book. "Well, it will certainly sell," I said finally. "It's got a lot of fights, and some humorous scenes. Of course, it's not the truth."

"That's why they call it fiction," Davy said.

I sighed. "Billy Kendall deserves better than this," I said at last.

"Well, Miss Peggy," said Davy, "if you want to tell the people the truth, you'll just have to write it yourself."

So I did.

Authors Notes

"The Guilty Client" is a work of fiction, and most of the characters and incidents in it are fictional. However, a few actual persons of the era made their way into this tale.

Alexander "Clubber" Williams was a well-known figure in New York City in the 1870's. I have taken some liberties with historical fact, and moved him from the East Side to the West Side somewhat ahead of time, to put him into the district where he made the famous remark, "I've been living on chuck for long enough, now I'm gonna get a piece of the tenderloin."

William Marcy Tweed, Jr, also called Young Tweed, was appointed Assistant District Attorney, and made a name for himself by courting the newly enfranchised Black voters.

Abe Hummel was the more sedate partner in the firm of Hummel and Howe. He was known for his heavy German accent and for bending the Law to suit his clients.

The New York County Courthouse, still called the Tweed Courthouse, began construction in 1868. By 1870 the building was more or less habitable, and was put into use. In 1872, William Marcy Tweed was tried in one of the courtrooms in this building.

The corruption and incompetence of the New York City Metropolitan Police Department in the 1870's and '80's is well-documented.

For more information:
Boss Tweed, by Kenneth D. Ackerman (Carroll & Graf, New York, 2005)

N.Y.P.D: A city and its police, by James Lardner and Thomas Repetto (Henry Holt & Co, New York, 2000)

Low Life: lures and snares of Old New York, by Luc Sante (Farrar, Straus, Giroux, New York, 1991)

ABOUT THE AUTHOR

Roberta Rogow has been writing since she could hold a pencil. She has had stories published in both science fiction and mystery anthologies. She is the author of four mystery novels in which the Reverend Mr. Charles Lutwidge Dodgson (better known as Lewis Carroll) and young Dr. Arthur Conan Doyle collaborate as detectives. She is presently reviewing juvenile mysteries in Mystery Scene Magazine. Roberta has recently retired after a 37-year career as a Children's Librarian in public libraries in New Jersey.